She would get over this attraction.

Her reaction was a normal one to kindness—that was all. Nothing more serious. In a day's time she'd wonder what she'd ever seen in him. A gladiator, one of the *infamis*. A man outside polite society. A man whose profession was death.

'Julia,' he said thickly, and put his hand on her elbow. She felt the sparks sizzle up her arm.

She would have to make sure that Valens knew and understood that she was not one of those bored woman of Baiae, the notorious beach resort near Naples, where the wealthy went to play and party, ripe for the picking. Her reputation was of paramount importance.

Although born and raised near San Francisco, California, **Michelle Styles** currently lives a few miles south of Hadrian's Wall with her husband, three children, two dogs, cats, assorted ducks, hens and beehives. An avid reader, she has always been interested in history, and a historical romance is her idea of the perfect way to relax. Her love of Rome stems from the year of Latin she took in sixth grade. She is particularly interested in how ordinary people lived during ancient times, and in the course of her research she learnt how to cook Roman food as well as how to use a drop spindle. When she is not writing, reading or doing research, Michelle tends her rather overgrown garden or does needlework, in particular counted cross-stich. Michelle maintains a website, www.michellestyles.co.uk, and a blog, www.michellestyles.blogspot.com, and would be delighted to hear from you.

The Gladiator's Honour is Michelle Styles's début novel for Mills & Boon® Historical Romance™

THE GLADIATOR'S HONOUR

Michelle Styles

MILLS & BOON®

First published in Great Britain 2006
Large Print edition 2006
Harlequin Mills & Boon Limited,
Eton House, 18-24 Paradise Road, Richmond, Surrey TW9 1SR

© Michelle Styles 2006

ISBN-13: 978 0 263 19074 8
ISBN-10:   0 263 19074 9

Set in Times Roman 15 on 17¾ pt.
42-0906-83938

Printed and bound in Great Britain
by Antony Rowe Ltd, Chippenham, Wiltshire

THE GLADIATOR'S HONOUR

To my long-suffering family
and to Helen French, without whose
support and enthusiasm this
would never have been written

Chapter One

Rome
65 BC

Who was that man? And, more importantly, why did she know him?

Julia Antonia risked another look at the man standing in the portico of the baths. It was not his bronzed muscular legs emerging from his almost too-short tunic nor the breadth of his shoulders that captured her attention, but rather the planes of his shadowed face. She knew those features as intimately as she knew an old friend's and yet, when she heard him speak to his companion, she knew she had never heard his voice before.

His gaze caught hers and it seemed as if he could look into her soul. He arched an eyebrow and nodded. Did he recognise her as well? Her fingers pulled her russet shawl more firmly about her head and shoulders and smoothed the folds of her green wool gown, making sure she was dressed in a manner appropriate for a Roman matron.

Sabina Claudia, her stepmother, gave that high-pitched cackle she always used when she tore some unsuspecting matron's reputation to shreds and threw the scraps into the swollen river of Roman gossip. Sabina's friends leant forward, their shawls quivering, eager to hear the latest juicy morsel, crowding out Julia's view of the stranger. When she had the time to glance back, the man had gone, vanishing into the busy marketplace as if he had never been there.

Where had she seen him before? His features were so familiar and yet she was positive she had never encountered him before. She'd have remembered that low rumble of a voice. The answer was on the tip of her tongue. She stared at where he had been, willing the answer to come or otherwise it would bother her for days.

'Where can that litter be? I told them I wanted to be picked up at the fifth hour, not at half past,' Julia's stepmother's annoyed voice broke through Julia's concentration. 'You can't get decent help these days for love or money.'

Sabina's harpies sighed in agreement.

'Shall I go and check? It sounds like a crowd has gathered up there.' Julia pointed to one of the side streets. It would do no good to remind Sabina that her husband was using their one litter for court and had promised to send it when he could. 'It could be held up. In any case, then we will know why the crowds are there.'

She hurried away, without waiting for an answer. No doubt, Sabina Claudia had turned back to her cronies with a sigh and the complaint: 'Poor creature, with no tire-woman to do her bidding, but what can one expect if one chooses to divorce a senator?' No doubt, the women would agree and it would signal another long gossip about Julia's failings and the scandal she had caused.

Julia held her head higher and quickened her pace. She did not regret divorcing Lucius Gracchus with his three chins, flabby fingers that curled into hard fists and lightning-quick temper. The wonder was that she had endured it for three and a half years. Every night, she went down on her knees and thanked Minerva that she had finally had the courage to leave.

'Excuse me,' she asked a porter balancing a basket of fish on his head, 'do you know why the crowd has gathered?'

The porter's eyes slid passed her and he moved on without answering. Julia wrinkled her nose, torn between discovering the reason for the gathering crowd and returning to the safety of the portico. The crowd was the most interesting thing to happen to her in days, other than catching sight of that mysterious man.

'Gladiators,' came the answer from a smooth rich voice from behind her right shoulder.

Julia spun round and found herself staring at the man from the portico. Close up, she could see the way the fine white linen of his tunic strained against his massive chest, and the bulge of his arm muscles as if he spent hour after in the gymnasium or on the practice fields. If only her mind would remember. She tilted her head. 'Gladiators?'

'That crowd are waiting to see the gladiators arrive. Julius Caesar, in his capacity as Aedile in charge of all public entertainment, is assembling the largest troop of gladiators Rome has ever seen. He is offering the games in honour of his late father. Today is the day they start entering the city of Romulus.'

'Is that so?' Julia's heart sank. She had forgotten today's promised spectacle. The news would not improve Sabina's temper. Her stepmother disapproved of the games and the time her father spent watching them. It was about the only thing she and Julia had some sort of mutual agreement on. 'I had forgotten. Not everyone follows the games, you know. Is that why you are here?'

'In a manner of speaking.' A smile tugged at the corners of his mouth. A twinkle shone in his eyes.

'But I would rather speak about you. Why you are here—and why you followed me from the portico.'

'I didn't,' Julia protested. 'I wanted to see what the disturbance was.'

'Ah, yes. It is all coincidence.' He looped his thumbs through his belt. 'You try to attract my attention, signalling with your eyes to meet out here and then you deny it ever happened. Bold but intriguing.'

Julia gulped. Had her actions been misinterpreted? She had only wanted to know where they had met before and why she seemed to know him. She stared at her hands. Now was the perfect chance. Once she had worked out where she knew him from, then the rest could be dismissed with a laugh and shrug of her shoulders. It would do no good to deny her actions. She was finished with that sort of behaviour.

'Do I know you from somewhere?' Julia asked in a rush before her nerve failed. She had to put her mind at rest. She fixed her gaze on the bright red awning of the market stall, rather than risking another glance upwards at his dark fringed eyes. 'I saw you outside the baths and thought we had met somewhere before, but could not remember where.'

'I'm Valens.' The man gave a slight bow. 'In the flesh—and you are?'

'Julia Antonia. Should I know your name?' Julia forced her lips to curve upwards and arched an eyebrow. 'Perhaps you could give me more of a clue to your identity. After all, Rome is the largest city in the world and there are very few who can go by one name.'

'I'm Valens the Thracian,' he said and shifted somewhat uncomfortably as if he were a child caught in the act of stealing honey cakes, instead of a hardened survivor of more than a dozen gladiatorial combats. This was not how the conversation was supposed to go, how he planned on it going when he heard her ask the porter the question. He had noticed her earlier and thought from her reaction that she had guessed who he was. His interest had been stirred when he thought that she had followed him after flirting with him with her eyes.

'If you are a gladiator, why are you here?' Julia Antonia crossed her arms. 'Why is no one crowding around you? Maybe you are one of the untried gladiators.'

Valens rubbed the back of his neck. Having his identity as a gladiator questioned was a novelty. 'I had business to conduct for the owner of my gladiatorial troop, arrangements about using the bathing facilities.'

'And so…'

Valens looked at the young woman standing before him with her face half-covered by a russet shawl and attempted to think of an answer, an explanation for his behaviour. Normally women were quivering puddles at his feet once they realised who he was, begging for some token for their husbands and sons or, worse, offering him their bed.

'Some say I'm one of the best gladiators in a generation or more,' Valens said, choosing his words. He hated to brag, preferring to let the skill of his sword in the arena speak for itself, but this woman left him little choice. 'Surely you've seen the posters. They are plastered all over Rome—from the Forum to the Circus Maximus. Figurines of me and the other gladiators are on sale from any street corner vendor.'

He watched for the inevitable swoon. Nothing but a slight curve to her full lips. He waited. A tiny frown appeared between her eyebrows.

'Oh, that explains it. I had begun to wonder.' Her voice held a note of relief. 'I must have noticed the figurines. It all makes sense now. We have never met. How silly of me. I thought…it doesn't matter what I had thought. Of course not. It had to have been the figurines. Funny, though, I never really look at them. It just goes to show that one notices more than one thinks.'

Valens stared at her in disbelief. Who was this Julia Antonia? Why was it such a relief that she had noticed him from a figurine, rather than having actually met him? He should walk away, should never have engaged her in conversation. Yet, there was something about her, the tone of voice, the way she held her head. With her clear eyes and heart-shaped face, she possessed a classic beauty, not one derived from pots of paint and the skills of her make-up artist. And her figure, from what he could see of it through the layers she wore, had the curves of a woman. Layers his fingers itched to unwrap, to free her like a butterfly emerging from a cocoon for his eyes only, to see the beauty he felt positive was hidden underneath.

As she gave a slight tap to her sandalled foot, he realised there was something more, a challenge to her eyes. She was treating him as a person. It had been a long time since anyone, let alone a woman of her social standing, had dared speak to him like a human being.

For the past four and a half years, since winning his first bout as a gladiator, he had either been treated as a god worthy of simpering worship, or a slave beneath contempt. He was neither. He was a man, doing a job. And she was the first to treat him as such, to remind him that there was more to life than the arena.

Another cruel twist of the Fates' thread, just as he had reached the pinnacle of his career—to remind him of what he had lost, what had been torn from his grip.

'I thought you'd recognised the badge on my cloak, there in the portico.' Valens tried again. He held out the insignia, emblazoned gold against the deep blue wool, for her inspection.

She examined the badge. 'A lion with a spear. I'm sorry, it doesn't mean anything to me.'

'It is the symbol for the School of Strabo. One of the foremost gladiator schools in Italy.'

Still that amused tolerant expression, but this time with a liquid laugh, a laugh that made him feel bathed in sunshine. Valens relaxed a little. Maybe now they could begin to break the impasse. He could retire from this battle with his honour intact. She would think he was more than a man beset by demons, given to accosting women. She'd understand him to be what he was—a gladiator who'd made an honest mistake. He was surprised that it mattered, but it did.

'Now I begin to understand. It starts to make some sort of strange sense.' Julia forced her smile to brighten as her mind raced. It would have to happen to her. A gladiator, the nearest thing in Rome to a living god, thought she had flirted with him. For the time the gladiators fought, their names were on everyone's lips, their pictures emblazoned on plates and cups and their images moulded into small statuettes that were avidly collected by the games' many supporters.

Without having to think hard, she knew a dozen women who would offer their best *stola t*o be in her sandals right now. But they weren't here, she was. And she intended to teach this gladiator a lesson. Not every woman he locked eyes with wanted to arrange an illicit meeting. She felt rather foolish for not having realised where she knew his features from earlier. All this could have been avoided. Juno's gown, what it must have looked like to him?

'What makes strange sense?' he asked, crossing his arms, making the material strain even more across his chest.

'Why you might think women would arrange assignations with their eyes. I understand many women are mad about gladiators. But I have to disappoint you again. For the entire twenty-one years of my existence I have found it possible to restrain myself from such behaviour and have chosen to remain in ignorance about gladiatorial games and the merits of gladiators in general.'

He lifted an eyebrow as if he did not believe her.

'Not everybody does, you know.' Julia gave a pointed cough. 'I merely came out to discover where my stepmother's litter was.'

'You don't follow the games?' Valens's eyes widened and he put a hand to his forehead. 'I refuse to believe it.'

'Is that some sort of crime?' Julia asked, beginning to enjoy herself. It was liberating to be frank. His face showed his absolute amazement. He appeared to have shrunk slightly, to have become a man. 'Where is it written that everyone must be passionate about the games?'

'Not a crime,' he said, running his hand through his thick dark hair. 'By the gods, no, just a surprise. Rome is such a gladiatorial-mad city. It seems all the conversation revolves around the games.'

'Does it, indeed? I had rather thought conversation in Rome revolved around the Senate or perchance the army and its recent victories over the pirates. There is life beyond the games. I, for one, have lived all my life in Rome and have never seen any need to visit the games.'

A silence. Julia resisted the urge to clap her hands together in triumph. She had done it. She had emerged from the long shadows of her marriage and had answered back. He had no ready quip to shoot back at her. She had won. She had proven to herself that she was indeed the new Julia Antonia.

'They were light-hearted remarks. I meant no harm by them.' His smile turned beguiling and her heart contracted. He touched her right elbow with feather-light fingers. 'Forgive me?'

'Apology accepted.' She'd end the conversation here. On a high note. Before she melted from the heat of his charm. 'Now, if you'll excuse me, I need to see about getting home. Another conversation that will not involve gladiators.'

She stepped backwards and her sandal slipped, sending her to the ground and scattering her bathing things. Warm hands gripped her elbow and helped her to stand.

'Are you all right?' His face showed concern, while his hands held her steady and for a breath she rested her head against his chest. 'Your foot landed between two paving stones.'

'I'm fine.' Julia moved her arm and he released her. She dropped to her knees, starting to pick up her scattered belongings—her bath *strigil*, ivory comb and four carved hairpins. She jammed them back into her shoulder bag. Where was the fifth? She scanned the ground for the hairpin and her alabaster perfume flask. Her heart sank when she saw where the hairpin lay. Julia gingerly plucked it from the top of Valen's sandal. She made a face. Why she had thought today would be different from any other day, she had no idea. Once again she had ruined a perfectly good exit. Try to teach a man a lesson and end up falling at his feet, literally falling. Without a doubt, it could only happen to her.

She glanced over to the portico of the baths, but Sabina and her entourage had disappeared. The litter had probably arrived and her stepmother had left. Julia could already hear Sabina's rising screech of a lecture when she did make it back to the villa. 'I've lost my alabaster jar, but, other than that, I will survive.'

A small gasp of pain came from her throat as she put too much weight down on her ankle. Strong hands grabbed her arm and steadied her.

'You've hurt yourself. You're limping.'

Without waiting for an answer, Valens knelt down and wrapped his warm fingers around her ankle. Julia felt the warmth radiate up her leg. She should object, but the words refused to come. He pushed aside the cloth to reveal her sandal, and the reddened skin. His fingers hovered just at her ankle.

'Have you grazed your knee? Or is it just your foot?'

'Not my knee, you stopped my fall,' she stammered, remembering the feel of his chest against her hands.

'Yes, I remember.' His gaze held hers, until she looked away, pretending a sudden interest in the wool merchant across the road, festooned in an array of brightly coloured cloth. 'I'm not likely to forget. What I want to know is how badly you are hurt.'

Julia's heart turned over. She hated to think how long it had been since anyone had asked a question about her with care in their voice, much less touched her with gentle hands. This stranger asked after her health, with more warmth in his voice than Lucius had had in all the time they were married. She bit her lip and tried to swallow the lump in her throat.

'I twisted my ankle in the fall. Nothing to worry about.' Her words tumbled out. Her eyes were drawn to the way his black hair curled on his neck just above his tunic as he bent over her foot. Giving her head a quick shake, she attempted to recapture her wit. 'I'm sure I can cope. I wouldn't want to deprive any woman who might be looking to arrange an assignation with you…'

Valens kept his hand on her leg. Instead of letting go, he touched the area above and below her ankle with careful fingers, turning her foot this way and that, but never enough to cause real pain. Julia again felt the heat from his hand course up her leg. It terrified her and excited her.

Now she started to understand why the poets went on about instant attraction. She had never felt this warm melting for anyone before, and she knew little to nothing about this man, this gladiator. She stared at him, wondering how a turned ankle could make her so light-headed, breathless.

'I think I've had my quota for the day,' he said, answering her joke with one of his own. 'Besides, I wouldn't have wanted to miss the opportunity of holding such a pretty ankle.'

The intimacy of his smile made her knees weaken and her hands itch to bury themselves in his hair. She had to take control of the situation or her actions would echo her thoughts, and she'd be little better than the women who stood around the gladiators' entrance after a match, hoping for a glimpse of their hero. And swooning with great long sighs whenever any gladiator appeared.

Julia withdrew her foot from his hand.

'You are an idle flatterer. It is the first time in my life anyone has praised my ankles.'

'Maybe it is time somebody did.' He laughed and then his face sobered. 'How bad is your ankle? Is the pain better or worse than when you first turned it?'

'It is nothing. I'll shake it off in a few steps.'

She forced herself to ignore the pain as she rotated it, but the world blurred in a haze. She could do this. She was strong enough to withstand it. She forced her back straighter.

'It looks more than a twisted ankle to me. You can barely put weight on your right foot.' Valens stood up, then reached out and lifted her chin. 'Your lips are white from pain.'

Julia's breath caught in her throat. For a heartbeat, she could only stare at him, watching the rise and fall of his chest. His eyes seemed to swallow her. Her lips ached, parted of their own volition. He might kiss her…in public. The thought acted like a plunge into the cold-water pool at the baths, bringing her to her senses. She ducked her head, hiding her face deeper in her shawl and made one last attempt to keep her dignity.

'The pain is lessening.' Julia took a step backwards and forced a smile on her face. She was a Roman matron, not a courtesan or a prostitute. Roman matrons had pure thoughts and a steady heartbeat. Keeping those thoughts uppermost, she folded her arms across her breasts. 'The Forum is only a few streets away, after that it is not too far to Subura and home. It should hold out if I go slowly.'

She shut her eyes and tried to believe her words, tried not to count the number of steps it would take.

'What, and collapse on someone else? Subura is at least a mile from the Forum. And how far do you think you'll get on your own, limping like that? You'll be a target for every thief and cutpurse in the city,' he said gravely.

Julia's heart started to race faster and she clenched her fists to prevent herself from throwing them around his neck. She had help. She wasn't alone.

'Julia, Julia, what in the name of the Good Goddess do you think you are doing?' Sabina said, rushing up to her and grabbing her arm. Julia put out her hands to keep her balance. She felt Valens's hand on the small of her back steady her. 'The litter is here at last. Your father did remember after all.'

'I…that is…' Julia gulped. Sabina would have to appear, just as things were starting to become interesting.

'It came just after you went on your little walk. I have been searching for you everywhere!' Sabina said, her voice rising in a piercing shriek. 'It is bad enough that your father uses our one and only litter on the day I promised Livia I'd meet her at the baths, but you have to go off on some excursion of your own, just when we need to leave. If you won't think of your own reputation, Julia, at least think about your family's.'

'I hurt my ankle and this gentleman has been helping me.' Julia said, hoping her stepmother had not seen Valens's hands on her leg. 'You were obviously too busy to notice.'

Julia watched Sabina's eyes narrow as she regarded Valens, taking in the short tunic and the expensive cloak slung around his shoulders. Julia resisted the temptation to bite her nails.

'And you are?' Sabina's voice could have been chipped out of marble.

'Valens the gladiator at your service, ma'am.' He gave a slight bow. 'Rescuing fair maids in distress is a speciality.'

'Julia, how could you? A gladiator,' Sabina whispered furiously. 'You promised—no more scandals. You're not to give Mettalius any excuse to wriggle out of your wedding.'

'Since when is falling a scandal?' Julia stared at Sabina. An edited version of the truth was in order if she was avoid a lecture—something that skirted around Valens's early banter and her replies to it. At Sabina's narrowed eyes, Julia widened hers. 'It's the truth. Valens kindly helped when others would have ignored me.'

'Please spare me.' Sabina cast her eyes heavenwards, before turning towards Valens. She made a shooing motion with her hands. 'It's all right now. My maid and I can see Julia Antonia safely home. We do have a litter. Thank you for helping.'

There was a pause as Valens lifted his eyebrow and Julia watched her stepmother's cheek colour.

'Would you like something for your trouble?' Sabina asked through firmly pursed lips. 'Galla—'

'Keep your money,' Valens said stiffly. 'A simple act of kindness, such as I would do for any.'

Julia wished the ground would open and swallow her. How could her stepmother be that rude?

'Thank you. You were very kind. I appreciate it.'

He caught her hand and held it, encasing it in his warmth. Their eyes locked and Julia felt her heart begin to race again.

'Julia, we have to go. Are you aware of how many things I have to do today?'

Julia started and withdrew her hand, scorched from the heat.

'It was my pleasure. What else are gladiators good

for?' Valens gave a lopsided smile. 'If I come across your flask, I'll try to return it to you.'

Julia returned his smile, before she limped off with Sabina and her maid flanking her on either side. One bright spot in her otherwise gloomy day. As if on cue, the rain started drizzling down, sending the market stall owners scurrying to close up and cover their goods.

She ignored Sabina's litany of complaint and concentrated on thinking about Valens's smile, indulging in a daydream of how he'd find her perfume flask and use it as an excuse to see her again.

Chapter Two

Valens watched the trio hobble off until they were submerged in the growing throng—Julia's head the highest of the three and her shawl easy to follow in the crowd. She was quite unexpected. The odour of her perfume lingered in the air—a light floral scent of lavender mingled with roses and somehow suitable for the woman.

He ran his hand through his hair. He had a thousand things to do, to prepare, and wasting time speculating about a woman was not going to help. This one last fight on the biggest stage in the world, and then he'd retire…with honour. But he'd seen far too often what happened to those who failed to concentrate.

Valens pulled his cloak more firmly around his shoulders and hunched his head against the rain. Out of the corner of his eye, he spotted a small stone flask wedged between two paving stones. He picked it up—I.A. was faintly scratched on the top. Julia Antonia? He glanced towards the direction he had last seen her, weighing the flask in his hand.

'Excuse me, excuse me but is that a gladiator's badge?' a young boy lisped, pulling on his cloak. 'I saw some gladiators fight last year in Capua with my father. And the spectacle was fantastic. Which sort of gladiator are you? I collect the figures. I have a Samnite, a *rentarius* and my mother just bought me a Valens the Thracian figurine whose arms can move.'

Valens glanced down at the boy's upturned face, glowing with admiration, and then back to where Julia had disappeared. He shoved the flask into his belt. There would be time later to find her if the Fates were willing. Back to being a god.

Julia chewed the end of her stylus, trying to think of a way to describe her encounter with Valens the gladiator to Claudia. Without a doubt, Claudia would have a hundred questions that as a dutiful best friend she should answer before she was asked. The problem was she had little idea of how to answer. She only knew he was a Thracian gladiator, but not if a Thracian was a great or little shield. Claudia was an avid supporter of the great shields, the ones who were nearly covered in body armour and carried the oblong shields, if she remembered correctly. Thracian would have to do. She sighed and pushed the tablet away.

'I know, Bato,' she said to the elderly greyhound who whined at her from his place by the brazier. 'But what is the point of writing when I am ignorant of so many things Claudia will demand to know?'

The dog gave a sharp bark and covered his nose with his paws. Julia laughed.

'Exactly what I'll do when Claudia demands further and better details.' She picked up her stylus again and started to write. Before she had written three words, a loud banging and shouts sounded outside. 'What is that unearthly racket, Bato? Have a whole host of Furies descended on the courtyard?'

She limped to the door, only to have it pulled out of her hand by Sabina, her stepmother's face contorted in fury.

'Now you've done it, Julia. You have done it. Listen to that racket! Just you wait until your father gets home.'

'What is it, Sabina?' Julia crossed her arms and stared at her stepmother. Julia's mind raced, trying to think what she had done to cause this red-faced anger. Nothing. But that small fact seemed to have escaped the older woman. 'Ever since we arrived back from the baths, I've been in that room, resting my ankle and writing letters. I'm totally innocent of whatever is happening out there.'

Sabina's mouth opened and closed like a codfish several times before she emitted a piercing shriek.

'That gladiator you talked to this morning, outside the baths. He's at the gates.' Sabina shook at finger at Julia. 'I will not have your brutish friends intimidating the porter. I won't have it, I tell you. You may speak to them in the marketplace, but I refuse to have an *infamis* in the house. Gladiators are the lowest of the low. They are even worse than actors. And, by Juno's necklace, you know how many times I have refused to allow them in my house, even for entertainment!'

'Is he?' Julia's fingers went to her throat. Valens here! A warm glow filled her as she remembered the way his hands had engulfed her ankle. She tried for a casual shrug of her shoulders. 'He's probably found my missing flask of perfume and is returning it, that's all. There is no need for you to put the house in an uproar.'

'He thinks you invited him to stay.' Sabina had a triumphant gleam in her eye. 'Julia, your father will be furious with you. I dread to think what Senator Mettalius will say when he finds out. You take his proposal of marriage too lightly, Julia. Many women would be delighted to ally their families with Mettalius. He's a rising star in the Senate.'

'Where is my father?' Julia asked, thinking fast as her stomach hit the tops of her sandals. Had she said something, anything Valens could take for invitation? She went back over the conversation. Nothing.

'He retired to the gym two hours ago. Perhaps, your luck will hold, but I'd make a shrewd guess and say you have less than a half-hour to get rid of your lovelorn gladiator friend before your father returns and Mettalius comes for dinner.'

'Mettalius is dining with us. Nobody told me.' Julia wrinkled her nose and her mind raced to think of a suitable excuse. This day was getting worse with each passing word from Sabina's lips. Perhaps her ankle would be too painful and she'd retire to bed.

'He sent word at five hours, just before we left for the baths. I want you to look your best. I will not accept any excuse. Your last one about your dog being ill was utterly transparent. Your father knows what is best for you and the family. Think of Mettalius's power, his influence.'

His bad breath? His high-pitched voice? Julia resisted the temptation to add these attributes to the list.

'Furthermore, if you cross me on this, I will...I will have that dog of yours put down.' Sabina's eyes narrowed.

Bato bared his teeth and gave a low growl.

'You wouldn't dare.' Julia curled her fingers around Bato's collar. She gave a wild look at Sabina, standing there, one hand on her hip, the other pointing at Bato. 'Hush, Bato, be good. She's only having her little joke.'

'Try me.' Sabina made a shooing motion. 'Now, go and get rid of the gladiator. Then we'll talk, and remember what happened the last time you tried to get the better of me.'

Julia clenched her jaw. She remembered all too well what happened—Sabina had consulted her favourite augur and she had been married off to Lucius before she had had a chance to voice a protest.

She covered her letter to Claudia with several scrolls, then placed her stylus on top. The last thing she needed was Sabina prying into her private letters. She snapped her fingers. 'Come, Bato. We have a gladiator to disable.'

Valens stood with his tablet in his hand, his foot blocking the porter from shutting the huge iron-and-oak door. The pain between his eyes had reached a crescendo. After he had answered an ever-growing crowd of supporters' questions, he arrived back late to the School's temporary headquarters only to discover the memories of Spartacus's rebellion cast long shadows. The Senate had passed a law forbidding more than three gladiators to be housed in one place. And Strabo wanted the situation sorted out yesterday.

Now, all he wanted to do was leave his gear, find

the nearest public baths before they closed and try to soak some of today's problems away. It was highly unlikely that this family would have its own private bathing suite, because as far as he could tell, they were equestrian, rather than senatorial in stature.

It had seemed straightforward when he left Strabo and Caesar. Unfortunately, the place where he was supposed to stay seemingly had no knowledge of him.

The fine drizzle dripped on the back of his neck, echoing his mood.

'But I'm expected,' he explained again to the grizzled porter cowering behind his table. For Hercules's sake, he had kept his voice low and deadly calm. The man behaved as if he had tried to strike him. He only wanted to go to his room.

'I know nothing about this—' the porter said in an officious tone.

'It's fine, Clodius. I will handle this,' a firm but melodious voice said.

Valens raised his eyebrows in surprise. The matron from the marketplace. Julia Antonia. Another sign from the gods?

A shaft of sunlight appeared through the clouds, lighting the doorway and the woman standing in it before vanishing. She looked lovelier than he remembered. No longer covered in a mantle, her hair had a dark black sheen like the wing of a blackbird he had once owned as a boy. Her movements reminded him of that bird—quick, sharp, nervous. At first, the bird had pecked his finger, but after his mother had shown him how to be patient, the bird had taken crumbs from the palm of his hand.

'At last, someone with a bit of common sense.' Valens made his voice sound playful but there was no relaxation of her shoulders, no answer to his smile. If anything, she looked more wary. There had to be something he could use to recapture the camaraderie of the marketplace. He frowned and reached into his satchel. 'I found your perfume flask. It had rolled a little way along the gutter.'

He held it out as if he were holding crumbs for his blackbird. At the sight of the flask, a cloud seemed to lift from her face, and she gave a smile that could have lit a thousand lamps. Cautiously she stretched out her hand. Her cool fingers closed around the flask, touched his and sent a jolt up his arm.

His eyes traced the relaxed curve of her neck before locking with her sober hazel eyes. Valens's lips curved upwards into a smile of triumph—he had her tamed.

A slim greyhound peered from behind her skirts, and then raced forward, breaking Valens's gaze, returning him to the present. The dog's cool muzzle touched Valens's hand, his tongue lapping at his palm.

Valens reached down and stroked the dog's ears. Instantly the dog gave a whine of pleasure, turned over and wriggled on its back, exposing its belly and nudging Valens's leg.

'Bato, come back here,' Julia said, tugging on the dog's collar and her face growing bright red. 'I'm so sorry. He's normally very wary of people, men in particular. I can't think why he should behave like that. Bato, sit!'

The dog gave another lap of his tongue—this time to Valens's sandal.

Valens went still. For a breath, he thought he knew the dog. It reminded him of one he'd left with his father before he went off to fight in North Africa more than five years ago. But that would be too much of a coincidence. He shook his head at his folly. The poor thing probably smelt the pie he had had for lunch. Mystery solved.

'It is quite all right. No harm done,' he said. 'I like dogs, in particular greyhounds. I used to have one as a pet when I was a boy. Have you had Bato since a puppy?'

Julia gave a wistful smile and her shoulders tensed. The blackbird look was back.

'He belonged to my ex-husband, but Bato tired of my ex's uncertain temper, decided he was my dog and took to defending me against my ex. When I left, he came with me. Except when I am at the baths, he is rarely more than a few feet from me.'

Her words held a wealth of hidden agony. It was no wonder she looked poised for flight, Valen thought.

'A wise dog.' He lifted one eyebrow and watched her cheeks stain with colour. A small laugh escaped her lips.

He regarded Julia with the practised eye of someone whose life depended on reading other people correctly.

The muscles had relaxed and she held her shoulders less defensively. He followed the line of her softly caught-up hair to where the curl brushed her neck. Her lips curved into a soft smile, rather than the rigid expression she had had when she had first appeared in the doorway, but her eyes were wary.

One or two more nuggets of carefully controlled conversation, and she should be at her ease. After that he'd introduce why he was here. He hoped she actually knew how to read.

He gave Bato one last pat. 'A very wise dog to stay so close to your mistress.'

Julia tilted her head to one side, and stared at him, trying to assess the situation. She had to find out why he was here. It had to be more than the flask she held in her palm. They could not stand here making polite conversation about Bato all day.

His blue cloak billowed slightly and she could see his massive chest, barely contained in the white woollen tunic. The damp had made his dark hair curl at his temples. Her eyes travelled up to his face and met his dark brown eyes. The gaze held for a breath before she dropped her glance and examined the flask in her hand.

He looked as if he were free from furies and demons, but appearances could be deceptive. She had thought Lucius was kind and considerate until they married and she had had to witness his rages.

She played with the lid to the flask, twisting it back and forth, as she waited for him to state his reason for being here. Silence. She peeped again at his shoulders, and thought of the strength that must be in those arms, the way he could slay men with a single slice of a sword.

A shiver ran down her back. Perhaps she ought not to have come out. She should have let Clodius handle it. It was his job, after all, to vet callers. But Clodius had disappeared, leaving her exposed and vulnerable.

She took a step backwards towards the safety of the house and winced as pain shot through her bad ankle.

'I forgot to ask—how is your ankle?' he said, putting his hand on her elbow and steadying her.

Sensation darted up her arm, making her heart pound faster. Her breath came in short gasps, as if she had just finished an arduous exercise session at the baths.

'My ankle?' Julia swallowed hard, warmth spread

like a fire from his hand infusing her body with its sweet languor. He wasn't supposed to ask about her ankle. He had returned her flask. He was supposed to máke his excuses and leave. 'It is getting better. I rested it this afternoon.'

'Have you had someone look at it? It might need treatment. I can arrange for—'

'There is no need—' Julia broke in.

Out of the corner of her eye, she saw Sabina advancing, her stiff curls shaking with rage. Julia pressed her lips together and shook her head. If she needed reinforcements, she'd call for them.

'But it is no bother,' he pressed. 'Proper medical treatment can make a world of difference. Too often in my line of work I've seen men die, because they trusted the soothsayer or augur rather than the surgeon. Thankfully, the gladiator school I belong to employs a medical team to oversee all aspects of training. I'll ask my surgeon to have a look at it for you. He's an expert on breaks.'

Julia rubbed the back of her neck. Dismissing him was proving far harder than she had anticipated. Her heart kept whispering to her to prolong the encounter, to enjoy feeling that someone might be interested in her welfare. But was it worth risking her father's wrath?

The beginnings of a headache pounded between her eyebrows. She shook her head and refused to let confusion take hold of her tongue. She had to get rid of the man, no matter how much her heart wanted him to stay.

'Thank you for the offer but I would hate to think I put you to any trouble.'

'It will be no trouble at all. Apollonius will be visiting here later. He has to make sure my diet will be adequately catered for. The problems this new law has caused. Luckily Caesar spotted the Senate's move before it happened.'

Julia felt an ice-cold finger creep down her spine at his words. His diet catered for? The headache crashed over her in full force. She swallowed hard and reached out a hand to grasp the doorframe.

'I'm sorry, but I think I misheard you. Why would we be catering for your diet?'

'Because this is where I am staying.' Valens looked at her as if she had lost her mind. 'It has been all arranged.'

Julia stared at the tall gladiator, unable to believe what she had just heard. She had begun to hope that perhaps Sabina had been mistaken. But his words confirmed her worse fears. Somehow, she had inadvertently invited him. She'd have to bluff it out, get rid of him before her father returned. Make him understand it was a mistake.

'Pardon me? Is this another one of your not-so-amusing jokes? If so, it is even less likely to raise a smile than the last one. I never invited you here. Of course, if you want something for bringing my flask back…' Julia started to fumble with her arm purse.

She paused. Her actions made it seem as if she came from the same mould as Sabina. He wasn't some servant or a street child to be given a token in exchange for a small service. He was a successful gladiator.

'There is no need for that. It was my pleasure. I was only too glad to find it.' Valens waved his hand and then stared at a tablet. 'This is the villa of Julius Antonius, the lawyer, isn't it?'

'It is.' Julia folded her arms and braced her legs. He'd have to move her from the threshold, before she let him cross.

'He is a client of Julius Caesar, who is the current Aedile in charge of the games and public entertainment, the man sponsoring my gladiatorial school?' Valens spoke slowly as if she were some half-witted child.

She released a pent-up breath in one great whoosh.

'Caesar is our second cousin, but I don't see what that has to do with anything,' she said carefully, her mind starting to whirl.

There was more going on here than a simple misunderstanding. Her hand twisted the necklace of blue stones around her throat. How like Sabina, not to give her the full story and to send her to accomplish a task Sabina didn't have the stomach for. If Caesar was involved, it would be unthinkable to refuse, even if she wanted to. Caesar was her father's most important patron, providing most of the clients for his law practice. Her father always acceded to Caesar's wishes.

'The Senate has decreed this morning that large groups of gladiators living together pose a threat to the city's security, citing Spartacus's rebellion of seven years ago. Caesar looks on this as a direct attack on his integrity as Aedile and feels it is an attempt by his rivals to discredit him. Therefore, he has requested your father to house a gladiator for the duration of the games,' Valens said, holding out a tablet. 'I am that gladiator.'

Julia took the tablet and read the words in Caesar's very distinctive script. She reread the words and glanced back at Sabina, whose face was growing more thunderous.

Not this time, Stepmother dear. If she wanted to cross Caesar, she did it herself.

'My father knows about this?' she asked, tapping the tablet against her lips.

'I was given to understand he did,' Valens said, lifting one eyebrow. 'Caesar is the most efficient man I have ever served. Within two hours of the law being passed, he had found places for over a hundred men. I see no reason to doubt his word.'

Julia bit her lip. What to do? She could see Sabina watching from inside the courtyard, making ever-increasing shooing motions. Julia shook her head at her for a second time. Let her father deal with Sabina's shrieks and wails when he came home. How like her father—desperate to avoid a confrontation with Sabina, he had disappeared until the storm had blown over, leaving others to sort out the mess. Her father and Sabina could be infuriatingly similar in their ways of dealing with uncomfortable situations.

'I can understand that—'

'Is there some sort of problem?' Valens asked, his eyes showing concern and something else. 'If you'd like, you can always send a runner to check with Caesar's house. I'm sure you will find everything in order.'

'There will be no reason to trouble Caesar with this,' she said in an overloud voice. 'I have seen his hand before. If Caesar requires his clients to house gladiators, who am I to question?'

Out of the corner of her eye, she saw Sabina shrink back at the invocation of Caesar. Despite her pretensions, Sabina was well aware how much their present prosperity was dependant on Caesar's continued generosity. How Sabina's most-prized possession, the bathing suite with its expensive mosaics, was a direct result of Caesar involving her father in several lucrative lawsuits. Lawsuits that would vanish overnight if her father crossed him.

'It will be our pleasure to honour Caesar's request and provide a room for you,' she said, turning back to Valens.

'I knew you were a woman of learning as well as sense,' he said and his voice flowed over her.

Valens's smile made her pulse race and drove all coherent thought from her mind. Her hand shook as she tightened her hold on Bato's collar. It was no good telling her heart that he smiled like that all the time. Her heart was certain it was for her and her alone.

'Thank you, thank you very much,' Julia stammered out and then tried to calm her thumping heart. 'I shall take it as a compliment.'

'It was meant as one.'

'First my ankle and now my intellect. Does idle praise always slip off your tongue with such ease?'

'I beg to differ. I merely state the obvious.' His eyes twinkled. 'I always tell the truth about such things.'

Julia pretended to reread the tablet. She was no good at flirting games. She had to change the subject, get her mind off him and onto the problem at hand—this gladiator's accommodation.

Caesar gave no indication of the rank he was supposed to hold in the house. She could hardly place him with the slaves and run the risk of causing offence to their most important patron. She wanted something to enhance their reputation with Caesar and to make up for the welcome Valens had so far received.

She tapped the tablet against her hand, her lips curving upwards. She'd teach Sabina to threaten her. She'd enjoy watching Sabina squirm for once.

'Clodius, please show our guest to the best chamber.' Julia made sure her voice carried and watched the colour drain from Sabina's face. 'What Caesar asks for, we should grant. He'd hardly go to all this trouble unless he wanted us to treat Valens as our honoured guest.'

'Julia.' Sabina's indignant whisper carried as she marched over to Julia. The sound of her sandals striking the paving stones echoed throughout the courtyard. 'Did I hear you order Clodius to show this gladiator to our best bedchamber? Surely the stables would have been good enough for one such as him.'

'Caesar's request, Stepmother.' Julia waved the tablet under the older woman's nose. Threaten to put Bato down, would she? 'I'm sure anything less would be looked on as a slight by Caesar. And I would hate to tell my father we slighted his greatest patron. But if those are your orders…'

'You are right. Of course you're right.' Sabina wrung her hands and looked distracted. 'I know you're right. What am I to tell Mettalius Scipio? I had rather hoped he would stay the night…'

Mettalius Scipio. Valens froze. The name opened cracks in his memory, sent his mind along forgotten paths. Images of forts and the tribune issuing orders, of the dark night and the breath of his men as they waited, of the ambush and then finally of the hook-nose pirate who had captured him and then spat in his face, crowded into his brain. Images he thought he had buried years ago when he first wielded the gladiator's sword.

'Mettalius Scipio, son of Mettalius Agrippa?' Valens asked, making an effort to keep his voice steady.

'Why, yes,' Julia's stepmother simpered. 'Do you know the senator? Julia is about to become betrothed to him.'

'We've met…several times.' He knew instinctively his words would be interpreted as meaning recently when in fact it was five years since they had last spoken. Valens closed the door to his memory with a bang. He refused to remember anything about the time before.

'That puts a rather different complexion on the whole thing, doesn't it? I mean, if you are a friend of senators…' She held out her hand, batting her false eyelashes. 'I'm Sabina Claudia, the wife of Julius Antonius. Julia is my stepdaughter, in case you didn't guess. I must apologise for her—Julia can be too cautious at times, too apt to judge people by their standing, if you know what I mean. Too proud for her own good.'

'Not at all like you,' Valens said and made an effort not to wince as he said the words.

Sabina Claudia was one of those dyed blondes with paint so thick on her face her very features were obscured, one of those women whose sole purpose was to grasp the next rung of the social ladder, kicking anyone and everyone as they scrambled over them.

'I am positive you are the soul of tact,' Valens added pointedly. 'A reflection of the true Roman-matron ideal.'

Bato the dog gave him a strange look, and Valens bowed back. He ignored Julia's questioning glance.

'Julia, why didn't you tell me your gladiator was so perceptive in addition to having such a fine Italian accent? He could almost pass as someone other than a gladiator,' Sabina cooed, hooking her arm through Valens's. 'Now you must try our bath suite. It has the latest word in luxury—a hot plunge bath. I made certain of that, and that is undoubtedly why Caesar chose us for your lodgings. He knew we could provide the facilities you needed, unlike others I could mention.'

Valens detached himself as unobtrusively as he could. Julia looked as if she was about ready to explode. At him? At her stepmother? Valens gave a slight nod in her direction, but Julia looked away, chin very firmly in the air.

'He's not my gladiator, Stepmother. I explained to you already that we had barely met.' Her voice dripped ice.

'A figure of speech, my dear,' her stepmother

replied airily. 'At least you had the good sense to run into a gladiator who is well connected.'

'I...' Julia said and then turned on her heel and limped off.

Valens watched her go, the skirt of her gown swishing at her heels. He admired the way she kept her head held high and did not stoop to dignify her stepmother's remark with an answer. She reminded him of the sort of woman he had dreamt of marrying years ago. The sort of woman who had helped make Rome great and who was for ever beyond his reach. One who did embody the ideals of Rome.

'I had no idea Julia Antonia was betrothed to Senator Mettalius,' he said, turning once again to Sabina, his anger growing at the stupidity of the woman, at his folly for wanting something he could not have and at his desire to remember the past.

'Of course, nothing is settled yet, but we are very hopeful. The senator appears to be willing.' Sabina's voice dropped to a hushed whisper. 'All things considered, Julia can not be choosy.'

'Indeed?'

'I am sure you will hear anyway, seeing as you will be staying here. The servants will talk.' Sabina gave a large mock sigh. 'Julia left her husband. She divorced him, claiming he had beaten her. She even took his dog. Her father was most upset. He had to take her back in, of course. She couldn't be left out in the street and she is his responsibility. I did tell him when they married that she is a flighty over-indulged child and might do this. Would he listen and marry her with *confarreatio*, giving her to her husband for ever, relinquishing all authority over her? No, he gave into fashion. Now he is faced with an unmarried twenty-one-year-old with the wisp of scandal clinging to her *stolla*. All the best alliances have gone. What sort of man wants a wife that will argue back?'

Mettalius, obviously, Valens thought but resisted the temptation to say it aloud.

'Now, if you'll have a servant show me to my quarters and to your bathing suite, I'll trouble you no further. I've had a long day.' He gave a slight bow.

'But you will join us for dinner.' Sabina gave a coquettish smile. 'We're having sow's udder. It is a speciality of mine, a recipe handed down from generation to generation. The senator always compliments me on it.'

'Regrettably, no, I follow a very strict diet in the weeks before a bout, eating mainly barley and beans.' Valens bowed and forced his tone to hold a note of regret. Sow's udder had never been a favourite, even in the days before he'd been a gladiator. 'I tend to take my meals on my own. Or with the others from the gladiatorial school. Caesar has no wish to trouble you any more than he has to.'

'Some other time.'

'Perhaps, but I will give you longer notice as I don't wish to put you to any trouble,' Valens said smoothly, making sure nothing betrayed his disquiet.

He had no idea how he'd react if he had to confront Mettalius over the dinner table. Already the memories of those last days in North Africa were crowding again into his mind, driving other thoughts away. Valens frowned, and concentrated on turning his thoughts towards the games. His future depended on forgetting his past.

Chapter Three

Julia woke in the silver-grey half-light before dawn. The sounds of the servants beginning to stir and the rumble of the carts in the narrow road outside the house filled her tiny room. She stared up at the rough-hewn plaster ceiling, reliving the events of yesterday evening.

Her father had arrived shortly after Valens, red-faced from his exertions at the gymnasium. Far from being unwelcoming and upset at having to house a gladiator, he had gone to the gym to get some sword practice in before their guest arrived.

Julia chuckled, remembering Sabina's face as her father went on and on about the honour Caesar had given him by letting him house one of the top gladiators in the Republic.

Her luck had held. After the first course, her father had accepted her excuse of a painful ankle and allowed her to retire. She avoided both the sow's udder and a prolonged exposure to Mettalius. Surely, the heated argument about the merits of the former dictator, Sulla, that wafted through her window meant the wedding was less likely. Venus, the special protectoress of the Julian family, had at last begun to listen to her prayers.

'It was a good day after all, Bato,' Julia said, sitting up and hugging her knees through the thin wool blanket.

No answering whine or lick to her face. Julia stretched a foot out, but failed to encounter the usual lump at the end of the bed, weighing the bedclothes down.

'Bato?' she called. Nothing.

Julia swung her feet over the side of the bed and checked the small room. No dog. She frowned and tried to think how he could have escaped. Surely, the window was too high and narrow to escape that way, even if he had smelt food.

The door creaked on its hinges.

She passed a hand over her eyes and tugged her hair in frustration. The means of escape was all too clear. Her heart sank further as she thought of the kitchens. If he was caught stealing again…

Julia belted her undertunic with a narrow cord. There wasn't time to get fully dressed, not with the clanking she already heard. Hopefully, she'd find him before he got into any major mischief.

'Bato? Here, boy,' she called as loudly as she dared.

She ran down the stairs and peeped into the large underground kitchen. Several rabbits hung on the far wall and a large piece of meat sat alongside an array of cakes and buns on the counter, waiting for the oven to get hot enough. No sign of the dog, just the back of the kitchen boy as he relit the stove. Julia let out a sigh of relief. Bato was safe from the cook.

Within a heartbeat, relief turned to panic. What if the dog had gone into the wrong bedroom? And licked Sabina's hand? Julia raced up the stairs, taking them two at a time.

Her hand twitched on her stepmother's door handle. Bato would never go in there. He had more sense than that, surely. Her stomach knotted.

She opened the door a crack.

All was peace with only the faint sounds of snores. She closed the door with a click, and tried to puzzle out where Bato could be.

The door to the guest bedroom lay slightly ajar. Julia's breath caught as she thought of the man lying asleep in there. What did he wear in bed—his tunic or nothing? Her fists clenched as she tried to rid her mind of the thought.

She placed her ear against the door, hesitating with her hand on the doorknob until she heard the telltale thump of Bato's tail.

She peered in and whispered, 'Bato, come here, boy.'

Bato looked at her from his place on the bottom of the bed, but refused to move.

Julia opened the door wider and snapped her fingers.

'Bato, now, come before the household wakes up.'

Bato stretched, leapt off the bed and started to move towards her, slowly.

Julia released her breath. Minerva was with her. She'd get Bato back to her room before anyone noticed…and provide an apology to Valens when she saw him later that day, should he mention it.

She screwed up her face. No doubt, he'd mention it in some sort of joke. Not content with leaving her flask behind, she had sent her dog as an excuse to get to know him better. Her cheeks burned.

'Come on, Bato,' she whispered as the dog stopped in the middle of an ornate bedside mat, sitting down to scratch his left ear.

He had to get out of there now!

Julia crouched low and started to crawl across the floor towards the dog, making soft encouraging sounds in the back of her throat as the skirt of her undertunic bunched up around her knees.

'Is there a problem?' Valens's low rumble resounded in her ears. 'I hope I haven't disturbed you.'

Julia froze, hand outstretched, knee on top of the central tiger motif on the mosaic-tiled floor. She glanced to her right and saw Valens standing, arms lifted as if he had been in the middle of an exercise session. If she had thought his tunic short yesterday, this one left little to the imagination.

And his feet were bare.

Her eyes traced the outline of his leg. The full length, from ankle to calf to thigh, was exposed. Her mouth went dry. Her heart started to thump in her ears as she realised her night-time imaginings had not been vivid enough. Reality was much more…

'No, no, you didn't disturb me,' she gasped out, thinking what a lie that was. Of course, he disturbed her. Even his scent—sandalwood and something else—this morning did strange things to her insides. 'My dog somehow seems to have ended up in your bed…I mean your room. I was trying to get him out.'

She scrambled to her feet, wishing she had more covering her body than her thin linen undertunic that she should have replaced a year ago and tried to smooth it lower. She should have thought about their guest, taken the time to get properly dressed, to do her hair and put her face on. There was nothing for it except to pretend she wasn't embarrassed. She lifted her chin.

'He came in during the night,' Valens said with a shrug, 'and went straight to sleep on the bed. I assumed it was where he always slept. The thought crossed my mind that this might be your room.'

At the sound of Valens's voice, Bato the traitor

padded over to Valens and laid his head against his legs. Valens reached down and scratched behind Bato's ears.

'It's the guest bedroom. Mine is two doors down the corridor,' Julia said, forcing the words out as she stared at Bato and Valens, her attention caught by the way Valens's fingers stroked the dog's fur. 'I have no idea why he is behaving in such a fashion. Normally he is devoted to me and is very wary of men. He refuses to let my father touch him.'

'Perhaps he knows an animal lover when he sees one. The dog I had as a boy used to like his ears scratched in the same fashion.'

Again, their eyes met and held. Julia felt a curl of warmth start in her belly. She had to get away from here, or she'd end up in his arms, behaving like the worst female supporter and demanding he share her bed.

Some day when they met, she would be poised and not off balance. Right now, she was conscious of the cold stone from the mosaic floor against her bare feet, her hair falling to her shoulders, and the fact that her undertunic, despite her efforts, only reached her mid-calf.

She watched his fingers stroke Bato's ears in the same way a starving man watched his first meal in weeks being prepared. She dug her nails into her palms, attempting to rid her mind of the image of his long fingers touching her.

'I am terribly sorry about—' She gestured to Bato, who now lolled his head against Valens's leg.

'It's quite all right.' His hand paused. His eyes stared straight into hers. 'Bato and I are friends. I enjoyed the company. Until I became a gladiator, I had a dog. It made a welcome change to have one sleeping at the bottom of the bed. I hadn't thought you'd be worried or I'd have sent him back to you.'

'I don't want Bato to make a nuisance of himself,' Julia said, snapping her fingers, hoping Bato would come to her so she could bury her burning cheeks into his soft fur. 'My stepmother is not overly fond of animals. She has threatened to send him away if he is caught doing anything untoward.'

Julia knew she ought to go. She ought to think of the scandal if she was caught in his bedroom dressed like this. No one, particularly not her father and stepmother, would accept the innocent explanation. It was an innocent explanation.

She had no desire to taste his mouth…

Her feet stayed rooted to the spot and her eyes refused to look anywhere except at his lips.

'That says it all,' Valens said. 'You can tell a lot about a person by the way they treat their animals.'

'I always think so.' She bent down and held out to her arms to Bato. 'I think this dog has bothered you enough. I don't want to impose.'

'He's welcome any time.' His voice dropped and his eyes seemed to imply there was something more.

Julia returned his smile and then shifted uneasily. Did he mean her as well as Bato? She smoothed a lock of hair back. She ought to go, but something held her there, pinned under his gaze. Her stomach knotted so much it hurt. She wanted the conversation to continue, but her words kept slipping away or else sounded inane. She refused to stand there like a mute gazing adoringly into a god's face.

'What are you doing up so early and dressed?' she blurted out, then wished she had kept silent. She turned her face towards the vine-leaf fresco so her blush was hidden. Always she said the wrong thing. She made it sound as if she expected to discover him naked!

'Training,' Valens said, withdrawing a royal blue wool cloak and a pair of sandals from his trunk. He fastened the cloak around his neck and proceeded to tie his sandals, lacing them around his calves. 'The morning session begins at dawn, but I like to arrive early in order to stretch properly. I was about to leave when you opened the door.'

'Do you know the way to the front door?' she said impulsively.

Immediately she mentally groaned. How transparent. Less than a day since meeting this man she had started to throw herself at him. He was probably certain now she had sent Bato to him. He looked at her with a quirked eyebrow and an amused smile on his face.

He did think that! Oh, help.

Julia swallowed hard and plunged on.

'The villa is a bit of a labyrinth, in case you hadn't noticed. It started off quite small, but successive owners have added to it.'

A babbling brook, that was what she was. Julia wished he'd say something. She twisted a lock of her hair around her forefinger and tried to think of how to recover. So far, in their short acquaintance she had tumbled into him, denied him a room and set her dog on him. She had her runaway tongue to blame if he thought her touched in the head. Julia realised with a jolt that she wanted him to think more of her than that. She wanted him to like her, to be attracted to her in the same way she was attracted to him.

'I noticed that,' Valens said, his voice flowing over her jangled nerves like a balm. 'Perhaps you'd be good enough to show me the way. It will save me getting lost or having to find one of the servants.'

Words of apology died on Julia's lips. He wanted to spend time with her.

With the next breath, ice washed through her veins. He had probably accepted the offer because he needed to leave quickly before his training began, before he had to ask her politely but firmly to leave.

He was trying to let her down gently, behaving as a guest should towards the daughter of the house.

'As it will save time, it will be my pleasure.' She swept out of the room with her head held high, eyes firmly fixed on the hanging lamp in the corridor.

His sandalwood scent enveloped her, holding her as surely as if she was in his arms. Julia felt some beads of sweat begin to gather on her forehead as she concentrated on putting one foot in front of the other.

'If you walk quickly, I'll lose you,' he said and tucked her arm in his.

Every nerve sizzled where her bare skin brushed his. Julia swallowed hard. Her whole body tingled from his nearness.

'It is easy to find your way, once you know how to go.'

Valens watched Julia's face as they walked along. This morning, her dark hair curled softly about her shoulders. No need to wonder at the outline of her curves. The thin off-white tunic clung in all the right places. He felt his body harden at the sight of it moulding to her calves as she walked.

He watched the way her body moved as she strode down the corridor, intent on showing him the way out, a way he already knew.

Despite his resolve to forget her, her face and her voice had haunted his thoughts last night and he had

had a dozen conversations with her in his head. He watched her sleep-kissed mouth, and the curve of her slender throat, and wondered where he should begin.

In many ways, it would be easier if she went into worship mode. He was used to that. He could ignore it. He was used to women offering him their bodies.

He wanted more from her than just a quick meaningless meeting. He enjoyed talking to her as an equal, being himself and not Valens the Gladiator for once. He'd almost forgotten he had an existence before the arena, before the spectacle of life and death. Only in nightmares did he remember.

'How much training do you do?' she asked as they started down the stairs.

'In the run up to the games?' Valens replied, relieved to be talking about something he knew, something he could discuss with authority. If he kept the conversation on training, he'd be less inclined to notice her lips or the way her thin tunic hinted at her thighs. His body demanded to know what she felt like against him.

'That's right—in the run up to the games.' She smoothed a lock of hair from her face and revealed more of her creamy neck.

Valens averted his eyes, concentrating on the middle distance.

'We're training nearly all the time. Making sure

the moves flow like water. There is more to a gladiatorial contest than simply waving a sword about. Each move has a countermove. The public are there for the spectacle, to see the danger of controlled combat. They want more than two amateurs hacking at each other. They'd sooner watch a spinning contest than that.'

Her laugh rang out at his rather feeble quip. He risked another peek at her face and found his eyes glued to her mouth as her floral perfume tickled his nose. He wanted this woman, he realised, with a great fierce longing. He wanted her in a way he had not wanted a woman for a long time. He reached out a hand to draw her towards him.

'Will you be training here or elsewhere?' Her voice drew him back from the abyss and his outstretched hand dropped to his side. 'I know my father hoped to watch some of your sessions. He was a keen amateur gladiator in his youth. Or at least that's what he said to Mettalius Scipio last night.'

Her innocent words felt like a sword plunging into his body. He knew why he could not have her, why women like her were for ever closed to him. Every nerve in Valens's body tensed and he waited for the next blow Fate had in store for him. Would she now confide how much she cared for Mettalius? Her hopes and dreams for the future as a senator's wife?

A surge of anger went through his body.

An intelligent woman like Julia was wasted on a man like Mettalius Scipio, a man who could barely move his feet and his sword at the same time.

'Is your betrothed a keen follower of the sport?' he asked and strove to keep his voice light, to not show how the man affected him.

'Please, he is anything but that. It is my stepmother's fancy.' Julia place a hand on his arm, her face turned up towards him with an earnest expression. 'I haven't divorced one feckless fish fancier to be saddled with another one, whatever Sabina thinks. Not without a fight. For one thing, the man smells of garlic.'

'I apologise. I misunderstood.' Valens noticed his heart beat faster.

He allowed his eyes to feast on her lips. The first faint light of dawn appeared in the sky, bathing everything in its soft glow. With each passing breath, Julia's face seemed softer, her lips more enticing.

Mettalius was not her choice.

He should be well on his way to practice by now, but her denial kept running through Valens's brain. He found it impossible to move from her side and refused to think of the consequences.

'Apology accepted.' She inclined her head, but her eyes glittered defiantly. 'To answer your question— I believe he considers himself to be an ardent supporter of the games. The way he was going on, you'd think it was his troupe of gladiators that were appearing in Rome.'

'Did he say anything about me?'

Julia stopped and peeped up at him through her long lashes. 'I could tease you and say no, but it would be unfair. He has seen you fight and was very impressed, inspired. You are technically one of best Thracians he has ever seen. Training-manual perfect, I believe he said.'

'I'm honoured to have such a distinguished senator as Mettalius supporting me.'

'Mettalius isn't very—' She stopped mid-sentence and gave a laugh, putting a hand over her lips. 'Oh, you said you knew him. I'd forgotten.'

'I am honoured,' Valens protested, but as soon as he said it he gave a deep laugh, joining in with Julia's infectious giggle. 'I may have exaggerated a bit. I will bow to your superior knowledge of the man. Senatorial support can be invaluable in the arena.'

'Why?'

'The patrons of the games are more often than not senators and quite literally have the power of life or death over a gladiator. It is good to have one or two on your side. For one thing, it increases the appearance fee and makes death less likely.'

He watched Julia's eyes sober. Should he have

dressed the truth in a polite series of lies for her? The patron of games held the life of each fighter in his fist. The thumb turned up or down was all that mattered at the end of a fight. It was all he looked for as he listened to the screams of the crowd.

'Better a senator than a dictator,' she said, with a small tremble in her voice. She turned her body away from him, bowed her head and seemed to gather her thoughts. Immediately she turned back and met his gaze full on. 'I may have only been a child, but I remember Sulla's rein of terror when we all became like gladiators, living on the whim of Sulla. In the end the Republic was restored and long may it last.'

Valens wanted to reach out and enfold her in his arms, to hold her and tell her that everything would remain as it had always been except for those years under Sulla. Instead he tightened his grip on his belt. He needed no distractions from his work. Worrying about Julia and the traumas she had been through was not going to help him win his next bout in the arena. He straightened his shoulders and strode more purposefully down the corridor, ignoring the questions in her eyes.

'Long life and prosperity to the Senate and people of Rome, I'll agree with that,' Valens said, when he had his breathing under control and they had entered the main courtyard. 'With men such as Julius Caesar, I have no doubt the Republic will endure for another seven hundred years. He is a man who knows the value of putting on good entertainment for the crowd. With the crowd on his side, who knows how far he can go?'

'My father has certainly found favour with his patronage, but Rome's politics are worse than the arena, I think. Many have risen to the top, only to fall back. Just look at my great-uncle—Marius—lauded as the saviour of Rome with honour after honour heaped on him, only to be reviled as a traitor and hounded to his death by Sulla.'

'Caesar is a prudent gambler. He will keep his feet.'

'I hope so. He is the best hope the Julian family has had in generations. We all need him and his good will.'

Valens closed his eyes and remembered when those words had been said about him—the time when he had been his family's best hope.

It was what made the fall so much harder—the knowledge he had let his entire family down. And the men who depended on him to keep them safe. His father had been right to turn his back on him, not to pay the pirate ransom.

He gave his head a shake as a tendril of Julia's hair caught his attention.

The cock crowed and Valens knew he needed to leave.

He'd stayed too long as it was. For once, the other gladiators would be there before him, practising, dedicating their lives to the games and forgetting they had ever had another life.

'I'm sure he has been a good patron to your father,' he said quietly, 'but he will be less than pleased with me if I arrive late to this training session.'

At Valens's words, Julia started, and looked at her hands. She had swayed towards him, her lips parted, convinced he was about to take her into his arms. Confusion swept over her.

'Absolutely, you must go.' She brushed her hair back with her hand. The simple act seemed to restore some normality to her thoughts. She drew a deep calming breath, taking in the damp earth smell of morning. 'How foolish of me! Keeping you here asking questions and prattling on about the Republic and its future when you are needed elsewhere.'

She turned to go, keeping a firm grip on Bato's collar. She would get over this attraction, this silly crush. She was a grown woman, not a girl in her early teens with her hair falling about her shoulders and dolls lining her bedroom shelves. She had dedicated her dolls to Venus the day she had married Lucius and left her childhood behind.

Her reaction was a normal one to kindness—that was all. Nothing more serious. In a day's time, she'd wonder what she ever saw in him. A gladiator, one of the *infamis*. A man outside polite society. A man whose profession was death. Someone who more than likely could not read or write. Even as she thought the words, she knew they were a lie fit for Sabina.

'Julia,' he said thickly and put his hand on her elbow. She felt the sparks sizzle up her arm as the attraction started to ignite in her. 'I… I've enjoyed speaking with you. Thank you.'

She halted, felt her grip loosen on Bato's collar, but kept her eyes straight ahead, focused on the fountain in the middle of the courtyard, refusing to look at the planes of his face. The warmth in the pit of her stomach grew with each thud of her heartbeat.

'It was my pleasure. Thank you for taking care of Bato,' she said, managing to keep her voice steady, ignoring the way his fingers ran down the bare skin of her arm, drew small circles on the inside of her wrist.

Then she met his gaze, and her look tumbled into his, captured, unable to do anything but stare back. She tried to form a witty sentence, but the words died on her lips at the sight of his intent expression. His face was so close, she could feel his warm breath fanning her cheek. This time he had to kiss her.

He leant forward and his lips brushed hers, lingered. A whisper of a kiss like the finest wool caressing her body. She wanted more. Her body demanded she have more. She swayed towards him, allowed him to gather her body in his arms and his lips claimed possession.

Her breasts brushed against his hard muscular chest, as she arched closer. Her lips opened and she tasted the sweetness of his mouth.

Chapter Four

The kiss sent shivers down Julia's spine. Valens's tongue glided over her lower lip and then touched the parting of her mouth before retreating. In her ears, she heard the thump of a heart—hers or his. Her body moulded itself into his hardness. It felt as if nothing had existed before and nothing would exist after.

There was only his mouth against hers.

His head lifted and he rubbed his thumb along her kiss-swollen lips, sending a fresh wave of sensation through her.

For a heartbeat, neither said anything. Gradually she noticed small things—the damp ground against her feet, the way his breath fanned her cheek, the touch of his hand against her back holding her, the slam of a door far away, but she found it impossible to tear her gaze from Valens's. Every fibre of her being wanted to taste his lips again. She lifted her face towards his.

The cockerel crowed a second time and broke the spell.

He stepped back from her, smoothing a lock of hair off her forehead as he did so. The cold morning air rushed between them, cooling her body. Julia swallowed hard and tried to gather her thoughts. Modesty demanded she object, but the words refused to come.

'Why did you kiss me?' she whispered into the silence and ran her tongue experimentally over her lips. They felt full and thoroughly kissed. Kissed in a way she had never been kissed before. The way she dreamt kisses felt like.

Before she had suspected something was wrong with her for detesting Lucius's invasions of her mouth, but now she knew—with the right person, kissing was another matter entirely.

'For luck,' he said with a lopsided smile. 'We'll be training later at Caesar's compound, if your father wants to watch.'

He lifted the latch of the heavy door and was gone before she could answer him.

She leant her cheek against the cool stone wall of the villa, waiting for the pounding of her heart to subside, reliving each movement, each word. The faint scent of his bath oil lingered—sandalwood mixed with something indefinably masculine. She knew hardly anything about this man, but her whole being cried out for his touch. She shivered as she ran her hand along her arm where his fingers had rested, reliving the experience.

The cockerel crowed a third time.

Julia put her hands to her cheeks. What was the matter with her? Standing here in the courtyard, half-naked. Had she taken leave of her senses? Despite the early hour, she could have been spotted. She could hear Sabina's squawks for hot water, and knew if someone had seen her, the betrothal to Mettalius would have happened before a toga had time to dry.

The next time they met, she'd have to make sure that Valens knew and understood that she was not one of those bored women of Baiae, the notorious beach resort near Naples where the wealthy went to play and party, ripe for the picking. Her reputation was of paramount importance. She was a sober, well-adjusted Roman divorcée, not some sex-crazed glad-iator supporter. She tried saying the words aloud, but, somehow, her mind kept returning to the kiss as her tongue traced the imprint of his mouth on her lips.

When Valens reached the Julian compound in the centre of Subura, the Roman sky was filled with streaks from the rose-gold dawn. Already, the narrow maze of streets teemed with men making their morning rounds to their patrons. The suffocating atmosphere of waiting men and high-rise tenements gave way to space as he entered the Julian compound with its tinkling fountains, gardens and range of ancestral statues.

The sound of wood clashing and bodies hitting the ground resounded in Valens's ears as he bent down to untie his sandals in the main courtyard.

Practice had already started.

He swore under his breath. He should have made the journey quicker, but had wanted to savour the feeling Julia's lips against his and the way her body had moulded to him and the honey-scented taste of her mouth—sweet and clear like a cool drink of spring water as her tongue teased his. A breath more and he'd have found an excuse to miss the practice. The thought· shook him and he concentrated on untying the knot in his sandal.

'You're late.' The gravelly tones of his usual sparring partner were unmistakable. 'We've been at this for a full hour already.'

The other gladiator wiped the sweat from his battered face with a linen towel as he approached where Valens knelt. His fair hair was plastered against his head. Valens moved his sandals to prevent them from being dripped on by Tigris's dark blue tunic.

'Nobody informed me of the change of time.'

'I find that hard to believe.' Tigris gave Valens's

shoulder a playful swat with his towel. 'You always know everything in this school, before it happens!'

'Enough of that! I am not a god.'

'You should try telling that to your legion of supporters. Would that I had as many people sighing for me! Everywhere I go in this city, that disreputable figure of yours is on sale. I have the sales of my own figure to consider.'

Valens reached out and grabbed the towel before Tigris could swat him a second time.

Tigris and he had entered Strabo's school together. Ever since they had fought each other to a standstill on the second day, Tigris had become the closet thing Valens had to a true friend. Thankfully, although Tigris wore a slightly different style of armour, it was only a friendly rivalry. They would never meet in the ring, would never be locked in mortal combat with each other.

'Tell me—what is the reason you are late?'

'As far as I knew when I left yesterday afternoon, everything was set to begin on the first hour,' Valens explained.

'Strabo sent one of the second halls with a message for me.' Tigris's face looked puzzled and he scratched a scab on his arm. 'Perhaps Strabo felt he didn't have to tell you. You are always the first one to practice.'

'But not today,' Valens said without elaborating, hoping that Tigris would drop it.

'And why not?' Tigris asked and raised an eyebrow. 'Have you found some Roman bird to feather your nest?'

Valens looked at Tigris, wondering if he should respond to the jibe. His friend's grin widened under his gaze and Tigris held up his hands before he continued.

'No, I forgot your creed: nothing is allowed to interfere with your work—not servants, animals and certainly not women.'

'I see no reason to leave behind a grieving wife and two fatherless children.'

Valens watched Tigris's face sober and knew he had hit a raw nerve—something they refused to agree about. Valens tightened his jaw. He would not apologise.

Straightening, he handed his cloak and sandals to a waiting servant. He would practise as he always fought—barefoot. When the time came, it was easier to stay upright. He'd seen too many meet their death wearing sandals as they slipped on the blood and dust in the arena.

'There is more to life than death,' Tigris said quietly, his eyes accusing Valens.

'Maia is already spoken for.' Valens gave Tigris a clap on the shoulder. 'Why should I settle for anyone but the best?'

A bit of mild flattery should divert the conversation away from his private life and towards Tigris's favourite subject—his wife and twin boys.

'Ah, now Maia is a grand woman.' Tigris gave a huge smile. 'I'm the lucky one. Only the Fates know what lies ahead for each of us, and when I die, I know my time on earth has been a little better because her and our children. You should try to find someone like her, Valens, someone who cares about you as a man.'

Tigris had married Maia a year ago just after he became a gladiator of the first hall and took every opportunity he could to advocate the joys of sharing your life with someone. Normally, Valens let him prattle on, but today his words bothered him, revealed an emptiness in his life that he thought he'd dealt with. He found he envied Tigris his joy in Maia.

What would it be like to wake every morning to a woman like Julia? To have her sleep-kissed eyes be the first thing to greet him each morning and the last thing he saw each night? To sleep with his limbs intertwined with hers? Valens shook his head and tried to get his thoughts away from the girl. There was something in the air in this city and his preoccupation with Julia was a symptom.

His past was sending tenacious ropes as surely as his usual type of opponent, the *rentarius* who casts his net in the arena, seeking to ensnare him in its coils.

He should never have come, avoided the promises of a large fortune and perhaps a wooden sword before one of the largest crowds the world had ever seen.

Valens gave a wry smile and glanced at the lion tattoo on his forearm. The choice had been taken from him. Strabo had wanted him to go. He was a slave, a slave who had considerable property of his own, but he belonged to Strabo. He bore Strabo's mark.

'That may be so, my friend, but why take the chance?' Valens gave a bitter laugh. 'I could end up with someone like Hylas's wife whose legs open on command to any man with a bit of sand on his feet and a sword in his hand.'

His words came out more forcefully than he intended. Who was he trying to convince—Tigris or his own heart?

'There is time enough for living after I have won back my wooden sword, my *rudius*.'

'You sound positive you are going to win one,' Tigris replied. 'I can count on the fingers of one hand the number of gladiators who have won their *rudius* in the last seven years. The tight-fisted patrons have no desire to part with their cash for such things. Although they are quick enough to condemn a man to death and pay that fee if the crowd bays for it.'

'I am a gladiator of the first hall. My record is beyond compare. If not me, who else?' Valens said with a wry smile that hid his inner determination. He had to win one. He'd go on fighting until he won. He wanted to leave the profession honourably—and that meant either the *rudius* or death. To retire or purchase his way out was not an option.

Tigris gave a cough. 'Speaking of wooden swords, they are one of the reasons Strabo started early. He wants the testing ceremony for *tiros* over and done with by three hours, so that Caesar can inspect his troupe at four hours.'

Valens stared at Tigris. He was joking, surely. Valens had been there when the contracts were drawn up. Strabo had been quite insistent on when inspections were to be allowed. He did not want the training interfered with by well-meaning amateurs. And Valens agreed whole-heartedly with the assessment. The morning was for training, the afternoon was for exhibitions, ceremonies and presentations.

'But it was in the contract—no inspections before five hours,' he said, ignoring Tigris's jerk of his head.

'Caesar wanted to make a special presentation to the troupe. I've made an exception,' a gravelly voice behind him rumbled. 'You are late, Valens.'

Valens turned to see Strabo, his squint more pronounced than usual and his scarred face like thunder. Before starting his school ten years ago, Strabo had been a gladiator, and was rumoured to have defeated

Spartacus, the rebel gladiator, in the arena, to win his wooden sword. Now instead of his shield and short sword, Strabo carried a scroll in one hand and a beaker of Flavian wine in the other.

Valens clenched his jaw. He refused to apologise for being late. Had practice started when it was supposed to, he'd have been on time or at the very latest he'd have just missed the start of the warm-up session. Strabo should have sent word.

They stared at each other, neither giving way. Strabo waved Tigris away.

'You're late, Valens,' Strabo repeated. 'It will be a thirty *denarii* fine for you unless you have a reasonable excuse.'

'I understood the starting time to be about now.'

'Did you get the note I sent you last evening?'

'No scroll arrived for me. Or none that I was given.' Valens looked at the leader of his gladiator school with a steady eye.

Strabo frowned and clapped his hands. A servant appeared instantly at his side.

'Did I or did I not send a scroll to Valens yesterday evening?'

'You did, Master. Aquilia took it along with his.'

'Is Aquilia here?'

'Yes, Master Strabo. He is practising in the centre ring.'

'There you see, Aquilia is here and you are late. You should have offered an excuse while I gave the chance. Next time you check the time and not merely assume. I was about to send guards to fetch you and bring you here, in chains if necessary.' Strabo shook his head. 'I hate to do this to you, Valens, but it will be a fine. First-Hall gladiators should set an example and be on time.'

Without waiting for an answer, Strabo strode away. Valens picked up a blunt sword and started to fence with Tigris.

'What's bothering him?' Valens asked, staring after the *lanistra*. 'My lateness was an innocent mistake, an inevitable consequence of the housing arrangements.'

'Strabo probably had a thousand problems and you weren't here to solve them. You got off lightly with thirty *denarii*. He has already sentenced two second-hall gladiators to whippings and one *tiro* to the hole in the ground.'

'Who was the *tiro*?' Valens asked, mentally running through the list of gladiators who were set to face their first real challenge in the arena.

'Leoparda. Apparently he argued back to Aquilia, refusing to act as live bait for Aquilia's net practice. Aquilia demanded Strabo take action.'

Leoparda. Valens knew the name—a Nubian who moved with the grace of a cat. He had the potential, but being confined to a cell with barely enough room to move your legs did something to a man. Valens well remembered the rat-infested pit he'd been confined in during his captivity.

'Strabo has never resorted to the pit for such a trivial offence before. Who is this Aquilia character who suddenly runs the show?'

'He's on loan from another school. A *rentarius* of the first hall, one of the few.'

Valens looked to where Tigris pointed and cold sweat formed on the back of his neck. He tightened his grip on his sword.

The emblem of Alexander was emblazoned on Aquilia's right forearm and he strode around the practice yard as if he was striding on the deck of his ship. Valens's stomach clenched. There was no need to hear the oddly high-pitched voice that floated on the breeze or see the distinctive hooked nose. He knew instinctively who Aquilia had been in his previous existence—the pirate responsible for Valens's capture.

'How the mighty have fallen,' Valens remarked, forcing his arm shield to meet Tigris's next blow.

'Do you know him?'

Tigris paused in his attack. Valens launched a counter-attack and sent Tigris's sword spinning to the sand. Valens reached down and retrieved it.

'The last time I saw Aquilia,' he said, handing the sword back with a flourish, 'he sold me to the African slave trader who sold me to Strabo. He was a pirate then.'

Tigris whistled. 'How the mighty have fallen indeed.'

Almost as if Aquilia could hear them talking, he turned and stared at them. Valens stared back. If it pleased the gods to match them in a bout, then he would take his revenge for the sixteen members of his patrol who had died in the pirate's pit.

'We had best to get to practising,' Valens said, deliberately turning from Aquilia without acknowledging him.

'So you are not going to tell me what happened this morning? And why there is a whiff of perfume about you?'

'You are imaging things, Tigris,' Valens said and blocked Tigris's next parry. 'The point is to me, I believe.'

As they squared off for the next round, Valens found himself thinking about Julia, the way her hair had felt under his hands and the softness of her honey-scented skin. Thirty *denarii* was not too steep a price to pay for the kiss, the taste of her mouth. If he had to do it again, and had known about the change in time, he'd still have stayed for the kiss.

The thought terrified him.

* * *

The spindle bounced across the floor as Julia's thread broke for the fourth time that morning. Years of practice generally ensured that her thread was smooth and straight. But today her mind kept returning to the time she spent with Valens in the early morning light and the thread kept breaking.

'Bato, drop,' she commanded as the dog started to nose the spindle.

Bato gave the spindle one more sniff and retreated back to his place by her feet. Ignoring Sabina's filthy look, Julia stood up and retrieved the spindle. She undid a bit of thread, fluffing up the strands, pulled some wool from her distaff, and started the spindle spinning again.

'You seem to have lost your touch, Julia,' Sabina said. 'You should have remembered that your father is not as wealthy as Lucius and you would have to help with the spinning.'

'I spun when I was married to Lucius,' Julia said, biting back the sarcastic words about Sabina's clothes, all of which were of the finest wool and linen. 'The wool doesn't seem to have been carded very well. That's all.'

Julia rolled her eyes. As if the thought of spinning would have put her off divorcing that misbegotten worm. Spinning was far from a loathsome task when put in the proper context. Julia tried to make the thread smooth, enjoying the feel of the wool against her fingers, the steady rhythm of spindle turning. The sound of Bato's snoring filled the room.

'That's about all I have time for.' Sabina started to put her spinning away. Julia noted Sabina had done about half of what she had in the same amount of time. 'I promised to meet some friends at the baths. Flavia may have heard more about the affair Lucia Pulia is having with her porter. The one I was speaking about yesterday. You are welcome to join us, Julia.'

'I think I will stay here and get on with my spinning. After all, you did say we needed new blankets.'

'As you wish, but remember I did offer.' Sabina swept from the room.

Julia breathed in the silence. Immediately, it was broken by the sound of doors slamming. Julia was unable to keep her heart from leaping. *Valens?*

'Julia, I have returned from the glorious south,' Claudia said, bursting into the room in a cloud of expensive perfume with gold bracelets tinkling musically on each arm. She reached down and gave Bato a scratch behind his left ear. The dog responded by thumping his tail vigorously against the floor. 'How has this scamp been? Found any more good ham bones, Bato?'

'Claudia, don't encourage him. I am trying to very

hard to forget that incident.' Julia felt her heart rate return to normal. 'Claudia, when did you get back? I thought you were still in Pompeii—soaking up the sun and enjoying the sights.'

'You must be joking!' Claudia's throaty laugh rang out. 'Me stay in Pompeii when possibly the largest gladiatorial bout ever known to womankind—or mankind, for that matter—is about to take place in Rome? Do you know how much flesh will be on display at the opening ceremony? When those men ride those chariots into the ground with their armour gleaming and their muscles bulging…'

'That's what the main attraction of the games is, and here I thought you enjoyed the contest.' Julia gave the spindle a vigorous twist, lengthening the thread with an expert hand.

Claudia tossed the end of her sky-blue veil over her shoulder and tilted her chin upwards.

'I am only displaying a healthy widow's attitude towards the games. You have to admit gladiators are better looking than the majority of senators.'

'That is not hard to do, Claudia.'

They both laughed and Julia reflected how much she had missed Claudia these past six weeks. Her friend leant forward and stopped the spindle.

'Put the spinning away. It's distracting me,' she said with a wave of her be-ringed hand. 'I want to talk to you, and you might be able to talk and spin, but I can't listen with that thing going round and round. What does Sabina find it impossible to do without this time?'

'Blankets for the beds,' Julia said, breaking the thread and wrapping it around the base of the spindle. 'We apparently need more and Sabina is determined the women of the house participate, to set an example for the servants.'

'I gather Sabina is not here, helping out as it were.'

'She talks a good spindle,' Julia said with as straight a face as she could manage. 'When did you get back?'

'Last night, and the less said about the journey, the better. All roads may lead to Rome, but do they have to be so rocky?' Claudia leant forward and touched Julia on the knee. 'Enough about me. Do tell your news. Have you managed to avoid the dreaded Mettalius or has Sabina's augur struck again? I need to know all.'

'We have a gladiator staying with us.' Julia kept her voice casual as she ended recounting her activities of the last few weeks. 'Valens the Thracian.'

Claudia leant forward, her eyes widening. 'I had heard that Caesar had housed the gladiators with some of his clients, but I'd completely and utterly forgotten your father might be one of them. You got Valens. Lucky, lucky you.'

'What do you know about Valens?' Julia asked, making an effort to lean back, not forwards. To emphasise how casual the question was, she started to wind the thread on the spindle.

Claudia gave her a long considering look with narrowed eyes. Julia's hands faltered and she felt the blush begin to creep higher on her face.

'I take it,' Claudia said with a twinkle in her eye, 'given your lack of interest in anything remotely sporting, you aren't interested in a blow-by-blow account of his prowess in the arena.'

'Claudia, he's staying with us and I want to be able to converse with him at supper and so on.' Julia made an expansive gesture with her hands and sent the spindle crashing to the floor. 'I was curious, that's all. For example, where is he from? That sort of thing. Just in case I need topics for conversation because, as you know, my knowledge of gladiatorial combat is pitiful.'

Claudia raised a perfectly plucked eyebrow. A tiny smile played on her lips as she reached down to pat Bato.

'I have had the pleasure of seeing Valens and his legs, Julia. You had better come with me to the Julian compound. Caesar has invited me to a presentation ceremony. You might as well see all the gladiators before you settle on one to cheer for.'

The main courtyard of the Julian compound overflowed with people. Julia spotted white-togaed senators freely mixing with the short-tuniced tradesmen. There were a surprising number of women, senators' wives included, displaying more flesh than Julia considered necessary.

Despite arriving before the ceremony started, Julia and Claudia were forced to stand at the back beside a life-sized statue of Venus, the patron goddess and supposed founder of the Julian family.

Although Caesar's voice rang out clearly across the courtyard, Julia had difficulty making out more than a shoulder or the top of a head. She kept tight hold of Bato. Had she realised what the crowd would be like, she'd have left him at home, locked securely in her room. Claudia had clambered on to the statue's plinth for a better view and now stood on her tiptoes with one arm around Venus's waist.

'What exactly is Caesar giving out?' Julia asked, attempting to peer around the bright red parasol of the matron standing in front of them for the tenth time. Every time she thought she had a good view, the parasol shifted.

'Armour—silver-plated armour. The gladiators are going to look magnificent in the arena.'

'Is this usual?' Julia struggled to make herself heard over the noise of the crowd. Bato cowered against her legs as another enormous roar went up. She reached down and gave his ears a stroke.

'No, no. It is the first time I have heard of it.

Normally a gladiator fights in whatever his school provides.' Claudia balanced on one foot. 'I think it will be your gladiator's turn to receive his armour now. They have almost finished with the gladiators of the first hall. Do you want to have a look?'

'Bato is with me,' Julia replied doubtfully, but her heart skipped a beat at the thought of seeing Valens, even if he failed to see her. But she wished Claudia would stop calling Valens her gladiator.

'Hurry and climb up. Bato will stay where he is told. He's a good and clever dog.'

'He can be a scamp.'

Claudia climbed down, took the lead from Julia and gave her a gentle push towards the statue. 'I'll keep an eye on him. See, I'll stand right beside him.'

Faced with Claudia's stern face and her own growing desire to see Valens, Julia gave in. She motioned for Bato to stay and then scrambled up on the plinth. Rather than holding on to Venus's waist, she clutched her upraised arm and looked out over the crowd. The raised podium was clearly visible now.

A thrill went through her, making her knees feel weak as Valens mounted the steps with firm footsteps. A faint breeze ruffled his dark hair as he strode across the stage. Julia could see his muscles rippling in the sun as he walked. He looked every inch in charge as Caesar handed him his armour. His size made Caesar seem small.

Here was an athlete in his prime, the very embodiment of what a gladiator should be like—strong, rugged and with the ability to hold the crowd in the palm of his hand.

The crowd hushed as Caesar handed Valens his equipment. Julia heard the lone rattle of a scroll being rolled up on the other side of the compound. In the quiet, Valens held a shining sword and helmet aloft and the cheers rang out, screaming his name.

'Valens seems to have the support of the crowd,' she said, listening as the cheers and shouts of approval continued long after Valens had stepped back into the line of gladiators.

'That he does, and if the crowd is for you, it makes things much easier in the arena,' Claudia replied. 'He might win the *rudius* he was denied at Pompeii. It was hard to credit that the patron of those particular games in the cradle of the gladiatorial tradition should be that pinched-purse to ignore the wishes of the crowd, but Crispanus was. No need to consult the soothsayers. He will lose the next election because of it.'

After the noise had died down, the commentator announced the next gladiator—Aquilia. A polite round of applause. But before the first ripple of applause had died, a few hoots of laughter and cat calls rang out. Julia stood on tiptoe, attempting to see where Valens had gone.

'Julia, quick, quick, tell me what you see. There seems to be a bit of a commotion on the stage. And this woman keeps moving her parasol.'

The sounds of laughter increased.

'Something happened. Valens had to go back on stage and retrieve something,' Julia said, shielding her eyes with her free hand. 'But I am too far away.'

'Julia, you have to be my eyes. Describe everything. This red parasol is a nuisance.'

'The cheering is not as loud as for Valens, but I can't see anything is seriously wrong. He's received his trident now and is stepping off the stage.'

'If you move over, I can get a better look.' Claudia scrambled up next to Julia and perched on a corner of the plinth. 'You're right—nothing, but it's Tigris now and he's one of my favourites. His legs are marvellous. I particularly like his knees.'

'Claudia, you are incorrigible,' Julia said, but made no move to get down. From where she stood, she could see part of Valens's back and a shoulder.

'I think the main attraction is over now,' Claudia said, shielding her eyes and standing one foot. 'Shall we go before we are crushed by the hordes trying to get out the door? I doubt we'll able to get near to the gladiators with this many people milling about.'

Julia looked back at the stage. The gladiators were parading in their new armour, holding their weapons aloft, and Caesar waved to the crowd with a benevolent expression. Already both men and women were pushing their way towards the gladiators. Her chances of getting near Valens were slim to none.

'Yes, of course you're right,' she said with one last look at Valens, standing in front of Caesar, as remote as any god, and climbed down from the plinth. 'There is little point in staying around.'

'I certainly didn't think it would this busy. Caesar will gain a lot of popularity with these games,' Claudia remarked. 'He will be unstoppable at the next election. I wonder which post he will stand for. Imagine what silver armour must have cost. Who do you think is funding him? Crassus?'

'I hadn't thought about it, but I guess you're right. Bato—time to go.' Julia reached down to grab Bato's collar. Empty air. She scanned around—no greying muzzle or wagging tail. Time stopped and everything went quiet. Julia swallowed hard. She snapped her fingers and gave a low whistle. No Bato.

'Claudia, Bato has gone.' Julia tried to keep her voice from panicking. There had to be a simple explanation. Silently she cursed herself for being interested in what Valens looked like on the podium.

'Gone? What do you mean gone? He's right there,

sitting like a good dog.' Claudia pointed to a now empty spot. 'I mean, he was right there. By the gown of Venus, Julia, I only took my eyes off him for an instant.'

'Oh, Claudia, what I am going to do?'

Julia twisted the end of her belt around her hand and tried to call Bato again with a whistle. This time, she made the whistle louder. Still nothing. The crowds of people started to empty from the courtyard.

'We'll have to wait for the crowd to thin a bit. And try not to worry. Have you ever known Bato not to appear eventually? He's devoted to you.'

Julia felt the squeeze as Claudia's arm went around her shoulders. The most she could manage in response was a brief smile.

'Do you think we'll find him? Claudia, I don't know what I will do if I lose that dog…'

'Don't panic, Julia. He's probably followed his belly to the kitchens. As I said let's wait until the crowd has thinned a bit and then we can find him. It's impossible to move in this anyway.'

Julia tried to ignore the pit growing in her stomach. She knew Claudia was being practical, but it wasn't her dog that was lost. Julia imagined all sorts of terrible fates for Bato.

Her lips muttered prayers, entreaties to any god that might be listening, as her eyes scanned the emptying courtyard for a trace of the dog.

Chapter Five

'Excuse me, I believe this imp belongs to you,' a now-familiar voice behind Julia said.

The rich tones seemed to bath her nerves in balm and at the same time make her insides ache. 'He decided to take part in the ceremony, much to Aquilia's displeasure. However, I caught him before he asked Caesar for his armour. I think he is a bit small to fight.'

She quickly turned, but the smile she had made sure was on her lips faded as she took in the scene.

For a heartbeat, she regarded him in his full gladiator regalia—silver breastplate hugging the contours of his chest, a grieve on his left wrist and a leather belt studded with bronze medallions over his tunic. His shining helmet emblazoned with a war scene hung from his right hand. More like a god than a man.

So different from the man she had kissed this morning and yet the same. If she'd seen him like this the first time, she wondered if she'd have found courage even to speak to him. The way he strode towards her, Bato trotting by his side, he seemed to be in command of the courtyard.

Behind him, she saw a group of labourers as well as one or two matrons she vaguely knew from the baths watching him, watching her. Bato the traitor was heeling at Valens's footsteps, gazing at him with huge adoring eyes.

'Thank you,' she said, but her voice came out no louder than a whisper. Julia swallowed hard, pressed her hands together until the knuckles shone white and tried again. 'Thank you, I was worried about him. He means so much to me.'

'I thought you might be concerned, but the scamp seemed to know where you were.'

He made a motion and Bato streaked to her side. Bato flopped down at her feet, his wet nose pushing at her sandal. Julia knelt down and buried her face into Bato's fur. She felt an enormous wave of relief wash over her. Something else stirred as she glanced up into Valens's face. Her eyes fastened on to his lips, and the memory of this morning's kiss jolted through her body.

Immediately she reburied her face. Better for Valens to think her utterly besotted with her dog than to see the bright redness of her cheeks.

'Bato, you naughty, naughty, naughty dog,' she said, holding Bato's face between her hands and looking the dog directly in his eyes. 'When you are told to stay, stay.'

'I suspect he became frightened in the crowd.' Valens's voice flowed over her like honey when it was first taken from the hive. 'I wonder that you brought him here.'

'Normally he is fine in crowds.' Julia glanced up, her eyes lingering over the perfect contours of his body, tracing the outline of his broad shoulders.

Had he held her in his arms this morning?

It seemed like a dream now. She ran her tongue over her parched lips and tried to keep her composure. Her knees were like water, but Julia forced herself to stand and look him directly in the eyes.

'I tend to take him everywhere with me that I can. Otherwise, he howls as if the harpies are chasing him, much to Sabina's displeasure.'

'Surely not this rogue?' Valens reached down and fondled Bato's ears. Bato leant towards him. 'He'd never do a thing like that.'

'If you only knew…' Julia said with a laugh.

She watched his eyes crinkle and wished she had worn her dark green gap-sleeved gown that fastened with bronze brooches at the shoulders—the one that Claudia said brought out the green flecks in her eyes.

And she could have worn it without the undertunic in this heat, revealing just a hint of her shoulder, under her shawl. Something so that she shone like the courtesan standing just beyond Valens, something so that he'd look at her with more than friendship.

The thought shook her to the core. She needed something to warn her to keep her distance before she threw herself at his feet.

It was all too easy to see now with these women milling about ogling him why he had made the mistake of yesterday. How many of them had figurines of Valens locked away in their private cupboard next to their jars of ointment, pots of white lead and caskets of wine dregs?

Julia bowed her head.

'Did you see much of the ceremony?' he asked, making no move to leave. If anything, he stood closer. 'I thought it went down rather well.'

He reached down a hand, caught her wrist, pulled her upright, then let go. Julia felt the sparks radiate upwards.

'I…I came with my friend Claudia. She is Caesar's niece.' Julia motioned to Claudia, who gave a small gasp and sank into a curtsy. 'And a great supporter of the gladiator contests, a real aficionado. She collects figurines.'

Valens raised an eyebrow and gave a slight bow. Julia wondered if her own face was as beet-red as Claudia's.

'Claudia is not of the same persuasion as you? Perhaps between us, we can convert you to the games.'

'I saw you at Pompeii three months ago,' Claudia gasped, grabbing on to Julia's arm with a vice-like grip. 'You fought magnificently. I mean, I normally support the Great Shields, but you fought so brilliantly. I loved the way you did that last slash of your sword and knocked the *renarius*'s trident away so he had to ask for mercy. I thought you deserved a *rudius* for your performance…'

'Thank you.'

Valens made a small salute with the hand holding his helmet. Almost identical to the salute he'd given at the end of the ceremony. Was it her imagination or did Valens look vaguely uncomfortable? Julia silently wished Claudia would not gush.

'Did you enjoy the presentation ceremony, Julia Antonia?' he asked when Claudia had paused for a breath.

Julia patted a stray lock of hair into place as she tried to think. She wanted to say something intelligent, but not fawning. She'd refrain from gushing.

'It was fairly impressive. Everyone should look splendid—fighting in their new armour.' Julia rolled her eyes as she listened to her voice, dripping with honey. She sounded worse than Claudia.

'Certainly for the opening parade when we ride the chariots out,' he said, his voice flowing over her again, sending tingles down her spine, 'but I'm superstitious, as are most of my colleagues, and prefer to fight using tried and trusted equipment.'

Julia gripped Bato's collar tighter. She stared at him, locking eyes, wondering what else she could say, what words she could use to prolong the encounter. In a breath, he'd be gone. Venus knew when she'd have a chance to speak with him again.

'Julia,' Claudia said, cutting across her thoughts, 'I've just remembered—there's something I have to do. Someone I have to see.'

Julia felt a weight roll off her shoulders. The gods had decided for her. Some god had taken pity on her, decided she had embarrassed herself enough for one day. Julia scooped Bato up in her arms.

'If you want to leave…'

'No, no, you stay and talk to *your* gladiator.' Claudia patted Julia's shoulder and disappeared in a cloud of expensive perfume and jangling bracelets before Julia could protest.

Bato wriggled out of her arms and went to sit by Valens. Julia stared at her sandals, rather than meeting Valens's eye. He was sure to have the same knowing smile of yesterday plastered all over his face. She was certain she appeared to be one of those Roman matrons who ran after gladiators and paid them for their services.

If only the ground were to open up and swallow her, Julia thought. Even her dog and best friend were conspiring against her.

'I am glad I have a chance to talk to you,' she said at last, breaking the silence that had descended after Claudia's departure.

'Yes?' he said with a lifted eyebrow—the tone of his voice implied he was tolerating her and looking for a way to end their encounter.

Julia squared her shoulders and tilted her chin upwards. She had to say it before she made a spectacle of herself, before the attraction she felt growing inside of her took firm root.

'About this morning…' she began. After two tries where no words came, she transferred her gaze from his face to the ground, keeping her eyes trained firmly on his sandals. 'I wanted to say…that is…I am not the sort of woman who behaves in that way. I am a Roman matron who keeps to her ideals.'

There, she had said it. She thought she'd feel much better, but she felt worse.

He lifted her chin with gentle probing fingers. Butterflies fluttered in her stomach. His brown eyes seemed filled with some emotion. After searching her face with intent eyes, he let go of her chin and his face became inscrutable.

'Forget it. I already have,' he said.

Valens moved back a little from Julia, trying to regain some measure of calm and distance. Her very scent of flowers and honey threatened to overpower him and the resolutions he had made this afternoon. He hated himself for lying to her and seeing the flash of hurt in her eyes.

All throughout morning practice, he had found it impossible to get her out of his mind. It was far better to stop things here before they started. The last thing he needed was an added distraction. And Julia Antonia was definitely that.

Despite his resolutions, his heart had beat faster when Bato appeared from nowhere to clamber on the stage. It made the ceremony more special to know that Julia was somewhere in the crowd, that she was watching him receive this armour.

He had pushed the thought away. Why should he care? He thought about shooing Bato away, but then the dog started to play tug of war with Aquilia's net and he refused to abandon the scamp to Aquilia's wrath. He had planned on returning him quickly, but the sight of Julia enveloped in her deep red layers made him want to linger. He knew the underlying curves, curves that had moulded to his body this morning.

The brief look of bewilderment in Julia's eyes made things harder. Valens shifted uncomfortably and wanted to take back the words. He had stated it badly.

He wanted to reassure her, but the words made him sound callous.

'Have you had anyone look at your ankle?' he asked.

'It is much better,' she said with a voice chipped out of marble.

Valens ran his hand through his hair, confused between his determination to keep his focus on his work and his desire for Julia. He should be rejoicing that she was annoyed with him.

'That's not what I asked. Have you sought proper treatment, like we discussed yesterday?'

'It appears to be healing on its own,' she said, pulling her shawl tighter around her shoulders, 'I see no need. Now, if you'll excuse me…'

Valens reached out a hand and caught her shoulder, holding her back. He should let her go, leave her to the Fates, but his conscience refused to let him.

'The surgeon is over there.' Valens pointed to where the school's surgeon stood, examining the shoulder of a young *tiro* who had won his proper sword this morning. 'It will only take him a little while to determine what is wrong with your ankle and if you will need further treatment.'

She jerked her shoulder out of his grasp and stood staring daggers at him.

'I think I am the best judge of how my ankle is. I

have managed quite comfortably all day. Now, if you will release my arm, I will go and take Bato home.'

Valens clenched his fist and contemplated marching her over to the surgeon. Had he ever met a more stubborn woman? Why did she refuse to do what was best for her?

'You are not going anywhere until you get that ankle looked at.'

'Under whose orders?' she snapped back, tilting her chin in the air and crossing her arms. Her green-shod toe was just visible under the hem of her gown, tapping away.

Valens groaned and shifted his helmet to his other hand. The weight of his new armour pressed down on him, reminding him where his duty lay.

'It's for your own good, Julia.'

'I think I know what is for my own good, Valens, and my ankle is fine.' Her voice was quiet, but determined. 'Now, if you'll excuse me, I believe I need to find Claudia. When I need your help, I'll ask for it.'

Valens stared at her. Julia positively bristled with indignation as she rearranged her shawl so that it covered her face. What had he done? The way she acted, it would be easy to imagine he had indecently propositioned her! He balanced on his toes, uncertain of his next move in this game.

'Whose dog is this?' Valens heard the high-pitched squeak of Aquilia demand.

The hook-nosed gladiator was bearing down on them, displeasure and menace oozing from every pore. With each step he took, he slapped his net against his thigh.

Valens took one look at Julia's fear-widened eyes and moved between her and Aquilia. His hand lightly gripped his sword.

'Aquilia, we've already had words about this—'

'You keep out of this,' Aquilia snarled, pushing at Valens's shoulder. Valens swore as he stumbled to one side, annoyed with himself—he should have anticipated the action.

'What happened up there was an accident.' Valens struggled to keep his voice even and reasonable. He could see Julia's hand start to tremble as she drew her dog closer to her.

'That dog was sent on purpose.' Aquilia's voice reached ever-higher squeaks with each word he uttered. 'Somebody wanted to humiliate me, and I demand to know who.'

Valens glanced at Julia, whose arms had tightened around the squirming Bato, the faint sheen of fear showed on her face. Bato gave a soft growl in the back of his throat. Aquilia's sneer increased. He raised his net above his head. Valens tensed. If Aquilia went for the dog, he'd have no more than a blink of an eye to react.

'The dog is mine,' she stammered. 'It…it was an accident, as Valens said. My…my dog escaped.'

'Your dog ruined Caesar's ceremony and made me, the greatest gladiator of an entire generation, the laughing stock of Rome,' Aquilia said with a curl of his lip.

'There appears to be a dispute on who is the greatest gladiator,' Julia retorted with blazing eyes. 'I had not heard your name bracketed with that title.'

Valens felt a glow of pride at her words. He could see from her white lips that she was terrified. But she refused to cower in front of Aquilia like so many women and men he had seen. A Roman matron from the tales of old, a woman to honour.

Aquilia gave an inarticulate roar. Julia flinched and turned her head into Valens's shoulder. At the sight, Aquilia gave a little laugh.

'The truth will out,' Aquilia said with speculation in his eyes. 'Tell me how long have you belonged to this…man?'

A deep welling anger built up inside of Valens. What right did Aquilia have to frighten Julia? He nearly lashed out, but managed to hang on to his temper.

In his three months in the pirate's custody, he had seen Aquilia behave in the same fashion to the others who had been captured with him, enjoying the fear. Back then, full of pride, Valens had struck back blindly. Retribution was immediate and harsh. Two legionaries, raw recruits barely two months out of Rome, men he as a junior tribune had been responsible for, died because of his foolhardy actions. Valens had vowed, kneeling on the deck, his mouth full of blood, never again to let Aquilia see his anger—he did not intend to start now.

'You had no need of a dog to help you become the laughing stock, you did it all on your own, my comrade.' Valens said, making his voice drawl. Before he moved away from Julia, he reached out and touched her hand, hoping she'd recognised he was trying to draw Aquilia's attention to himself. 'You know what they whisper—Aquilia is little better than a dog. Caesar must have had a hard time deciding on whom to bestow the armour.'

Valens caught the full force of Aquilia's furious glance. The dead-eyed stare made the flesh on his neck creep. Valens forced himself to stare Aquilia calmly in the eyes, but his hand fingered the hilt of his sword. This time, he knew how to fight.

'Who are you, gladiator? As brave in defending your lady love with your fighting skill as you are with your words?' Aquilia spat. '*Tiros* should be seen and not heard until they have bloodied their swords in the arena.' Aquilia's curled lip showed the insult was deliberate and designed for maximum offence. There could be no doubt Aquilia knew Valen's status.

'If it is necessary, yes.' Valens looked his opponent up and down. He refused to lose his temper, despite the calculated insults. 'This should not take long. I have seen you fight.'

'Have a care—I am a first-hall *rentarius*. I could order you whipped for your insubordination.' Aquilia snapped his fingers. 'Perhaps I will. It should be fun to watch.'

'Valens, a first-hall Thracian, and not some untried *tiro*,' Valens said, making an elaborate bow, but keeping his eyes trained on Aquilia's shoulders. Should Aquilia decide to strike, there would be a slight movement in the shoulders, giving a clue as to the direction. 'May I suggest *you* have a care, as you so aptly put it. You are no longer in command of a ship. Thracians come before *rentarii* in the gladiator world, and Strabo does observe the order.'

Valens waited for Aquilia's reaction, knowing what he had done. It was a code of practice among gladiators not to name previous deeds. Part of the initiation ceremony was to be reborn as a gladiator. The only thing that existed was the arena and the games. The muscles in his sword arm tensed to breaking point.

Aquilia smiled, showing an array of broken teeth. He pulled a scroll from his belt.

'Valens…ah, yes, I have a message for you.

Practice this morning is brought forward by an hour. Caesar's orders.'

'I discovered.' Valens drew on all of his self-control and kept his face blank. He returned the gaze steadily without blinking. No emotion. Nothing to give Aquilia the satisfaction of seeing the anger. He forced his shoulders to relax. 'Had you delivered it earlier, I might have been able to act.'

'I am no messenger boy.' A dagger flashed in Aquilia's hand. 'Especially not for a Thracian.'

'You are what Strabo says you are,' Valens shot back. 'Next time, if he asks you to deliver a message, do it on time.'

Aquilia blew on his nails. 'Care to make me?'

Valens tightened his grip on his anger. He knew that Aquilia expected him to lash out blindly. He refused to give him that satisfaction. He forced his hand from his sword.

'I save my fighting for the arena.'

Behind, Valens heard Julia gasp. He was vaguely aware of a growing crowd starting to surround them.

'Now if you'll excuse me…'

He heard the hiss of the net and moved before it could strike his chest. It fell harmlessly to the ground.

'That was very foolish, Aquilia. Very foolish indeed,' Valens said as he put his hand on his sword and crouched low.

Aquilia stood tall and strutted, languidly retrieving his net. Valens's eyes flicked over the other gladiator, searching for his weak point.

'After I am finished with you, I shall take your woman to bed. It will be my pleasure to pleasure her.'

Keep your temper, my boy, Valens heard the voice of his first trainer echo in his mind. *Your opponents will probe for a way to make you lose it, lose control and lose the match. You stay alive by keeping in control.*

Valens glanced over at Julia now. She no longer even attempted to hide her fear. One hand grasped Bato's collar while the other clutched at her throat. All colour had drained from her face.

Valens knew, from her reaction, that Aquilia's hissed words had carried. He felt his control begin to slip.

How dare Aquilia start in on Julia! Gladiators protected defenceless women.

With one movement, he fit his helmet to his head, closing the visor with a click and unsheathed his sword. He readied his stance, every nerve on fire, every muscle waiting to move. A red mist filtered over his eyes.

He heard Julia gasp and paused, his sword raised. He needed to meet the aggression with controlled violence, not with a headlong charge.

The crowd around them made a ring. He heard someone shouting out the betting. Valens's eye flicked over Aquilia, searching for an opening, a way to knock him on the ground.

'Move away, make way.' Strabo squeezed through two bystanders to appear on Valens's right. 'What in the name of Hercules is going on here?'

Strabo's words broke the spell. Valens straightened and removed his helmet. The red mist receded. He looked at Aquilia, whose net dangled on the ground. The sneer of the pirate captain was more pronounced than ever.

'It appears Aquilia objects to being a messenger boy,' Valens drawled. 'He has just now delivered the message you gave him yesterday evening for me.'

Strabo scowled. 'Is this true?'

Aquilia shrugged, lifting both hands into the air.

'I am a gladiator of the first hall, not a messenger boy. If I see the man, I deliver the message. I did not see him until just now. Then I give him the message.'

Valens crossed his arms and started counting. He reached two when Strabo exploded, his face contorting as the words sank in.

'You are a slave, boy. And you and your trident belong to me for the duration,' Strabo growled and grabbed Aquilia's breastplate, shaking him. Then he released him and took a step towards Valens, but stopped short. His hand curled around empty air. 'Neither of you forget that. You fight when I say you fight.'

'Understood, my *lanista*,' Valens said calling Strabo by his official title of trainer-manager as he placed his sword in its sheath.

Aquilia merely bowed.

'Shake hands,' Strabo commanded. 'You are outside the arena now. Save it until you meet inside.'

Valens grasped Aquilia's hand briefly, promising himself, should the Fates declare they meet in the ring, that it would be a fight with only one victor. The crowd cheered and then started to disperse.

'Aquilia, forty *denarii* for insubordination. Valens, your fine is commuted to ten.' Strabo clapped his hands and two of the trainers appeared. He motioned to Aquilia, who had flecks of spittle around his mouth. 'Take him somewhere to calm his temper. Valens, I think I can trust you.'

Without waiting for an answer, Strabo strode off. Valens turned towards Julia, who was standing with her back against the statue of Venus. She looked white-lipped as her hands clutched Bato. The dog gave a slight whine of protest.

'He said such horrible things about me,' she said. "Lies everyone could hear! Lies that will fly around Rome within the hour. Rome loves scandal.'

'He was trying to goad me,' Valens said and didn't need to elaborate on how close he had come to succeeding.

'Were you about to fight him?'

Valens took Bato from her and set the dog down. He resisted the temptation to draw her into his arms and contented himself with brushing some tendrils of hair behind her ear. She gave a tremulous smile, one that made his heart skip a beat.

'If I had to, I would have. No doubt this little encounter has sealed my fate for the games,' he said to draw his attention from her lips, which were now back to their normal rose colour.

The words were easier to say aloud than to think them. Before him danced the tantalising image of beating Aquilia and being awarded the rudius for it. Victory would be all the sweeter for avenging the death of his comrades. He could almost hear the roar of the crowd. And what would he do afterwards? Valens jerked his mind away from the thoughts. Nothing must exist outside the arena. To do that would be tempting the Fates.

The other possibility he refused to consider. He would win because he had to win.

'How so? How is your fate sealed?' Julia crossed her arms and looked up at him with narrowed eyes. 'Even knowing as little as I do about the games, I thought the matches were decided on the day. A great play is made of stones being drawn out. Vestal Virgins are used.'

Valens decided to give her an edited version of

gladiator procedure, rather than the truth. He refused to believe that the Fates would place Aquilia in his path and not allow him to fight, to avenge his capture.

'I believe Aquilia and I will meet in the ring. Strabo saw the crowd, and heard the shouts. He might be annoyed now, but when he calms down, he'll see it as a commercial opportunity. Despite the nonsense of picking fighters from a hat on the day of the match, I believe the Fates have already decreed or at least been given a helping hand.'

Julia made an annoyed pushing-away motion with her hand.

'You make it sound like it was some sort of children's game. You could have been hurt. That man is frightening. I was quaking in my sandals.'

'Julia, that's my job, my profession.' Valens looked at her in dismay. 'Every time I enter the ring, I could get hurt or killed. Men like Aquilia don't frighten me—now.'

He looked into her face and realised it was a lie. What unnerved him was that Aquilia had instinctively found something that made him lose control—Julia.

Chapter Six

Julia tried to stop the trembling of her arms, her entire body as she stared at Valens. Now he seemed to have shrunk back to normal size, but when he had been arguing with that other gladiator he had seemed a giant consumed with anger. How could she explain to Valens that the entire confrontation terrified her? His reaction to Aquilia frightened her, as well as being so close to two such large men who seemed to be out of control.

As she had watched the two square off and Valens's angry retorts echoed in her ears, she had had flashbacks to her marriage when Lucius had gone into rages. Sometimes Bato's low growl had prevented Lucius from striking her and sometimes he hit her anyway. She swallowed hard and tried to rid her stomach of the empty hollow feeling. She had sworn to Venus, when she left Lucius, she would not have anything to do with men who lost their tempers easily.

Her eyes traced the line of Valens's jaw where shadowy stubble had appeared. She looked at the silver armour and tried once again to reconcile it with the man who had held her in his arms this morning.

'The arena is a foreign place to me. That sort of behaviour shocked me,' she said, taking care with her words.

Valens's face broke into a wary smile. 'It shocked me. But it was worth it to see his face when Bato tried to get the net, absolutely priceless.'

'You did that on purpose?' Julia stared at him in disbelief. 'How did you know that Bato would be here?'

'I didn't. The opportunity presented itself and I figured I could handle the consequences.' His eyes sobered. 'I had not intended to put you in danger, merely to teach Aquilia a lesson.'

'You picked a fight with that brute?' Julia asked, still unable to believe it. Her heart still thumped in her ears from the confrontation. What she was feeling wasn't exhilarating, it was something far more complicated. As for Valens, he seemed to treat it lightly. 'Why did you do that?'

Valens's face showed myriad emotions. His lips parted before pressing very firmly together. His face became a bland mask.

'Why, Valens?' she asked again.

'I've fought worse.' He laid a warm hand on her

shoulder, but she twisted away. 'The brutish ones are generally easier to deal with. It is the sly ones, the ones who use trickery, who are more troublesome.'

'I suppose you get used to it,' she said doubtfully. 'Perhaps it is in men's blood to fight. Women don't behave like that.'

'Some women fight in the arena.'

'Now you are teasing me.' Julia forced herself to laugh. She wanted Valens to stay and talk with her until she got over her fright. With each passing breath, her heart rate was going back to normal. 'Women would not fight in public. It wouldn't be dignified.'

'I've known several,' Valens said. 'They are what we call novelties, to whet the appetite of the crowd. I believe Caesar is using a two pairs of female glad-iators before the mid-day interval on each of the seven days of his games.'

Julia stared at him in astonishment. Women in the arena! Was this another of his jokes? She searched his face, but it bore a serious look.

'Are they any good?' she asked at last. 'It would never occur to me that women would fight in public. I thought the arena was the most masculine of places.'

'It used to be, but the public want novelty, some-thing new to whet their appetite. And the women gladiatrix I've seen can fight. All the ones I know have been prisoners of war. In some countries, women are trained from birth to fight. I believe they received their armour just after the *tiros* did.'

Julia shook her head. 'I was searching for Bato then.'

'You sound unconvinced. Shall I introduce you?'

Julia watched him closely. The world seemed to have shrunk to the two of them. She tried to tell herself that his attention was just because he felt guilty about subjecting her to that brute of a gladiator.

'Women can do many things if men will let them,' she said with a firm voice. 'They are capable of more than sitting at home, spinning and tending the household gods.'

'Ah, you are one of those independent-minded women. I should have guessed.' He lightly touched her shawl, allowing it to run through his fingers like water. 'Do you spend all your time playing games at the baths gymnasium?'

Julia's breath caught in her throat. *Independent-minded*—those words echoed the words Lucius threw at her when she finally said she wanted a divorce. He then called for his whip. She shuddered at the memory, tried to forget the sickening pain he had inflicted when she had let her tongue run on once too often.

'Julia, are you are all right? Look at me.'

She opened her eyes and saw Valens's face close to hers. Both his hands were on her shoulders.

'I'm fine. Please believe me,' she said and the

memory faded. 'It's the excitement and the worry about Bato.'

'I think you should get back to your father's compound right away.' Valens clapped his hands and a servant appeared. 'Fetch a litter, please. Julia Antonia is going home.'

'I can walk,' she protested.

'Nonsense. Let me take care of you.'

Take care of her? She knew all about the hollowness of those words. She knew what happened when she refused to follow orders.

Julia felt the pit open again in her stomach. No man would ever take care of her again. After what Lucius had done to her, she was determined to stand on her own two feet. She'd marry when she had to, when there was no alternative, but she'd never let a man have that sort of control over her again. Once she had naïvely thought her husband would look after her. She shifted her shoulders in remembered pain.

'I am perfectly capable of taking care of myself.'

Valens's eyes seemed to assess her before he shrugged carelessly with one shoulder.

'It is my way of repaying the debt I owe you. The litter is here.'

Julia saw a curtained litter emblazoned with Strabo's logo and hated to think of what Sabina would say if she arrived home in a litter that had been ordered by a gladiator, how Sabina would shriek about what the neighbours would think.

Her heart sank further as she realised this afternoon's events were bound to be discussed by everyone. The news would be all over Rome that two gladiators had nearly duelled over her dog, travelling at the speed of a whispered hush. Dear gods, the betrothal to Mettalius might be being drawn up as they spoke.

'You don't owe me any debt,' she said carefully.

'But I do. Or rather, I owe Bato a debt. Thanks to him, I have had my fine reduced by twenty *denarii*.' His smile sent her heart soaring. 'Now, do you get in or do I sling you across my shoulder and carry you there?'

'You would not dare.' A tingle went through Julia as she remembered exactly what being held in his arms felt like.

'Try me.' He crossed his arms and positioned himself straight in front of her. His gaze deepened and held her. 'Between your fright and your ankle, you are in no fit state to stumble back to your home. If you would prefer me to carry you…'

Julia took a step backwards and the plinth from the statue of Venus dug into the back of her thighs. She had no doubt about Valens's seriousness. He would carry her, kicking and screaming if necessary. The scandal would then be unstoppable.

'Very well, I accept your offer of a litter, because it

is the best way home for Bato. I can walk over to it on my own.'

Their gaze held and her heart whispered despite the possibility of scandal she would do it all again.

'May the gods go with you, Julia Antonia.'

'And with you too, Valens.' She turned and hurried after the servant.

Julia decided Juno, Minerva and Venus were with her when she arrived back at the compound. Neither her stepmother nor her father was at home and a quick check with Clodius the porter revealed neither had been home in her absence.

Perhaps it was all deniable, Julia thought as she picked up her spinning again. Bato flopped down on the mat next to the brazier and went to sleep, his nose buried beneath his paws.

'Julia, Julia Antonia!' her father bellowed from the courtyard. 'Come here, daughter of mine.'

She knew that tone of voice. There was little point in hiding or pretending she had not heard. She twisted the thread around the spindle's handle and placed it on top of the wool.

'Here, Father,' she called from the window. 'Shall I come down or you come up?'

Her father, dressed in the white toga he wore to court, shielded his eyes and gestured for her to come down.

Julia's heart sank to the hem of her gown. His face was thunderous. In his hand, he held a sheaf of scrolls.

As she ran down the steps, she tried to think of a reasonable excuse for this afternoon. Should she mention it first or wait for him to bring it up? Perhaps he wanted to see her about some other misdemeanour.

'What is this I hear about two gladiators fighting over you?' her father thundered as she entered the atrium.

Julia swallowed hard. How could she explain? She widened her eyes and began the explanation she had concocted. A white lie, but she knew another scandal might turn her father against her.

'Two gladiators fighting over me? Father, you know how the rumours fly in Rome—'

Her father cut her short with an impatient gesture of his hand.

'The entire Forum was buzzing about it late this afternoon. My very own daughter in the centre of a gladiatorial brawl! Bringing her family so publicly into disrepute! I never thought you would be involved in so vulgar of a display. Not my daughter I said, but Fabius Claudius swore it was you. And he has known you since the day you were born.'

'I wasn't at the centre, more to one side,' Julia mumbled, picking at the skirt of her gown.

'I didn't quite catch that, Julia. Look at me when you speak.'

Julia forced her gaze from her sandals.

'I said I wasn't in the centre of the fight,' she shouted.

Her father's eyes widened at her voice.

'But you don't deny they were fighting over you.'

'Over me?' Julia shook her head and said quickly before she lost her nerve, 'They were fighting over Bato.'

'Bato?'

Her father lowered his eyebrows and pierced her with his dark stare. The elephants began trampling Julia's stomach. Any hope of glossing over the incident or giving a polite lie vanished. Her father had adopted his inquisitorial lawyer pose.

She began to rapidly explain what had happened, her words tripping over one another in the rush to get them out. When she reached the end of the tale, Julia's voice faded away and she waited. If her father thought she had brought disgrace on the family, he was capable of banishing her or worse. Cold sweat began to prick the back of her neck. She should have run when Valens approached her. Her only hope was that she had told her version of events before Sabina had had a chance to poison him with the bath-house version.

'It was all down to this dog of yours escaping from Caesar's niece?'

'That's right,' Julia said. She twisted her belt around

her hand, feeling the cord dig into her palm. He had to believe her.

'That rascal.' Her father's face broke into a wide grin. 'I should have made you return him to your ex-father-in-law weeks ago when you first arrived back on my doorstep. Senator Gracchus should take care of the dog, if his adopted son refuses to. Rascal then and rascal now. I knew there had to be more to it than my daughter behaving badly. You have never given me cause to worry about such things before. In that case, I shall have to thank him with the largest bone possible.'

The words of protest died on Julia's lips. She looked at her father in amazement. 'I don't understand. You want to reward Bato?'

'That little escapade has resulted in three briefs coming in for me today. Everyone is discussing it. It has raised my profile no end.'

'Then you're not angry?' A great wave of relief washed over Julia.

'Had the gladiators actually been fighting over you, that would have been another matter entirely, but as it stands—it is another of Rome's rumours. The dog will do as an excuse. People can be reminded of whose dog he was to begin with. The name of Gracchus should strike fear into the scandalmongers' hearts. They wouldn't want to anger two powerful politicians from opposite ends of the spectrum—Caesar and Gracchus.

Julia felt the tension rush out of her, leaving her body tired as if she were the one to have fought a battle with Aquilia.

'Who are the briefs from?' she asked, a suspicion forming in her brain.

'They were sent from Caesar by special messenger. This morning, nothing—by late afternoon, I am back in favour.' Her father grinned and patted the scrolls. 'He is pleased that you, or rather your dog, raised the games' profile. You have ensured the match will be on everyone's lips. And Caesar wishes to reward me for it. Caesar always repays his debts.'

Julia stared at her father and offered a small prayer of thanks to Venus. When was a scandal not a scandal? When it resulted in work for her father!

'I am pleased Bato was of service,' she replied quietly, trying to hide her relief.

She stood, shifting from foot to foot, waiting for her father to dismiss her with a nod as he normally did.

'Shall we go for a walk?' Julius Antonius gestured towards the garden. 'Spend some time together? I see little of you these days.'

Julia released a breath. That was all? No explosion. No threats to marry her off. He wanted something, but what? She had at last something to bargain with.

'A walk with you, Father, would be a lovely idea.'

They took several turns about the enclosed garden,

speaking of nothing very much. Her father stopped by the portrait bust of her mother, hidden in a small nook between two clipped bay laurels.

'How like her you are,' Julius Antonius said, placing a hand on the statue's shoulder. 'It seems hard to believe that her shade has been in Hades these last five years.'

'I remember her as being very kind, a model of Roman womanhood.' Julia ran a hand over the smooth marble, tracing the outline of her mother's mouth.

'Sabina wanted me to get rid of the bust, but I refused. Had it moved here in this nook to where it can't be seen from the house.'

'Sabina took the news in her usual calm and collected manner?' Julia laughed, pleased that her father, contrary to appearances, did not give in to Sabina in all things.

'Her shrieks could be heard from here to the Aventine. The she refused to speak to me for a week. But she gave in when she realised I was determined. It cost me a violet gown though.' Her father gave a barking laugh and then his face sobered. He placed his hand on the shoulder of the portrait bust. 'Now that we are here, Julia, there is something I must ask you.'

'Yes, Father?' Julia's heart leapt. Would he ask her for her opinion about Mettalius? Perhaps In the wake of the briefs, she could convince him Mettalius was not the man she should marry. That his star was on the wane in the Senate…

'Is there anything going on between you and that gladiator?'

Julia's heart stopped. She pulled her shawl tighter about her shoulders. How to answer? If her mother were here, Julia knew she could explain the situation and her mother would understand, but would her father? He had changed so much since her mother's death and she knew what Sabina's reaction would be. Could she take the risk? She looked at his stern mouth. Later, she knew, she'd get down on her knees and ask the gods to forgive her for deceiving her father, but she hoped they would understand.

'We have met once or twice. First in the market-place, then here and when he returned Bato to me this afternoon,' she said, choosing her words and making sure her voice sounded strong. 'I'd hardly call that something going on.'

She offered a quick prayer up to Venus that no one had seen the kiss she and Valens had shared earlier this morning. Surely, since Venus was the goddess of love as well the protector of the Julius family, she'd understand and help her.

'You are willing to swear that on the shade of your mother?'

Julia looked directly into her father's eyes. 'I have done nothing to be ashamed of or to bring disrepute on this family, you know that. I am willing to swear it on her shade.'

That much was true. She had not done anything that would disgrace the family, nor did she intend to. She knew her father would misinterpret the answer, but she had no choice. The guilt she felt at the evasion threatened to close her throat and stop her breath. If he asked more directly, she'd have to confess. There was a difference between not answering the questioning and deliberately lying. She had learnt that from her father discussing his legal cases, but the thought held little comfort.

Her father's eyes assessed her for what seemed to be an eternity. Julia's palms became damp. She fought the urge to wipe them on her gown. Then suddenly his face cleared and he patted her shoulder.

'You know what your stepmother will say. She is desperate for an alliance with Mettalius. The betrothal should be announced without delay, according to Sabina. She wants to formally consult her augur on the appropriate day and time.'

Did he guess? Or had she fooled him? His words should make her feel better, but they made the pit in her stomach grow. She sank down on a bench and stared at the bust. Her mother's firm chin and the set to her jaw gave Julia courage. Her father must still have feelings for her mother, even though she had been dead for the past five years. 'If Sabina wants to marry Mettalius, she should do so herself.'

Her father gave a sharp intake of breath.

Julia refused to allow herself time to panic. She stood up and pressed her hands together. She had to act. 'Father, I will not be made the scapegoat of some made-up scandal in order to further Sabina's social ambitions.'

'Mettalius would be useful to the family, that is true, but others may make offers because of Caesar's favour.' Her father squeezed her hand. His smile was tender.

'Are you saying I don't have to marry Mettalius?'

A twinkle appeared in her father's eye and he looked more like the man she remembered from her childhood dreams than the stern figure she had encountered over the last few years.

'Your escapade this morning has changed matters, Julia. I intend to play a waiting game. See which way the wind blows. Other more suitable alliances may appear. Question me about the war with Spartacus? Champion that dictator Sulla! At my own dinner table! Who does Mettalius think he is?'

Julia sank down into a curtsy. 'Thank you, Father. I will not make you ashamed.'

The twinkle disappeared and her father looked once more like the man she had faced across the dinner table last night.

'Mind you, if I hear you have been consorting with gladiators in public again, I may be forced to take stronger measures.'

Julia went still.

'What sort of measures?' She pushed the question around the lump in her throat. She had to know.

'As I am sure you are a respectable matron like your mother, I will have no need. If you'll excuse me, I shall leave you to contemplate your mother while I dress for dinner.'

Julia ran her fingers over the bust of her mother and placed a smile on to her lips. Her heart felt as if it were breaking. She had no doubt of what her father's threat meant. In exchange for her freedom, she agreed to give up Valens and their growing friendship. It wasn't as if there was anything between them, she argued with her heart. Yesterday, she had been unaware of his existence. But the words did nothing to ease the pain in her heart.

Valens walked through the shadowy garden at dusk. The clipped bay laurels cast long shadows over the finely raked gravel paths. In a secluded nook, Julia sat by a portrait bust of a woman who shared the same firm chin, and determined mouth. She sat as remote and still as the statue, eyes fixed on a distant spot, seemingly oblivious to his entering the garden.

'Julia,' he called softly, trying not to startle her, the speech he had decided on forming in his mind. He'd apologise one more time, then leave. He had only sought her out in order to make sure she had arrived back safely and recovered from her fright. That was the end to it. Unemotional uninterest. He was focused solely on the arena. 'Julia, we should speak.'

She started and turned towards him. In the fading light, he could make out the anguish in her gaze. Valens's stomach twisted as if she had driven a knife into it. He wanted to take away the pain and turn the shadows into smiles.

All his thoughts about keeping his distance vanished along with the polite speech he had planned. He crossed the garden in ten steps to reach her side, drawing her further back into the shadowy nook.

'What's wrong?'

She gave a tiny shrug of her shoulders. 'Nothing is the matter. Why should anything be the matter?'

'You look as if you have lost your last friend, as if all the sadness in the world is about to over-whelm you.'

Valens reached out to take her in his arms, but she stood up and moved away. Valens allowed his arms to fall to his side.

'Sometimes I miss my mother. That's her statue.' Julia pointed to the bust.

Valens looked at the statue and back at Julia. There was more to this than missing her mother.

'How long has your mother been dead?'

Two bright spots appeared on her cheeks. Her hands twisted the end of her belt. 'Five years. She died when the fever swept through Rome.'

Valens caught her arm and turned her to face him. This time she didn't move away. She stood rigid. As he moved his hand up her arm slowly towards her shoulder, she laid her head against his chest with a great sigh. Valens stroked her head, the scent of her filling his nostrils and teasing his senses.

His body responded, hardening to her nearness; the temptation to taste her lips again was overpowering.

'I've spoken to your father about the incident at the presentation ceremony this afternoon,' he said in an attempt to draw his mind away from the way her body felt against his.

Immediately she stiffened and drew back. Her eyes flicked towards the entrance to the garden and the colour drained from her face.

'You've spoken to my father,' she said.

'Yes, I gather you already discussed the incident with him. I apologised for any embarrassment and explained about discovering your dog on stage. He seemed concerned about you and your reputation, but I explained the course of events.'

Julia felt another lump form in her throat. For that brief time, resting in Valens's arms, she'd been convinced he was about to kiss her again. How mistaken she'd been! He'd held her like a friend, not like a lover. Silently she cursed her treacherous mind and body.

She'd promised. She would not get involved with this man. Already the guilt of the small deception was eating away at her insides. But her father had said 'in public', and this garden nook was private. Julius Antonius never said anything without a reason. She pressed her fingertips together, relief building within her. He had not forbidden her to see Valens in private. If he had intended to keep them apart, he would have demanded Caesar remove Valens. She had been worried over nothing.

In her anxiety, she had managed to loosen the tight knot of hair at the back of her head. If she moved her head even an inch, her hairstyle would crash down around her shoulders. Not the impression she wanted to give Valens. She reached up and began to twist it back into a bun, taking out a hairpin.

'I've already explained to my father what happened, the truth about what happened,' she said carefully.

'He informed me before he and your stepmother left for dinner.' Valens's eye bore a distinct shine. 'He was pleased—your story matched with mine.'

Julia dropped a hairpin and she bent down searching for it. Keeping her eyes firmly trained on the ground, she said 'And why should they not match? I told the truth. The fight had nothing to do with me and everything to do with Bato and his escape plans.'

She spied the hairpin and reached out to grab it. Valens's hand reached out and closed around hers.

'Are you going to tell me what is bothering you, Julia? I thought you'd have been pleased your father is taking it so lightly. I heard the gossip in the streets.'

Julia withdrew her hand from his and stood up, jamming the hairpin back into her head so hard she winced from the pain.

'I have had an upsetting day. That's all. I nearly lose my dog, get in the midst of a violent fight and then, to cap it off, my father accuses me of having an affair with you.' She finished with a dramatic flourish and waited for his response.

Annoyingly Valens stared in the middle distance for a little while before he began to speak.

'What bothers you most—that your father accused you of having an affair or the fact that we are not having an affair?' His face wore the same look of yesterday when he accused her of following him from the bath.

The arrogant—Julia clenched her fist. 'How dare you!'

'If you desire an affair, it can be arranged, Julia.' His eyes held promises her body wanted to try. 'It

might save some time. You know we are both attracted to each other.'

Julia closed her eyes and tried not to think of this
morning and that kiss, the kiss that had sent shivers
through her soul. She stiffened her back and stared
straight into his face. When she had finished with him…

'You think, because you stole a kiss this morning,'
she said with narrowed eyes and crossed arms, 'then
had me sent home in a litter after a fight you engi-
neered, that I should fall into your bed.'

'It has happened before.' A dimple showed in the
corner of his mouth.

'Why, you—!' Julia reached up and drew her hand
back. His hand caught her wrist before she connected
with his cheek.

'Physical violence rarely solves anything outside the
arena, Julia.' His voice hardened and his eyes glittered.

'That is rich coming from a gladiator,' she shot back.

'I do what I have to do to survive.' His voice was
barely above a whisper now.

'And is this about survival?' she asked, intending to
draw her hand back. Her stomach fluttered. She
should flee now, but her legs refused to move.

'No, this is about desire,' he growled. 'Desire
between a man and a woman.'

His voice made her insides leap. She hesitated and
wondered what it would be like to feel his mouth

against hers again. She ran her tongue over her lips, which seemed to have grown full and swollen from just a look.

'You are mistaken,' she lied. 'This has nothing to do with desire. I had enough sense not to scream when a gladiator took me in his arms.'

She looked away. She ought to leave. The danger was too great. They might not be seen from the house, but a servant could walk down the garden path. Her knees were like water and her feet refused to move.

'You're lying. Shall I prove it to you?' His voice tickled her ear. 'That sort of challenge is impossible to resist.'

Valens brought her chin up, capturing her face between his hands. She stared at him, watching the banked fires in his eyes grow. Valens reached out and pulled her to him. His lips swooped and held hers. His kiss bore little resemblance to this morning's gentleness. It plundered, took and ravaged her mouth.

For less than a heartbeat, she thought about pushing him away, but, even as his tongue touched hers for the first time, she knew it was impossible and gave herself to the kiss, returning it measure for measure.

The nature of the kiss changed and became less punishing and more enquiring, seeking a response from her, a response her body longed to give.

Her body arched closer, feeling the hardness of him

as he ran a hand down her back, passing a hand over her buttocks and pressing her closer. Against her belly, she felt the telltale bulge of his desire and warmth spread throughout her, increasing in its intensity as it neared her centre point. Every muscle, every fibre of her being felt on fire and still he would not let go, would not end the kiss. She moaned in the back of her throat and brought her hands up to his head, running them through his crisp hair and then down his back.

As abruptly as the kiss began, he stepped back, ending it. She stared at his heaving chest, tousled hair and eyes dark with passion before lifting a hand to release her hair, allowing it to tumble down her back and over her shoulders.

His lips curved into a heart-stopping smile.

'I shall take that as an invitation.'

Julia made an inarticulate noise in the back of her throat. She knew she'd regret it, but, for now, her body demanded to feel his against hers. 'Please,' she whispered, not knowing if she was asking him to continue or to stop.

She felt his eyes trace the shape of her body. For a heartbeat, she thought he would draw her into his arms again. Then he shook his head, running his hand through his hair.

'I prefer a soft bed and privacy for seduction, Julia Antonia. Any time you are ready, say the word.'

Without waiting for an answer, he turned his back and strode off. Julia grabbed the hairpin and threw it after him. Her breasts tingled with unfulfilled longing. She could feel her nipples straining against the breast band and knew, if he so much as looked back, she'd melt into his arms.

Valens heard the hairpin drop on the ground behind him, and forced himself not to turn around. The kiss was supposed to teach her a lesson. It was supposed to frighten her. And it was supposed to be the end of it for him. The arena beckoned. He could not afford to let anything distract him from this next bout. Every time he came near her, he could only think about her.

He'd lied. A breath more and he would have seduced her there, without the benefit of the bed. His loins ached from the feel of her pelvis against his. Why had the gods sent her to torment him?

He quickened his pace as a second hairpin hit his shoulder. If he turned back now, he'd sling her over his shoulder and carry her off to his bed, refusing to let her out until they were both satiated with passion.

Chapter Seven

For the next two days, Julia kept her distance from Valens, checking her bedroom door three times each night before she climbed into bed to ensure there would be no repeat of Bato's escape.

On the afternoon of the second day, half-hidden by a pillar, and unable to stop herself, she watched him practising with several other gladiators in her father's courtyard. With each parry and thrust, his tunic strained to reveal more of his body, his muscles slick with sweat and gleaming in the sunlight. Julia swallowed hard and tried to force her legs to move on, but they stayed still, rooted to the spot.

She had been prepared to hate the sport, but she found, to her surprise, that she enjoyed watching the clash of the swords and the ebb and flow of the fight. Each time Valens landed a blow on his opponent, a silent cheer rose within her.

If one of the other gladiators made a mistake, he stopped and explained what was wrong, demonstrating how that cut or this blow worked better. At the end, when he sent the last of the trainees' swords flying, their eyes met and she drew back to the safety of the house, trying to forget the kiss in the garden that was imprinted on her brain.

The kiss haunted her dreams and she woke, drenched in sweat, burning with desire for his touch. She threw the blanket off and padded over to the window, throwing open the shudder to breathe in the cool night air.

The garden was bathed in moonlight. The bay laurel hedges were etched in silver. In the shadows near her mother's secret nook, she thought she saw a couple move, embracing the way she and Valens had embraced. She blinked her eyes and the couple vanished.

Her hands gripped the window ledge. She stumbled back to bed and stubbed her toe on Bato. Bato raised his nose, looked at her and padded over to the door.

'Fine, I suppose it is my fault for getting out of bed,' Julia said, grabbing a blanket to wrap around her undertunic before slipping her feet into her house sandals 'And I'll come with you to make sure you get back to the right room with no detours.

For once, Bato behaved himself, Julia thought with a pang as the early morning dew on the path seeped through her shoes. He showed no sign of wanting to go off and explore as he normally did. Julia heaved a sigh of relief and tiredness bit at her every limb. She tried to summon the energy to climb the stairs back to her bedroom. A muffled shout from above brought every nerve to attention. Valens! It had to be. Bato gave a sharp bark.

Julia raced up the stairs behind him. When Bato started whining and scrambling at the guest bedroom door, she threw it open.

A single oil lamp burnt on the table by Valens's bed. The cotton sheets were tangled about Valens's body as he lay on his carved wooden bed. In one hand, he clutched the heavily embroidered counterpane. His head, slick with sweat, thrashed about on the lamb's-wool-filled mattress.

He gave a moan and cried out again, pleading for someone's life.

Julia stepped into the room and closed the door.

'Valens,' she said softly, going to the bed and shaking his shoulder. 'You're having a dream, a nightmare.'

Valens's eyes flashed opened and his hand shot out, his fingers curling around her throat.

The nightmare had come again. Valens had known it would and waited for it, steeled himself for it. Each night as he closed his eyes, he wondered—would it be tonight? Then, when enough nights had gone by without the dream, and he had begun to hope, to consider sleeping without a light, it struck with savage intensity.

Valens knew how it started—innocently enough, a bright clear day with laughter. Then the ambush by pirates and watching eight of his men fall and the rest held captive. Then came the agony of watching the others perish—two, and finally the last six as Aquilia laughed. In the next act, it switched to the arena and the men he had fought and killed. Sometimes he fought back and at others, he was rooted to the spot, defenceless, unable to fight. Always it ended with him fighting a faceless opponent and waking drenched in sweat, gasping for breath with violently trembling hands, his nostrils filled with the stench of blood and rotting flesh, his ears aching from the screams of the dying. All the more terrifying for the repetition.

'Valens, Valens, you're dreaming. Let go of me.'

Through the cries of the crowd and screams of the dying, Valens heard Julia. His eyes snapped opened and his arm fell back on the bed.

He stared at the woman before him, feeling the sweat drip down his neck, but uncertain of the vision before him. His hand had encountered solid flesh but was it just another illusion? Here was a Julia unlike he had ever seen before except in his dreams, a Julia with her hair curling softly about her shoulders, and a dark wool blanket around her shoulders.

Was she real or was she some new twist on the nightmare?

Her subtle scent of lavender and roses enveloped him and he knew he was in the land of the living. He drank in her being as a man dying of thirst gulps in water. His body hardened as his eyes fastened on her breasts pushing gently underneath her gown with each breath she took. She shifted slightly and broke the spell.

'Julia, what are you doing here?' he said, annoyed at finding comfort in her presence, annoyed at his body's reaction to her. He pulled the soft wool blanket firmly around his midriff. 'You should be asleep in your own bed.'

'I heard you calling out,' Julia answered, rubbing her throat as she stood uncertainly by his bed.

Against the cream-coloured flesh of her neck, three broad red stripes stood out. He watched as they started to fade, horrified by what he might have done to her. 'You should have stayed away.'

'You called for help,' she whispered.

'It was a nightmare,' Valens explained and dragged his eyes from the hollow of her throat to the frieze of garden flowers on the wall behind her.

'I guessed as much.'

He glanced again at her throat where the red marks

had disappeared. His stomach turned over and knew the words were inadequate.

'I thought you were someone else. It would have passed if you had not come. It always does.'

'You sounded terrified as you shouted out, begging for help.' Her fingers held the blanket tight about her shoulders. Her body was half-turned towards the door.

Valens froze. How much had he revealed? He examined her in the soft lamp light. She looked wary, ready to flee with sleep-laden eyes and reddened lips.

In his mind, he listed all the reasons to keep away from her. All the reasons that had seemed so important when he first thought of them. They seemed much less important here with Julia standing beside his bed.

'Your name? I called your name?' He closed his eyes and knew he had, remembered doing so. The nightmare had taken a new and frightening twist. Besides his men, he had to save Julia, to keep her from Aquilia's clutches. If he failed in his task, she would be lost for ever, dying like the rest.

'No, others.' Her voice was soft and hesitant. 'You called for a centurion to help you. Then you told your men to get away. Finally you pleaded for help from anyone. At that plea, I ran.'

She gave a slight laugh. Valens opened his eyes and stared directly into her face. A small crease of a frown showed between her eyebrows. His shoulders relaxed.

She hadn't heard him call her name, but she had come anyway, only knowing he was in pain.

'I regret disturbing you.'

'You didn't disturb me.' In the soft lamplight, her cheek glowed pink. His gaze dropped to her mouth and his body hardened further, aching for her touch. 'I was awake.'

'I was in the army,' he said, anything to get the conversation away from her and his need for her. 'Years ago, before I became a gladiator.'

'As an auxiliary?' she asked in a puzzled tone. Her head tilted to one side and again Valens was reminded of his pet blackbird, ready to flee but curious.

He refused to lie to her. He would open the door to his memory the tiniest of cracks, and then shut it firmly. It could do no harm. 'As a legionary.'

He heard her gasp and knew she understood the significance. No citizen would willingly take the gladiatorial oath to be burnt with fire, shackled with chains, whipped with rods and killed with steel. After the oath and burning of the tattoo, a man became an *infamis*, an outcast. Society turned its back on him. A gladiator could never enjoy the privileges of an ordinary citizen unless he won the wooden sword. And even then, the upper reaches of society would be closed to him. He could never be the best hope for his family's success for generations after that.

'You were a citizen of Rome, a soldier, but now you are a slave. How could that happen?'

'It is a long and unedifying story about a young man who thought too highly of himself, and, like Icarus in the myth, flew too close to the sun.' Valens forced his lips to turn up into an ironic curve and lay back on his pillows. 'My main preoccupations were hunting, gambling and enjoying the company of loose women. The secondment to North Africa was a chance to break free from my father's lectures.'

'What did you do?' Julia took a step closer and her gown slipped off one shoulder to reveal the swell of her right breast. 'Why did you have to leave the army?

Valens's breath caught in his throat and he had a difficult time thinking of anything but the creamy expanse she had inadvertently exposed. His lips itched to taste the hollow between her breasts, to see if it did truly taste of summer as it had in his dream. With great effort, Valens tore his gaze from her bosom to look at the ceiling.

'My actions in North Africa led directly to the death of my men. Sixteen men, good and true, who expected more of me than I could give.'

'Please tell me, Valens. I would like to know more about you. How did you become a slave? Men have made mistakes in war before without being disgraced like that.'

He stared up, willing his breathing back to normal. The door in his memory he had kept closed for so long had been flung open.

He opted for a safe option, one that told the truth but not the whole truth. He could not bear to think of the look her eyes must surely give, if she realised the full height from which he had fallen and how he as much as anyone else had been his own master of his downfall.

If he had led his life differently, been more the son his father had desired, would his father have wanted him back?

The ransom Aquilia set was far from excessive. The question haunted him and made him more determined to succeed, to force people to acknowledge him as an honourable man. He wanted to return from the dead.

'When the pirates captured me in North Africa, my father refused to send the ransom. I suspect he thought I was dissolute enough to not waste any more money on me. Later I discovered he had adopted a man to take my place—someone more suited to his notions of propriety than I—almost before the ink on his response had dried. Someone less prone to fencing, gambling and gymnastics. The pirate was enraged and killed my men for sport. It tickled his sense of humour to sell me as a slave.'

Julia watched Valens's face twist as he said the words. His eyes bore a shadow of pain. She reached out and touched his hand, wishing she could say something that would take away that aching sorrow, and that she could gather him in her arms and hold him, much as a mother does with a young child. Her fingers longed to smooth the lock of black hair from his eyes.

She pressed her hands together, lacing the fingers and holding them back. She knew anything she said would sound trite.

Her blood became hot when she thought of what he must have suffered. To be disowned and without a family must be unimaginable torture. It was like taking away the centre of your being. Your family defined you and your status in society. To make matters worse, in losing his family, he also had lost his freedom, his citizenship and his identity. He had become a slave and had had to endure a kind of living death.

'I had no idea,' she said, pulling the blanket more firmly around her shoulders. 'How could a father behave like that towards what I think must have been his only son?'

He gave a bitter smile and a shutter came down over his eyes. The glimpse she had of his vulnerability was gone so quickly she wondered if she had mistaken it. His face with its clenched jaw was as remote as the statues that flanked Jupiter's temple on the Capitoline hill.

'It was over four years ago,' he said, 'and there was fault on both sides. I have forged a new life in the arena. There is a saying that you die when you take the gladiatorial oath and are reborn. If I had know then what I know now, I would have saved my men. We would never have been there in the first place.'

Julia heard the muffled sob hidden in the last words. She again longed to hold him, but feared his reactions. The last three and a half years with Lucius, when he had lashed out at her every time she sought to offer comfort, assaulted her memory. She contented herself with plucking at the folds of the blanket, pulling the folds tighter.

'I had best go if you have recovered from your nightmare,' she said after a long pause where the only sound in the room was the gentle snores of Bato. She bent down and slipped her fingers under Bato's collar, preparing to drag him away.

'Quite recovered, thank you.' He turned towards her and his eyes were deeply fringed by his impossibly long lashes. The knotting of her stomach was replaced by a different sort of fluttering. 'I regret waking you with my shouting.'

She shook her head. How could she tell him that the memory of him and the kisses they shared had disturbed her sleep?

'Bato woke me,' she said, opting for a half-truth.

'He wanted to go out. When I passed your room on the way back from the garden, I heard your cries.'

At his name, Bato gave a slight whine, thumped his tail against the mosaic tiles, but refused to move.

'Leave him. He looks like he has settled down for the night.'

Julia looked at Bato who put his nose back under his paws. She made an exasperated noise. She'd already embarrassed herself by going to Valens and now her dog was intent on making himself at home, throwing them together. It reminded her too much of the other time, the time when Valens had first kissed her. She felt a warm tingle and a flush begin to spread throughout her body.

'I don't know why he keeps doing this,' Julia said, transferring her gaze to Bato. 'Bato, you should know your bed is elsewhere. Valens doesn't want us here.'

Julia bent down and started to tug Bato's collar. The dog opened one eye and then shut it. Julia felt her gown and blanket slip further off her shoulder.

'I never said that.'

There was a new note in Valens's voice. Something more, something that called to her inner being. Julia swallowed hard and tried to ignore the flick of warmth building in her.

'We had better go.'

Valens leant forward, the covering falling off his chest and sliding with a soft thump on to the floor.

'Must you?' His voice held a different richer note from the hard one he had used when he recited his story.

Julia looked over her shoulder at the door, wondering whether her father would appear. Then she looked back at Valens with his hooded eyes and her feet seemed to have become marble.

'I need to go back to my bedroom,' she whispered. 'Somebody might see.'

Valens threw back the cotton sheet and stood up, dressed only in his loincloth, the naked flesh of his broad shoulders and chest gleaming in the flickering light. She could see his pulse thudding in the hollow of his throat. Julia gulped and her eyes slid down his chest to his flat belly, then down his long muscular leg.

The ripple of excitement built into a wave of desire inside her. She moved her arm and felt the old linen of her undertunic brush her breast. The nipple puckered and hardened as she remembered his touch, longed for his touch again.

'You could stay.' There was no question in his voice, merely a statement quietly made.

With her eyes, she measured the short distance to the door. Would her knees hold out until she reached the safety of corridor?

'You've recovered from your nightmare.' She twisted a tendril of hair around her finger, torn between wanting to keep her promise to her father and her body's desire for his touch.

Her breath caught as his eyes deepened and a glow came from deep within them. She found it impossible to look anywhere but at that hot gaze that scorched her soul, and caused the warmth in her belly to grow until she was engulfed in flame.

'Perhaps I am in danger.' His voice held her there, entangling her in its silken coils…

'What sort of danger? You said the Furies had fled.'

He stood next to her, so close she could see a thin white scar above his left eyebrow. He leant forward and touched her cheek with his finger. A shiver ran through her and she felt her back arch towards him before she regained control of it. She had to leave now! This instant! But her feet refused her mind's command to move.

'You chased them away, but that is not the danger I speak about.'

'I'm not sure I understand.' Her voice echoed in the room, hung there between them. 'Nobody saw me come here and nobody will see me go.'

Common sense told her that she should leave. Her father's words resounded in her ears. *No more scandals.* She had been foolish even to peek inside the door, let alone stand beside the head of the bed. She felt her cheeks begin to sizzle from his look.

'If you must go, may I have a kiss to see me through the rest of the night?'

Without waiting for an answer, his lips touched hers, his tongue gliding over her lips until it reached the tiny parting.

Julia felt her breasts brush his chest with only the thinness of the linen to separate the flesh.

She raised a hand and tentatively touched the silver-white scars on his chest. He captured her hand and brought it to his lips.

'From the ring?' she whispered, noting the slashes and ridges that criss-crossed his chest.

He nodded. 'Honourably won in combat.'

'And that?' Julia pointed to a tattoo of a lion with a sword in its paw on the inside of his right arm.

'My gladiatorial mark. They branded me with it when I took the oath. It too is honourable, although I did not think so for a long time.'

He ran his hands underneath her tunic. His hands stilled and she saw a frown appear in his eyes.

'What are those from, Julia?" he asked.

She stepped out of his embrace and, hugged her arms about her waist. Would she disgust him as she had disgusted Lucius? Her insides knotted into a tiny ball.

'I need to go now,' she whispered, and started towards the door. 'I've stayed too long.'

'Stay,' he said in a low voice. His hand gripped

her upper arm. 'Julia, who beat you? Who marked your skin?'

'Please, Valens, let me go. It was a mistake to come here.' She tried to twist away from him. How could she explain? How could she bear to see him turn from her in disgust? How could she have failed in her most important duty as a wife—to quicken with child?

'I know the marks of a whip when I see them. Tell me who beat you.' Valens turned her to face him. Her face was white-lipped. 'I won't do anything to harm you, Julia.'

Silence. Valens listened to the sound of her ragged breathing. The level of anger he felt surprised him. Not since the last of his men died in Aquilia's hold had he felt this strongly.

He clenched his fist and longed to slam it into a wall, or, better still, into whoever had done this. He felt the red mist begin to descend. The memory of Julia's reaction at the Julian compound broke over him. She had shrunk from him then as well. He contented himself with clenching and unclenching his fist.

'Who did this to you, Julia? Your father?'

Her eyes widened. 'Not my father. No one knows about this except you...and the man who did this.'

'Then who?' He touched her shoulder and felt her flinch. He withdrew his hand, unable to bear that she was frightened of his touch. 'I'm not angry with you,

Julia. I just want to know. What sort of person would strike you this savagely?'

Slowly she turned back towards him. Valens longed to draw her back into his arms and kiss away the hurt, but he had to be sure she would not reject him again or worse shrink from him.

'Lucius,' Julia whispered. 'I failed to pleasure him in bed. I tried, but my body disgusted him. Then I could never become pregnant. I prayed to the Good Goddess. Offered sacrifice after sacrifice, but my womb never once quickened. Each time I failed, his fists became harder.'

'Oh, Hades,' Valens swore. Why did it have to be her husband? No wonder she was shaking like a leaf. He'd behaved in an unforgivable manner. He'd nearly lost control as it was. Another caress and would he have been able to stop?

He wasn't sure who he hated more—her ex-husband or himself.

'Julia, please believe me. I have no wish to make you do anything you don't want or desire.' He reached down, picked up the blanket and put it around her shoulders. 'I think I had best take you back to your bedroom now.'

Julia watched as he pulled his tunic on and walked over to the window. Her flesh puckered from the cold. She should never have told him. She must disgust him in the same way she disgusted Lucius. But she hated to think of how he must think of her—a woman so devoid of everything that her husband had resorted to beating her.

'I did my best. I wanted to be a good bride and a good wife, the very embodiment of a Roman matron…' she began, but her throat closed, forcing her to stop. How could she explain how much she longed for children and how her failure to become pregnant had resulted in her husband's anger? He had said that others had his children but not his wife, accused her of practising black magic. Awful accusations when her dearest wish was to hold her own baby in her arms.

'I'm sure you were.' His voice sounded remote and she could see his knuckles gleaming white as they gripped the window ledge.

She took a deep shuddering breath and started again. 'At first, when I stood waiting for him, dressed in my saffron cloak and flame-coloured veil, surrounded by the scent of verbena and sweet marjoram from my wreath, I thought this was how marriage was meant to be. Sabina had assured me that all would be well. She and her mother before her had been married in the same fashion. But before the cries of "kiss the bride" faded into the night, I knew my father had done me a grave disservice.'

'How so?'

'Lucius had absolute control over me. He had everything and I had nothing. He took every opportunity to remind me...' Julia faltered, trying to forget what happened by the marriage bed, or in the months that followed. How she made it impossible for Lucius to fulfill his duty, despite everything she tried, from not moving a muscle as Sabina advised, to... She tightened her hold on her waist.

'But I thought your father retained control over you. Couldn't you have just divorced him?'

'My father would not listen. He thought I was being hysterical. Lucius was always polite to him.'

'But not to you.'

'In private? Never. He has a quick temper for those who cross him.' Julia's throat started to close again. She forced her back straighter. 'I disgusted him—too many curves.'

Valens was at her side, gathering her into his arms. He cradled her, stroked her hair, smoothed it away from her face.

'Why did you divorce?' he asked.

'One evening after the baths, I walked in and found him in our bed...with a boy. He beat me and I finally snapped. I could not stay in that house, so I walked out.' Julia pressed her hands together. There was no need to tell Valens the entire sordid story. 'I had had enough of the gilded prison. On this occasion, Sabina was in Ostia, visiting friends, and my father believed me. He wasn't happy about it, but I was able to divorce Lucius with my father's blessing.'

She waited to hear what Valens would say, but he looked at her with an inscrutable expression.

'I'm sorry,' she said, tightening the ends of the blanket around her shoulders and trying to swallow the lump in her throat. 'I'll go now.'

'Julia, I want to make love with you, but not like this.' His voice was strained.

Julia gave a small nod of her head. Perhaps this was for the best. She refused to beg. 'You're being sensible.'

The corners of his eyes crinkled. 'Not sensible, selfish. I want to have the time to show how it should be done properly. I can see the first faint streaks of dawn.'

'Until some other time,' she said, intending to sweep away, intending there would be no next time.

He caught her arm and pulled her close. She felt the hardness of his body and knew, if she stayed one heartbeat longer, she'd lose all her dignity and beg. He put his hand to his mouth, then his finger traced the outline of her lips.

'Until the next time.'

Chapter Eight

Sunlight streamed through Julia's window when she opened her eyes. The pounding in her head echoed the pounding on the door.

'I know you are in there, Julia, wake up!'

Claudia. Julia flopped against her pillow, wondering at the time. How late had she slept? The sun from the window had reached the bottom of her bed. Most days, she dressed before it crept over the window ledge.

She remembered lying awake for ages, going over the time with Valens, detail by detail, wondering, if she hadn't pulled back, whether they would have become lovers. But she must have drifted off.

She turned her head and saw a white rose, lying on her pillow. When had he left that there? Her fingers touched the petals, and she wondered at the meaning of the gift. Cupid gave a white rose to Harpocrates, the god of silence, to keep him from betraying Venus and her love affairs. Did it have to do with passion or was it a request that she keep silent about his life's story? She tapped the rose against her teeth.

'Julia!' Claudia cried again. 'Are you coming out or am I coming in? You can tell whatever man you have hidden under your bed to leave by the window.'

Julia pressed her hands to her flushed cheeks. Claudia's joke caused her body to tingle. What would it be like to have Valens in her bedroom and to experience his kisses again?

'Since when do I have a man in my bedroom?' Julia called, struggling to keep her voice light as she hurriedly placed the rose on her dressing table.

The door crashed opened and Claudia swept in, face perfectly made up and a gown of the finest green wool clinging to her every curve.

'I'd have a man in my room if I could,' she said with an impish laugh. 'I'd start with that gladiator of yours. By Hercules, he has broad shoulders. And his legs! Imagine how safe a woman must feel in his arms.'

Julia stood up and concentrated on dressing, wishing she dared wear something as suggestive as Claudia's gown and settling instead for a tawny gown and matching shawl and *stola*.

'He's hardly my gladiator,' she protested, wondering how many times she would need to deny it.

The lifted eyebrow from Claudia signalled she had

waited too long before making her protest. Julia tightened her belt just under her breasts. The last thing she wanted was more gossip, more scandal. The story about the brawl over Bato was starting to die down, but at least three people had questioned her about it at the baths yesterday.

'Please believe me…'

'Julia, I'm teasing you,' Claudia said, laying her hand on Julia's shoulder. 'You are such fun—you take everything seriously.'

Julia shifted under Claudia's gaze. She grabbed a pot of red wine dregs and started applying it to her cheeks with fierce short stabs of the brush.

'I told you what my father said. Even a little joke like that could send him back into the arms and plans of Sabina. He says he has told Mettalius "no". Am I to believe him? Sabina kept on and on at him at dinner. She wants him to agree to the betrothal as soon as possible. She has apparently asked the augur at Juno's temple and he believes the omens are right, but my father wishes to consult Caesar's augur. Mettalius tends to align himself with the older senators, rather than Caesar, so there is a slim chance that the augur might read the signs differently.'

Claudia leant forward and tapped a bit of the wine dregs off Julia's left cheek.

'If it is anything like the situation at my brother's

house, you barely see the gladiator. I fail to understand why you are making my light-hearted remark seem like the fatal blow in a hard-fought campaign. Your father heard rumours. All of Rome has. The betting is heavy on which one will win come the games.'

'Valens rescued Bato. You were there. I have scarcely seen him after that episode.' Julia set the brush down with a trembling hand. She knew if she continued to try to apply her make-up, she'd look like one of the mimes from the theatre. 'He's nothing special.'

Claudia pursed her mouth and raised an eyebrow. Julia had the sinking thought that perhaps she had overdone the denials and Claudia had reached her own conclusion.

'Then I guess you have more pressing plans than going to watch the gladiators train with me. It is a full practice today at the Circus Maximus. The opening of the games is but a week away and Caesar wants to take a measure of his gladiators' preparedness.'

A shiver ran through Julia. To see Valens so soon after their late-night encounter. Her heart pounded in her ears. She had to go.

'If you need someone…' Julia said, toying with a pot of face cream.

'Good, it's settled then. We'll leave as soon as you

have finished with your face,' Claudia said, clapping her hands and sending Bato scurrying under the bed. 'This time we will leave Bato with your porter, Clodius—to be on the safe side. Your reputation might not survive another brawl.'

'I never said I'd go.' Julia fastened a string of blue beads around her neck and slipped two gold bracelets on her right wrist, then contemplated her face. How could she apply the extra make-up to ensure she looked stunning without Claudia guessing the reason? 'There is plenty of spinning I should be getting on with, and several scrolls I wanted to read.'

'But you need to go. You must want to feast your eyes on the gladiators up close. Valens is not the only one with broad shoulders. When the games start, the gladiators will look like ants from where we have to stand. The only way you will be able to tell who they are is from their helmets.'

'Who said I was going to the games?' Julia's stomach twisted as if it were thread on a spindle. How could she sit and watch Valens fight, possibly to the death? 'There are a number of things I should be doing, like supervising the making of the new blankets.'

Claudia's mouth dropped open and her hands fell to her sides. Who was the one who disliked being teased? Julia resisted the urge to point this out.

'Julia, you can't say that spinning is more attractive than watching the games. You know some of the top gladiators, now. I'm counting on you.'

'One of the gladiators,' Julia corrected and tried to erase the image of Valens bleeding on the ground from her mind. A chill went through her.

'I still have a few days to convince you otherwise. I am determined to make a supporter of you. Say you'll come today,' Claudia looked at her with pleading eyes. 'It will give you something more to talk about...whenever you chance to meet him.'

Julia picked up a clean brush and started to dust her eyelids with powdered oyster shell, giving her eyes a luminous glow.

'Claudia, do you think any of the gladiators are Roman?' she asked finally, putting one last dab on.

Claudia frowned. 'They are mostly slaves. There might be one or two ex-criminals or maybe a man so down on his luck and deep in debt that he became a contract gladiator. But rumours of any patricians being gladiators are products of the playwrights' imaginations. Nobody becomes a gladiator without a good reason. Why?'

'I wondered about their backgrounds. That's all.' Julia tossed her shawl over her head and carefully arranged the folds. She made a face in her mirror before setting it down on her bedroom table.

'Gladiators are for feasting your eyes on,' Claudia

said with a knowing expression on her face, 'and other parts if you are lucky. Their backgrounds are of little concern. They are symbols, not people.'

'They are people. Valens—'

'Even your gladiator, Julia,' Claudia said sternly. 'Don't you think you are fooling me with your oh-so-casual approach. This is the first time I've seen you spend that much time over your make-up since before you married Lucius.'

'I had wondered, that's all.' Julia tried for an innocent voice. She placed a hand on her friend's arm and gave it a squeeze. 'I have heard this lecture in different guises at least six times in the past week.'

'I will keep repeating it, Julia, until you start listening. Gladiators are different from the likes of you and me. If you become involved with one, and it becomes public currency, you are asking for trouble. Marcia Augustina, the Consul's daughter, decided to ignore convention and move in with a gladiator. Now he's dead and she might as well be—banished to Spain, never to contact her family again. Imagine no family, no friends, no Rome. And for what? A few tumbles in bed with a gladiator who abandoned her. No man is worth that.'

Julia turned to face her friend, pleased she had kept last night to herself. Claudia would misunderstand and would more than likely run to her father for

Julia's own good. She crossed her arms and gave what she hoped was a carefree toss of her head.

'Shall we go and feast our eyes, as you say, or shall we stay here and wait for Sabina to come up with some little chore that has to be done?'

'I'm trying to look after you, Julia.' A crease appeared between Claudia's eyebrows. 'The last thing I want is for your new-found freedom to go to your head. I've seen it happen before…in Pompeii. It nearly happened to me. Widow or divorcée, you must keep to Rome's unwritten rules.'

'Let's get one thing straight, Claudia, old friend.' Julia put the top of her alabaster jar back on with a thump. 'I'm a grown woman and I can look after myself. I have no need for any protectors.'

The cold water from the jug trickled down over Valens's head and shoulders, cooling him off after the morning's practice. He allowed the droplets of water to enter his mouth, enjoying the sweet tang of the water.

'It was a hard session out there,' Tigris remarked after he downed his jug of water, the sweat pouring from every inch of his body. 'The Circus is a much larger place than I had thought. It would be easy to get overawed by the crowd.'

'Yes, Caesar has considered that,' Valens replied laconically.

The exercise had proved the outlet for his frustrations about Julia. His anger at her former husband had driven him to press harder and look for more openings. Perhaps he had been wrong to worry that feelings for someone would take away his appetite for the sport and reduce his focus.

If anything, this morning, it was all the keener. Standing here in the Circus with its rows of wooden seats, he was more determined than ever to win the wooden sword.

'I thought you were about to kill Leoparda.'

'He's a good fighter. In a few bouts' time, I have no doubt he will have earned the right to sit among the first halls and enjoy the privileges it brings.'

'If the gods favour him....'

'You're getting philosophical, Tigris,' Valens said, ducking the jug into the water butt for the third time.

'Missing Maia and the children, I suppose.' Tigris refilled the jug, took a long drink, then wiped his mouth with the back of his hand. 'I find myself thinking about them at odd times and wondering if Crispus has learnt his letters or the peas are coming up in the garden.'

'Spoken like a true farmer, Tigris.'

'I was a farmer once, before the war.' He gestured around the empty arena. 'Before all this.'

Valens rubbed the back of his neck. Tigris must be

unnerved for him to mention his previous life. For four years, he had avoided finding out what Tigris did before, and now he found himself wondering why fate had chosen them. Memory was a dangerous thing.

'There is a sizeable crowd of spectators today,' he said, changing the subject. 'Caesar is whetting the appetite of the mob, trying to ensure his games are a success.'

'Aye, that there is and your girlfriend is among them.'

Valens froze.

'What girlfriend would that be, Tigris?' Valens asked with a hearty laugh. He knew without looking whom Tigris meant, but it bothered him that Tigris had guessed so easily.

'The woman you and Aquilia fought over. He is still is raging about it, vows he will harm you and the woman.'

'She is the daughter of one of Caesar's prominent clients,' Valens retorted, surprised at his growing alarm for Julia's safety. 'He would never dare try to harm someone like that.'

'Since when has a little thing like that stopped Aquilia?'

'What are you talking about, Tigris?' Valens felt the bile rise in his throat. He hoped it was another one of Tigris's jests, a wind-up to see how Valens would react.

'Haven't you heard? Haven't you been listening to the gladiators' mess hall?'

'I have little time for myths and legends, Tigris.' The sweat on the back of his neck turned ice-cold.

'You should pay more attention.' Tigris's eyes were shadowed. Valens noticed how old and careworn his friend looked. 'Aquilia has a reputation for being ruthless, for going all out to win. He seems to know instinctively where an opponent's weak spot is. He has the uncanny ability to bewitch them, turn them to stone, so they say. Hylas barely blocked any of his blows when they fought in Capua two months ago, he stood just there with his shield down and you know his reputation for ferocity.'

'Old wives' tales. Hylas was unlucky that day and let his guard slip. His mind was on other things. Two nights before, armed men attacked Hylas's wife in her house and left her for dead.' Valens looked at his nails. 'I believe I have the measure of the man.'

'It is the other thing that bothered me.'

'In this business the arena must be everything. A gladiator must be able to focus solely on his work.' Valens wondered who he was trying to convince— Tigris or himself.

'You have no idea how much I worry about Maia and the children. Will I behave like Hylas in the arena when faced with Aquilia? And it wasn't just Hylas, you know, there were seven others who had it happen to them in the exact same manner.'

'Their women were attacked before the fight?' Valens looked sharply at Tigris as a stab of concern sliced through his body. He had to protect Julia. He'd sooner cut off a finger than have one hair on her head harmed.

'No, became like stone after Aquilia fixed them with his eye. He bewitched them. They say he has magic powers obtained from the demon goddess he worships. Tell me when a *rentarius* last made the first hall.'

'Tales best told around the brazier, Tigris, along with all the other myths.' Valens forced a laugh from his throat.

'But this time I believe them. Maia and the children need me.'

Valens clapped his friend on the back.

'You need not worry. Have you ever lost in the arena?'

'I can't help it. You wait until one other person becomes the centre of your being.'

'Aquilia will meet me,' Valens said forcefully. 'Not you.'

'It could be any of the first-hall Thracians he fights…'

'Do you think with the betting that is going on, Caesar will miss a chance like this?' Valens shook his head and laid a hand on Tigris's shoulder. 'No, my friend, stop staying awake during nights, Maia and your children will be safe. One day, Fortunata willing, all you will have to worry about is when the barley is ripe.'

'I pray to the gods you are right, but he has vowed vengeance on you and your girlfriend for the insult you paid him.'

'Aquilia should grow up.'

A liquid laugh floated on the breeze towards him. Valens turned to see Julia merrily chatting to her friend, underneath the shade of a green silk parasol. He started to go towards her, then checked his footsteps. He refused to put Julia into danger. He had to protect her in the only way possible. He had to make Aquilia think she no longer mattered. It was going to cut like a knife to do it, but he had to—for Julia's safety.

'You were wrong, Claudia,' Julia said, shading her eyes with her hand and peering out on to the sand-strewn ring. 'We arrived in time. They were taking a break. The gladiators are about to start practising again.'

'Thank the Good Goddess. We appear to have missed the third hall and *tiros* in their practice bouts. The best gladiators are yet to come. These are the ones I am interested in. Pay attention to their feet and legs. You can learn a lot about how the bout will go from the way a gladiator moves his feet.'

Julia watched the gladiators as they marched on to the sand and gave a salute before dividing into pairs.

She scanned the groups until she caught sight of Valens's broad shoulders. Her stomach gave a nervous jump.

He was dressed in his full regalia: armour, grieve and helmet. It was only from the set of his shoulders and the way he carried his sword that she recognised him.

He closed the visor of his battered helmet with a distinctive movement and crouched down.

'Are they going to fight with real swords?' she asked Claudia. 'I thought they practised with wooden swords.'

'The swords are blunt, but they are real,' Claudia answered in a distracted voice. 'It should give the public a good idea of who is in form for the games. Did you see the blow that Tigris just gave that second hall? It was superb.'

'I am not sure how you can tell them apart.' Julia kept her eyes on Valens as he circled his opponent, jabbing right, then left with his sword, probing. 'They all look the same to me.' Except for Valens, she silently added.

'Their helmets are all different. It is one reason for the popularity of the figurines. If you study the helmets, you can determine who is who. I've seen Tigris fight before and his is easy to pick out—it is in the shape of a tiger. Valens is that one over there. The *rentarius* paired with him is called Hermes. He is supposed to be fleet of foot—see the wings etched on to his breastplate.'

Julia gave a brief nod. The arena resounded to the ring of steel against steel as the gladiators clashed, parried and clashed again.

Valens's skill, which she had seen at her father's, seemed to desert him. Julia's heart leapt in her throat as Valens slipped to the ground, and had to use his shield to ward of the blows his opponent rained down on him with his trident. He rolled in the dirt, scrabbling to his knees.

Julia saw his opponent knock Valens again, and Valens half-staggered. She grasped Claudia's hand, wanting to look away, but was unable to tear her eyes from the scene.

When she was certain Hermes had beaten Valens, he lifted his shield and sent Hermes's trident spinning into the air. Immediately Valens counter-attacked and put his sword to Hermes's throat. Hermes raised his left hand, signalling his defeat. The bout was over. Valens had triumphed.

Julia sank down on a wooden seat, her heart thumping in her ears. Her arms trembled as if she had been the one in the fight, instead of being an interested bystander.

'That was quite a bout,' Claudia remarked with obvious satisfaction, twirling her parasol. 'Such moves and such skill.'

'Will they fight this hard in the games?' Julia asked

around the lump in her throat. At least three times she thought Valens would be severely injured. The memory of the gashes on his torso burned on her brain. From this distance, it was impossible to tell if he was hurt. She narrowed her eyes and tried to look for any red gashes or any other sign of injury. But Valens appeared to be fine. Julia drew a deep calming breath.

'Harder and faster. The thrill of the contest fills the very air you breathe. The weapons they fight with during the games are razor sharp. They are tested before the games begin to show the audience.' Claudia's eyes glowed. 'If you thought this was thrilling, wait until you experience the real thing. The excitement is unbearable when the gladiators walk into the ring. Whom will the gods choose to favour that day? Who will live and who will die?'

Julia looked back at Valens. He slapped his former opponent on the back and demonstrated a sword technique. She balled her hand into a fist, hating herself for enjoying the contest.

'At last,' Claudia continued seemingly oblivious to Julia's emotional turmoil, 'you can see why I think he deserves a wooden sword. Only one gladiator out of a hundred would have been able to pull off that last move without getting severely injured. Everyone will be looking for it come the actual fight. The wooden sword is there for him to win, and if he does that move successfully with a sharp sword, Caesar will be hard pressed not to give it to him.'

But at what cost? Julia questioned silently.

'Who are the gladiators without helmets?' she asked to divert Claudia's attention away from Valens.

'Those are the *rentarii* or fishermen. They fight with a trident and net and never wear a helmet. They are the only gladiators whose faces are well known. Some people look down on them for that reason,' Claudia said, pointing. 'I enjoy watching their skill with the net. Shall we go closer?'

The malevolent stare of the gladiator who had quarrelled with Valens caught Julia's eye. She shivered as he deliberately tripped his opponent. There were a few boos from the crowd, but the gladiator responded by casting his net over the man, kicking him with his foot and then triumphantly waving his trident. Some in the crowd seemed to delight in his antics.

'No, I think just here is fine. We can see the whole arena.' Julia swallowed hard as she realised that this cheat was the man Valens would most likely face in a life-or-death struggle.

'If you wish, but you ought to see the skill that Aquilia uses. He will be more than a match for your Valens.'

'For the love of Juno, he's not my gladiator.' Julia

knew the warmth on her cheeks was from more than the hot sun. 'He is a man staying at my father's house. I told you that before.'

'Shall we go talk to him anyway?' Claudia clutched Julia's arm. 'He looks to be finished. See, he's talking to that group of men.'

Julia regarded Valens, who was laughing and talking with a group of toga-clad admirers before he turned to a group of schoolboys standing open-mouthed with their tutor.

She trembled as she remembered the taste of his mouth and the touch of his hands. She watched him demonstrate the way he made the final thrust with his sword. It was hard to tell who looked more thrilled—the boys or their tutor. Suddenly, as if he felt her eyes on him, he turned his head. Their eyes met, and her heart stopped in her mouth. She started to wave her hand, but stopped, puzzled by his remote expression. His brows furrowed and he frowned before a school-boy tugging at his tunic caught his attention and he turned back towards the group.

'He's busy now,' Julia said, hiding her blush with her shawl. She busied her hands with arranging and rearranging the folds of her *stola*. Her mind started whispering reasons why she should have stayed away.

'Those boys are departing. That horror shaking Valens's hand is my second cousin on my mother's side,' Claudia replied. 'A proper little imp. Do you know he put frogs in the fountain just when his mother gave a dinner party for a potential patron? They hopped all over her table, ruining the arrangement of pastries. Let's go greet Valens before that group of soldiers get there.'

'This could be a mistake.' Julia hung back. 'I don't want him to think I'm one of those women who gather around the arena's gates.'

'Julia, stop it. He will be delighted to see a friendly face. You worry too much.' Claudia gave her a small shove forward.

Julia forced her feet towards where Valens stood, looking as remote as a god as he laughed and joked. The smooth strong column of his neck rose above his impossibly broad shoulders.

As they approached, he turned towards the water butt and said something to one of the gladiator school's servants before turning towards the group of soldiers.

Julia waited until the soldiers had departed for him to acknowledge her presence. A warm breeze blew across her face, making a strand of her hair fly into her mouth. Julia pushed it away, but although Valens had turned towards her, he said nothing and his eyes appeared as remote as a statue's. Julia cleared her throat.

'Valens,' she began with a faltering voice barely

above a whisper, 'Claudia and I thought you fought wonderfully well. It was exhilarating to watch.'

Her cheeks were as hot as if she had spent an hour in front of a brazier. She sounded exactly like a lovesick female supporter, sighing for the moon. He seemed to be staring off into the middle distance. Perhaps he had not seen her. She tried again, this time in a louder voice. 'Valens, aren't you going to greet me?'

This time he did looked down, directly into her eyes and her heart dropped to the bottom of her sandals. His face bore little resemblance to the passion-filled face of late last night. This face was haughty, almost cruel. His eyes were chips of black glass.

'Forgive me, I didn't see you there. Julia Antonia and Claudia Julia, how pleasant to see you both.' His tone implied it was anything but.

'Claudia thought it might be a good way to pass the afternoon—watching the gladiators practise.'

'You saw me fight.' His lips turned down at the corners.

'Yes,' Julia said, taking a step backwards. Birds flew in her stomach, pecking it and making it hurt. She tried to understand what she had done wrong. She drew a deep breath and started again 'Claudia invited me. She'll make a supporter of me yet.'

He gave an elaborate bow and a smile that did not quite reach his eyes. Julia tilted her head to one side, trying to assess his mood. He seemed so different from the Valens of last night. She bit her lip. Had she made some terrible mistake? The awful truth whispered in her mind—her body disgusted him like it had Lucius. She tried to keep the misery from swallowing her as she listened to Claudia gush about his skill at turning the trident away.

'You were right and I was wrong. Gladiatorial bouts have merit,' she said when Claudia stopped to take a breath.

'I'm pleased you enjoyed it,' he said with little warmth in his voice. His eyes seemed to dart around the arena. 'Now, if you'll excuse me, I need to speak with some more supporters. Duty calls.'

He gave another bow and was gone. Julia stared after him, stunned. She covered her mouth and nose with her hands, hiding her expression from the world. Last night, she had destroyed everything. She should never have pulled away. She disgusted him in the same way she had disgusted Lucius.

'Of all the nerve,' Claudia said with her hands on her hips. 'He might have at least greeted me pleasantly. He barely said two words to me. All the nice things I said to him. It would serve him right if I switched allegiances.'

Julia's backbone sagged, and she felt the urge to run away. Immediately she straightened. She had acted properly. He had been insufferable, but the only thing he had wounded was her pride. And her pride would mend…eventually.

'It has been a pleasant afternoon, Claudia, but I think the spinning is calling me. Sabina can be such a pain at times.' She rushed her words, hoping Claudia would understand. 'I won't join you at the baths after all.'

'I thought you were going to give me a game rolling hoops at the gym, to see if you could even the score up. I am leading the series—sixteen to fourteen.'

A few more hours pretending everything was fine, chatting and listening to Claudia dissect various gladiators' anatomies was impossible, torture of the worst sort. Julia pressed her lips into a firm line.

'My sleep was disturbed last night, Claudia. I feel a bit unwell,' she lied. 'I'm not up to going to the public baths today. I think I'll have a bath in Sabina's new plunge tub.'

She turned on her heel and nearly crashed into Aquilia's massive chest. She mumbled an apology and started to walk on, but he caught her arm.

'You're a very pretty lady,' he said with a thick accent. 'You Valens's woman?'

'I am nobody's woman,' Julia replied crossly, wrenching her arm free from his grasp and marched out of the gate without looking back.

Chapter Nine

Julia's anger dissipated as she lowered her body into the steaming hot water scented with white rose petals. She lay back against the rim of the tub and looked at the mosaics of dolphins that adorned the wall of the newly installed bath suite.

Her stepmother had spared no expense in the decoration, but the rooms were rarely used. Sabina preferred to keep the bathing suite as a showpiece.

Julia had scraped the arena's sand and dust off with oil and her *strigil*. If only she could scrape the memory of Valens's arms away so easily.

She would do this more often, she thought, allowing her body to float in the warm enveloping water. What was the point of a bathing suite that was for viewing only?

Her mind drifted back over the day's events. She trailed her hand along the water, trying to be realistic and unemotional. What had she expected—for Valens to sweep her into his arms and declare his undying love in front of that crowd?

The only thing that would have accomplished would have been a quick betrothal to Mettalius or somebody worse. It was far better she get over her obsession with this man and on with her real life. The only place anything with him would lead to was a quick trip to Sabina's tame soothsayer and betrothal to whomever Sabina felt would best benefit the family. She had to be practical. She must keep silent about what had passed between them, no matter how much her heart longed to shout it and demand explanations.

Julia drew a shuddering breath and reached for her towel. If she stayed in much longer, she'd turn into a prune with water leaking from her fingertips and no further on in her dilemma.

Her hand encountered a bare foot, rather than the cloth she expected. She drew it hastily back.

'Are you looking for this?' Valens's voice flowed over her.

She glanced up to see him holding her towel. The whiteness of his tunic contrasted with his skin, glowing golden in the lamplight. His broad shoulders blocked out the door, and she remembered all too clearly how they had felt against her hands this morning. She also remembered his angry words of a few hours ago.

'What are you doing here?' she squeaked, before sinking her body against the bottom of the tub, grateful for the rose petals and the flickering light.

'I could ask the same question of you.'

'I'm having a bath,' Julia retorted indignantly. 'Leave.'

'I was attempting to do the same. Your plunge bath looks inviting.' He dipped his hand in. 'Hot but not scalding, just the thing to soothe my aching muscles. I had a quick wash after practice, but wanted to ease my shoulder. I injured it three years ago and it can play up at times.'

Julia glared. How dare he act like this! He had no business being here. She had told him that he was unwelcome. 'I was here first.'

'And your point is…?'

'Knock and wait your turn.'

Valens lifted one eyebrow and stared at her with an amused expression on his face. Julia was acutely conscience that the white rose petals in the flickering light provided only the minimum of cover and that her discarded clothes lay in an untidy heap on the far side of the room.

'I did knock—you ignored me. I had assumed the bath suite was empty. It always has been before.'

'The instant you realised I was here, you should have left,' Julia retorted.

'If you had wanted privacy,' he said with a crinkle of his eyes, 'you should have bolted the door…like I did.'

Julia's heart stopped. He had bolted the door. They were here alone, and with only petal-strewn water between her naked body and his hooded gaze.

'If you had called out, I'd have come out as soon as I had finished…' she began and started to wonder how she could gracefully exit from the bath without revealing more than she absolutely had to.

'You were a pleasant surprise,' he said with a smile spreading over his face. 'I had wondered when we would next encounter each other.'

'There will be no encountering,' Julia said with grim determination. 'I had planned on ignoring you for the rest of my life. My towel, if you please.'

She held out her hand, but turned her face away from him. Her fingers closed gratefully around the cloth. If she held it up between her and Valens and then climbed out backwards, crouching down, she might be able to do it. She started to climb. Her right foot slipped and she nearly fell back in the water. Julia tightened her jaw and tried again.

'Julia, what is the matter? Are you injured? Is your ankle giving you problems?'

At the sound of his voice, Julia gave up trying to be dignified. She scrambled all the way out of the bath, stood dripping on to the fish mosaic, her back to

Valens, and wrapped the towel firmly around her body. She reached for another from the pile and draped it over her shoulders. Then picked up a third towel and started vigorously to dry her hair.

If I ignore him, he might leave.

'You can tell me.' He put his warm hands on her shoulders. Julia felt the flame of desire leap and cursed her treacherous body. 'Is there anything I can do to help? Any little thing?'

'You made your feelings quite clear this afternoon,' she said through clenched teeth, trying to ignore the pleadings of her body that became louder with every breath she took.

'And which feelings would they be?' Valens asked. His hardness pressed into her backside as he pulled her against him, leaving her in no doubt as to his aroused state.

Julia shivered and stepped away from him, wrapping the towel tightly around her body. She refused to allow her heart to be used as a plaything. Love-making was not a game for her.

'At the Circus Maximus—' she began.

'I was rude and impossible,' Valens finished her sentence and captured her shoulders again, turning her towards him. His finger lifted her chin. 'Believe me, Julia, I know and I apologise, but it was for a good reason. I had no wish to put you in danger. Think of what would have happened if Roman tongues began to wag again. Your dog was not with you this time.'

She gazed into his dark eyes, eyes that promised much, eyes that smouldered. The ice of this afternoon had become a smouldering fire of passion. She felt her nipples harden at his look. She wanted to believe his words, but this afternoon still stung.

'And that's it? I am now supposed to fall into your arms?' she asked sarcastically. It would be too easy to fall and give her body up to that passionate promise.

'That was the general idea.'

A dimple played in the corner of his mouth, tempting her, calling to her, making her want to taste him. She forced her lips to press tight and clenched her fist more firmly around the towel that was wrapped about her body. She refused to drop into his lap like a ripe plum.

'Did you have this thought in your mind before you came here or did it just form?' She made her voice as cutting as possible.

His hands pushed the towel off her shoulders before he trailed his fingers down her arms. The flame in his eyes leapt further, nearly scorching her in its intensity.

'It could be enjoyable for both of us.'

Her body swayed towards his and her breasts touched his chest. His arms came round and held her closer. So close she could hear his heartbeat thumping in her ears.

'Soft words are not required.' Her breathing sounded as if she had run a long race. More than half of her hoped he'd swoop to capture her lips. It bothered her. After all the hurt he'd given her today, Venus help her, she still wanted him. The fact troubled her. 'I need to know why. I am not some plaything, Valens, to be used and discarded at will.'

He ran his hand through her hair, tangling it and sending a series of shivers down her spine.

'I know you are not, but you need to understand, Julia—there is more to my life than keeping you happy. I want to keep you and your reputation safe. I have enough to worry about in the arena, without fearing for you.'

Julia shook her head, attempting to clear it of buzzing. She stepped away from his encircling arms, ran a hand through the rapidly cooling water and watched the droplets fall off her fingers. Nobody worried about her in that way. They only cared for her as if she was a glass soldier in a game of *latrunculi*.

'I hardly think anyone would get the wrong idea. I was not asking you to kiss me, Valens. I merely came up to say hello out of politeness's sake.'

'Julia,' he said thickly, 'there are those who seek to harm me through you, if they thought there was anything between us.'

'Who?'

'Aquilia for one,' was the immediate answer.

'He would never dare.' Then she remembered Aquilia's clammy hand on her sleeve and shivered.

'Underestimating him is a mistake I made once and have no wish to make again.' His voice held a note of determination.

'I thought you two had never met in combat,' she said in confusion. 'What sort of mistake did you make?'

Silence filled the chamber. Julia felt Valens's mood change. The passion in his eyes vanished and his face became colder, crueller. His being stilled and it was as if he had entered some private place in his mind, a place she could not follow.

Her impulsive questions had ruined everything, Julia thought. She needed to curb her tongue.

Julia fumbled with her clothes, attempting to pull her undertunic over her head without allowing the towel to slip. She needed to be away from here, before she ended up in his arms again. Her under-tunic clung to her body where it was still damp, as she pulled it past her knees. It would have to do. Julia started to tie the belt around her chest. She had to get away. The walls seemed to be closing in on her, pushing her closer to Valens.

'Five years ago, he was the pirate chief responsible for capturing me.' Valens's voice resounded in the small chamber, echoing off the walls.

Julia's hand froze and the belt slipped through her fingers, falling silently to the floor. She stared at him in amazement, all becoming clear. She thought of the nightmare she had seen, and his pleas for help against an all-too-real-enemy.

'You should have said something. That day when Bato disrupted the ceremony,' she whispered, 'was that why you goaded him?'

'I have seen him slay men for looking him in the wrong way. I have seen him rape women for the sheer pleasure of hearing their screams. I have seen him murder for no better reason than that he was bored.' He raked his hand through his hair. 'That day, I suppose I wanted to show him that he no longer held power over me. I regret involving you.'

His eyes looked past her to the shadows on the walls. Julia turned her head and she thought she could see the ships, the people and the murder in the flickers. She shivered and drew her undertunic tighter about her.

'He should have been crucified,' she said, forcing her gaze from the wall, trying to block out her imaginings. 'The arena is too good for people like that.'

'General Pompey and the rest of the senators in their wisdom decided to send him to the games.' Valens said laconically. He gave a shrug and a smile. 'Who is a mere gladiator to second-guess the wishes of perhaps the greatest general Rome has ever known?'

Julia remembered the curious dead-eyed glare Aquilia had given her that afternoon and how he had blocked her way when she tried to leave. A shiver ran through her, chilling her to bone despite the heat of the room. 'Do you think he'd still be able to hurt people, innocent people?' *Like me?* Julia crossed her arms and hugged her waist tight.

Valens crossed the floor of the small room in two steps. He gathered Julia into his arms and held her close. She rested her head on his chest and listened to the thumping of his heart. It told her far more than words ever could. Neither spoke.

'Julia, let me worry about Aquilia,' he said when he broke the silence. 'If it meant hurting you a little bit to save you from a greater injury, then I would do it again. It is for that reason only I seemed offhand. I did want to talk to you, but I worried that Aquilia would get ideas.'

'But why would he want to hurt me?'

'To strike at me. To put me off my stride. The man is determined to win at all costs. He has used the tactic before, I am certain of it. Not witchcraft, as Tigris claims, but good old-fashioned intimidation tactics. I wanted to ensure he had no reason to strike out at you, to harm you. If he had thought we were involved… Now say you forgive me,' he whispered against her hair.

Julia reached up and touched his face. 'I wished you had explained sooner.'

His answer was to brush her forehead with his lips.

Julia touched her mouth to his throat and tasted the slight saltiness of his skin. His arms tightened and the tenderness of a moment before was replaced with something else. It made Julia's heart beat faster and every muscle in her body feel alive.

'Your skin tastes of roses,' he said, his lips making trails of fire down her throat. Little flames of fire that grew and spread, until her body was alight.

'I thought you were only interested in soaking your aching shoulder,' Julia teased.

'It can wait.'

He touched her collarbone, pushing her gown off her shoulders. His tongue traced the length of her neck. Then he ran his hands down her body. She arched her back, pressing closer to him. His fingers stroked her breasts, fondling the nipples through the thin material until her body exploded with exquisite pain. Her breath came in short sharp gasps and her fingers plucked at the gown. Where before she had welcomed it as protection, now it imprisoned her body, prevented her skin from touching him the way she longed to.

'I think I shall begin to tutor you in what pleasure is about,' he whispered in a husky voice. His skin glowed golden in the lamplight.

His mouth touched hers and before she had a chance to draw back, he drew her forward so that her midriff touched his. His hands slid down her back to cup her bottom, and pulled her tighter against him. She could feel the strength of his desire and moaned in the back of her throat.

He eased her back among the discarded clothes and the warmth of the hypocaust-heated floor rose up to meet her. He slipped his hand under her tunic, running it up and down her curves. Her heart soared. He was touching her as if she was made of precious glass, with a slow sweetness. Her curves did not disgust him. He had acted that way because he sought to protect her. She felt wanted. This is what passion between a man and a woman felt like. She was alive in a way she had not been before, in a way she had never dreamt of being before.

With one fluid movement, he lifted and discarded both their tunics and Julia felt the smoothness of his skin against her. Nothing but the merest sheen separated them.

Where his hand had stroked, his mouth followed. She arched her back, driving upwards as his tongue lapped at her breast, drawing ever-increasing circles, before returning to suckle again. She closed her eyes and her body was rocked on a sea of sensation.

Tentatively she lifted a hand and ran it down the

length of his back, feeling the indents of long-healed scars. How much he had endured. She raised her head and kissed a white scar on his chest. His thumb traced the outline of her lips.

'Thank you.' His voice was a husky rasp.

She nodded, unable to say anything.

His gentle fingers continued their exploration of her body, building waves of desire that peaked and then crashed throughout her body, filling her with a burning need to be one with him. But a little voice kept whispering about her failures. She might be experiencing this, but was he? What if she disappointed him? She resisted the temptation to move.

His hands gently nudged her thighs apart and became entangled in her curls. One finger touched her innermost spot and then retreated. A stab of fear coursed through her. What would he find there? Would he become angry like Lucius had? Julia steeled herself for rejection. But he kissed a forefinger, then touched her lips. The need within her deepened.

She tugged at his shoulders and he moved back up her body until the tip of him was positioned between her thighs.

'Are you ready?' His voice was barely recognizable.

She stiffened, knowing what was coming next and fearing the pain that had always come with it. She worried her earlier experiences had spoilt her for ever.

And she hated to think that he might be disappointed in her. But how to tell him? She wanted to go on, her body demanded it, but she was nervous about the ultimate joining. She wanted him to experience what she was. Her fingers reached out and touched the smooth curls on his head where they caressed his forehead.

He raised his head, his dark eyes boring into her, reaching her soul. 'I only want to give you pleasure, Julia. You are giving me so much. See what you are doing to me. Feel what you are doing.'

He gently took her hand and brought it down to his shaft, urged her to touch it, to explore its smooth hardness. It felt like warm marble. A shudder of excitement coursed through her body. She had caused this. He wanted her. He was here because he wanted to taste her, to kiss her, to make love to her. He was not here because it was his duty. He was here because he desired her and wanted to give her pleasure.

She drew his face towards hers and recaptured his mouth, parting her lips and inviting his tongue to enter and take possession of her. He groaned in the back of his throat. Their tongues touched, tasted and tormented each other until she felt the warmth between her legs grow hot and slick.

With each stroke of his tongue, her fears receded until they became consumed in the flame he was stoking inside her. Every nerve in her body tingled as if it was on fire. She felt his probing fingers enter her secret place once again and shuddered with pleasure as they slipped in and out, faster and faster. Her back arched, demanding more. She wanted everything. Her legs parted. She moaned in the back of her throat and she felt the whole length of him enter her and her body stretched to envelope him.

Then he lay still, with his pulsating warmth buried deep within her as if that was all he desired. But Julia knew it was not enough. Not nearly enough. She needed more. She wanted to feel the pleasure that comes with joining. With an age-old instinct, she began to move her hips, feeling the length of him within her, increasing her need for him.

Always when she was married, she had dreaded this bit and had tried to lie as still as possible, but now she knew she wanted it to last for ever. She wanted to feel the rhythm of his body, this feeling of soaring and yet being as close to someone as possible. This is what the poets wrote about. This was why the gods came down to earth. This was what it meant to be a woman.

She moved her hips faster and he responded, matching her stroke for stroke. She rode the crest with him until the shuddering finish, a finish where she heard a cry and found it impossible to tell from whose breath it had been torn as he plunged deep within her body.

* * *

Later, in the circle of his arms, Julia trailed her hand in the cool water of the bath. A languor filled her; although her body ached in places she never dreamt possible, she had never felt this satisfied, this alive before. This was what lovemaking was supposed to feel like. At last, she understood why the poets praised it. Her encounters with Lucius had never made her feel this way.

She had assumed her failure with Lucius had been her fault, but she now knew that for a lie. She had not failed with Valens. What passed between them was beyond all her imaginings.

'It appears I have delayed you,' she said, her lips curving as she remembered the pleasure and it was pleasure he had given her.

Valens gave a smile and pushed a tendril of hair back from her forehead.

'Would that you could always delay me like this,' he said, pulling her close and running a hand down her body. Then he heaved a sigh and straightened. 'But I fear you are correct, the water will be only enough to wash the sweat from my brow. Luckily I found another way to ease my ache.'

Always. A thrill of excitement followed by a stab of fear ran through Julia. She wanted to think no further than his arms, but she had to. She wanted this to more than just one encounter. She knew that this was the man she wanted to be with for ever, but her father would never allow a liaison with a slave. It was a scandal for a Roman woman of patrician descent to be involved with a plebeian, a common man, let alone a slave.

The story Claudia had imparted about Marcia Augustina and her lover rose in her mind and a shudder ran through her soul. Exile, a living death and the lover had died. Julia gazed over Valens's naked shoulder towards the dolphins frolicking on the wall. Never to see Rome again or to hear her father's voice. To lose her identity and cease to be a member of the Julius family. Despite the passion she had just experienced, she wasn't sure she was ready for that. She had to be sensible.

Gladiators were for one night was Claudia's motto. It had to be hers as well. She would have to become like the other women who followed the sport. She stood up and started dressing, a small action to bring normality back to her world.

'You are thinking deep thoughts,' he said, catching her hand; his thumb traced small circles on the inside of her wrist, sending sensation after sensation up her arm. Her knees started to turn liquid and she was certain she'd press herself against him, demanding.

'Just thoughts,' she replied and wondered if there was anything she could do, any way she could get him to be a citizen instead of a gladiator. If he wasn't a slave, there was the slimmest of chances she could persuade her father to accept the union. Then she would not have to face the awful spectre of leaving everything she held dear. Her hands trembled as she tried to fasten her belt. 'Mainly about how we depart from this place and what happens after that.'

'You should go first. Now,' he said, his face turning grave. He took the belt from her unresisting hand and tightened it about her chest. 'Dinner will be soon and your stepmother will be expecting your presence.'

Their gazes met and held.

Julia swallowed hard. She should go, but her feet refused to move. She wanted to stay wrapped in this cocoon of safety, not to face what lay out there.

'I want to stay with you,' she whispered and lay her head against his chest. 'A little while longer.'

He shook his head before planting a kiss on her forehead.

'You must go.' He gave her hand a squeeze and rubbed his thumb against her swollen lips. 'There will be time to be together, I promise, but for now…'

Julia felt the colour rise in her cheeks. He made it sound as if this meant more to him than a quick tumble. For now, that was enough. It would have to be enough. Until she figured out a way. There had to be a way.

'Sleep tight, my gladiator,' she said, gathering her

things in her arms. 'May no Furies invade your dreams tonight.'

'Should I encounter one, I know where to find a cure.' He opened the bathroom door, and quickly glanced outside. 'Now go while there is no one about and before your stepmother decides to investigate where you are.'

Julia walked quickly away from the bath suite, vowing with each tap of her sandal that one day she would not skulk in the corners with Valens, but would stand by his side.

Valens stared after Julia's slim figure as she flitted across the courtyard. With each step, he watched the curve of her ankle appear and disappear. She stopped in the doorway and looked back, her gaze meeting his. The tide of passion began to rise again in Valens's body. He longed to go to her and bring her back into this enchanted room.

His fingers curled around the doorframe, holding him there. He had never expected to discover her here, and had allowed his desire for her to overcome his reason. The depth of his reaction frightened him. It was impossible to ignore that he had feelings for the girl and wanted her to be his.

He grabbed his *strigil* and used the blade to scrape his skin clean for the second time that day. He wished he could discover a device to peel off the layers of his life and send him back to before, and he could lead his life spotless up to the point where he met Julia. Valens pressed down with the *strigil*, bringing his mind back to the present. His past had no meaning for him. He refused to remember it. He walked in the sandals of a gladiator now—who he had been had no bearing on who he was or who he could be. He had learnt that lesson and it had kept him alive.

He wished he held a status worthy of her. There was no denying the hardest part would be when her father married her off to another, but to offer now would mean punishment—for both of them.

He had no illusions about what would happen or about the double standards of Roman life. Roman matrons were for Romans only—in public, at any rate. Men might enjoy the company of slaves, but women never—Roman women must be kept pure for breeding more Romans.

He slammed the *strigil* down and angrily bathed his body in the cool water. The wetness enveloped and soothed him.

There was little point in railing against what could have been. He had to be sensible. The only way forward was to carry on with his plan. Should the gods favour him, he'd win the *rudius*; if not, he'd die trying. Either way, he'd regain the honour he needed.

Valens closed his eyes and allowed himself to dream about what could happen, if all went as planned. He built villas in the air, imagining Julia with two small boys clinging to her skirts as they lived together on his estate near Pompeii, far away from the frenzy of the arena. He dribbled water over his head and smiled at his fancy.

Then he pushed it away. All that could come after he had defeated Aquilia, after he had won the *rudius* and was a slave no longer.

Julia stood at the entrance to the dining room, waiting to have her feet washed by one of the servants. The last bang of the gong sounded, and even though she anticipated Valens would not be there, Julia had decided to wear her rose-coloured gap-sleeve gown. It could help explain the high colour in her cheeks, she decided as she slipped off her sandals and prepared to enter the room.

The dining room with its frescoed walls of blue and green, depicting the perfect garden, was the one room her father had refused to allow Sabina to modernise. Julia instinctively sought out her mother's favourite fresco, a tree with two doves in it. But before her eyes reached it, her gaze fell on Valens. He raised an eyebrow and his lips contracted to give a silent appreciative whistle. She felt the colour rise higher in her cheeks.

His hair curled slightly from the damp of the bath, and he had dressed carefully in a longer pure white tunic, one that only revealed his calves. If she had been meeting him for the first time, she would have sworn he was a patrician, rather than a gladiator. She found it impossible to do anything but stare at him. The memories of what they had just experienced flooding her body.

'Ah, Julia, at long last you arrive.' Sabina's sneer cut across Julia's confusion. 'It is so pleasing that you have taken time out of your busy schedule and finally decided to make an appearance. I see the pile of wool is sitting untouched in the atrium where you left it yesterday.'

'I had a slight headache and was resting,' Julia answered calmly. 'It wasn't until I heard the gong that I realised the time.'

The truth, but not the whole truth. Julia trained her gaze on the ornate floral patter of the middle couch.

'Sabina, Julia is but a little late,' her father said. 'The other guests have just finished having their feet washed. And it is a pleasure to see her looking so pretty.'

'Try to keep better track of the time,' Sabina said, pursing her lips as if she had swallowed a glass of vinegar. 'You shall have to have the right couch with the gladiator next to you. I have already assigned your usual place to Livia.'

Julia vaguely listened while Sabina told the two other couples where they would be reclining. Her heart had leapt at the thought of being so near Valens so soon, but then had plummeted to the hem of her gown. She would have to be very careful not to betray her interest in him. This was the first time she had encountered him under the watchful gaze of her father. She had to remain calm.

At Sabina's signal, Julia went to the couch on the far right-hand side and started to arrange herself crosswise. Within a breath, Valens was reclining beside her. She ruthlessly suppressed a tingle as she felt his breath on her cheek.

'I thought you dined alone,' she said, forcing her lungs to breathe normally.

Valens reached over and put a cushion between her and his body. 'Are you disappointed that I am here?'

'Not disappointed, surprised. You gave no indication when... when...' Julia's voice trailed off.

'Your father came into the bathing suite just after you left and insisted I join him for dinner. It seemed churlish to refuse an invitation from the man who has provided me with all this hospitality.'

Julia's breath caught in her throat and she started to cough as she realised how fortunate she had been to escape from the bath suite undetected. Had she lingered a little while longer, her father might have burst in on them. Or he might have been waiting patiently outside when Valens had unbolted the door. She brought her napkin up to her face to hide the worst of the blush.

'I had not realised…'

'We understand each other,' Valens said smoothly. He took a napkin from the waiter, spread it in front of him and then washed his hands in the ewer of perfumed water that another waiter proffered. 'Your father is an honourable man and I can respect that honour. So it was with great pride I accepted his invitation to dine.'

Julia risked a glance at his profile, but she found it impossible to read. Did he mean that he felt he had somehow dishonoured her father's hospitality? Or was she trying to read too much into his words? She concentrated on arranging her napkin and ignoring the stabs of guilt and doubt. She risked a glance at her father, but he was speaking to one of the guests. Julia glanced down at her hands. The time was wrong for confessing.

'I see Senator Mettalius is not here,' Julia said, changing the subject.

'Your father said when he invited me that the senator had pleaded another engagement and there was a place spare,' Valens answered in an undertone. 'He wants to keep the guests to the number recommended by his soothsayer.'

'That could explain Sabina's bad mood.' Julia whispered back. 'A senator at the table would have given her superiority over Livia Gladiticus, the woman on my father's left and Sabina's great social rival. Sabina used to take great pride inviting Lucius, my former husband. Every second conversation was about how wonderfully he was doing in the Senate. Sabina's overriding ambition is to be greater than Livia. See how many times she has pointed out the new water clock and its ability to spit out pebbles on the hour.'

'And was your ex-husband a rising star? Another Pompey?'

'No, but Sabina ignored that. She only saw the broad purple stripe of his senatorial toga and smelt its stench from the Tyrian shellfish dye.'

'There is more to a man's character than the stripe of his toga and the odour of his clothes,' Valens said decisively.

'I know…' Julia sighed '…but try telling Sabina or my father that.'

As the first course of small pastries stuffed with dates and meat was passed around, she tried to concentrate on the ebb and flow of the conversation and ignore the movement of Valens's body, mere inches from her own. There had to be a way of making her father see beyond Valens's status to the good and honourable man she had begun to discover.

'What are dear Julia's prospects for remarriage?' Livia's voice boomed out as the servants wiped the marble table in preparation for the next course. 'I have been waiting for weeks for this fabulous announcement you have been promising, Sabina.'

'Go on, Sabina, you may tell our friends,' Julius Antonius said in a measured voice as he finished washing his hands in the perfumed water. 'You may tell our friends what we have decided to do…about Julia's marriage.'

Julia's hand trembled as she lifted her cup of honey-sweetened wine. She found it difficult to credit that her father would contract a marriage without consulting her. He had promised. All her happiness at this afternoon seemed to taste like ashes in her mouth. She wanted to weep. It took all of her willpower not to throw the napkin down and storm out of the room. She felt the gentle pressure of Valens's hand on her elbow, steadying her. It was difficult to believe this was happening to her. Her father had promised to wait.

'You know what men are like, Livia.' Sabina paused and theatrically rolled her eyes to the ceiling. 'It all depends on the augur and the omens apparently. Julius Antonius wants to consult the very best as we have no desire to have a repeat of the last time. You all know what a disaster for the family that was.'

Sabina's eyes narrowed as she stared directly at

Julia. She was left in no doubt whom Sabina blamed for the breakdown of the marriage.

'When are you consulting the augur?'

Julia's breath caught in her throat. She stared at the centrepiece of fruit.

'Tomorrow morning at three hours,' Sabina replied, patting her hair and pointedly turning away from Julia. 'Julius Antonius arranged it all without asking me. This augur, Apius, at the Temple of Venus, comes highly recommended by no less than Caesar himself.'

Julia felt her winecup begin to slip out of her grasp. The sound of Sabina's words echoed in her brain—tomorrow.

Valens eased her fingers away from the cup and placed it on the table. She gave him a grateful glance and he inclined his head very slightly. He had spoken of protecting her, but he could not protect her from this fate. Did he even want to? And what happened when she was married? She knew her sense of duty would never let her betray her husband.

The rest of the meal and the evening's entertainment passed in a blur. Each time she risked a glance at Valens, his face seemed to grow more remote and stone-like until it looked like it was chiselled out of granite. The warmth in his eyes seemed to have disappeared entirely by the third course, leaving only chips of black glass.

Julia picked at her cakes soaked in sweet wine, unable to concentrate as her thoughts kept circling back to one fact. Tomorrow her fate would be decided and she faced a future without Valens. She had to confront the stark truth. Their encounter had only been a brief interlude in her life.

Chapter Ten

Valens slammed the door to his bedroom shut with a satisfyingly loud bang. The dinner had been a mistake. He should have ignored the blandishments of Julius Antonius and had supper in his room as he had done every day since he had arrived in this household. But the desire to see Julia again had been too strong.

Reclining on the couch, he had been reminded that a Roman dinner party was very different from the parties he attended as a gladiator. He also remembered how his mother had lived for dinner parties, how she enjoyed supervising the cooks and fussing over the food. She had enjoyed the speeches after the food, the entertainment.

Even after five years, he heard echoes of her laughter in some of the stories. One or two jokes were ones he knew she would have smiled at. He also knew how she wilted whenever his father forbade the parties. She had been a pale imitation of herself on their estates in northern Italy, only coming to life when they returned to Rome.

From her flushed cheeks, and bright eyes, Valens knew Julia had enjoyed the dinner. What would it mean to her if such things were forbidden? If former friends walked on the other side of the road rather than greet her, as he knew must happen if their liaison became public currency?

The hardest part of the whole evening was listening to Julius Antonius calmly announce that his daughter's future was to be decided in the morning. In that bald statement, Valens knew he did not want to see her become a bride to another man. It had taken all of his willpower to refrain from asking for more time. All he wanted was the chance to compete for her, but that could not happen until he had won the rudius.

Or could it? There was a way he had not tried. He had refused to try.

Valens strode over to his iron-bound trunk and searched through his belongings for the cloak he wore to the opening ceremony. His fingers closed around the brooch pinned to the right-hand shoulder, the floodgates of his memory opening.

He should act now. Confront his father. Attempt to regain his birthright that way, an insistent voice whispered in his brain. It would be so easy. He stood to gain much. Once his father saw him in the flesh, he'd throw his arms wide and welcome him back, ignoring the past. Valens allowed the brooch to slip from his grip as he remembered his father's sneering remarks about gladiators. If he had been unwilling to ransom his son from a pirate's hold, why would he be willing to help now when his son had risen to the top of his disreputable profession?

To acknowledge him as his son, his father would have to admit that his own flesh and blood, a member of one of Rome's oldest families, was an *infamis*. The one consistent refrain of his childhood was that members of his family died before they disgraced the family name.

Valens bowed his head, hating what he had become, yet he knew he was a far more honourable man than the junior tribune who had left Rome on the troopship bound for North Africa, despite whatever Roman society might think.

His hand closed around the brooch. It was tempting, but he had to stick to his original plan. When he confronted his father, he wanted not to be in a position of having to beg. His father had left him to die once. Why should his father help him now?

Valens bent down and pushed the brooch and cloak to the bottom of his trunk. It had been a lapse to even think about such things. He had come this far without any help. He had found a way to solve his problems on his own and he would not seek help now.

He would try to buy time for Julia, but he could not look beyond the games. He would have to trust the gods, something he had found impossible to do. But what if they had a gentle nudge?

Julia entered the dank Temple of Venus the next morning with a heavy heart. She knew Juno and Minerva had ignored her prayers. The white rose on her dressing table had wilted. The smell of incense and roasted lamb assaulted her nose. Her father, dressed in his best white toga with its narrow purple stripe proclaiming his equestrian status, led the way towards the main altar. Sabina, the very picture of a pious Roman matron, followed closely on his heels. Behind her, Julia could hear the soft bleating of the newborn lamb her father intended to offer to the temple as a sacrifice.

Despite the number of layers she wore, Julia shivered as they waited for the augur to arrive. When a door beside the high altar finally opened and a bald-headed man dressed in priestly robes appeared, the only thing Julia wanted was for the ordeal to be over.

'The questions you wish the goddess to answer, please,' the augur intoned in a singsong voice after the initial ceremony finished.

Julia's father bowed low and withdrew a scroll from a fold in his toga. 'These are the questions concerning the fate of my daughter.'

The priest appeared to go into a trance as one of his apprentices waved heavy incense over the scroll. Another banged a drum slowly, the beats filling the cold temple.

Julia pressed her palms together and offered prayer after prayer to Venus. She had to understand about affairs of the heart.

'As to the first question,' the priest said, opening his eyes, 'the omens are poor for an alliance with Mettalius Scipio. The goddess has permitted me to see that his star is on the wane. Your family will suffer should such an alliance be pursued.'

Julia bowed her head against her hands. Venus had answered.

'But, but—' Sabina exclaimed. 'He's a senator.'

'Who is this woman who doubts the goddess's word?' The priest's face grew thunderous and Sabina shrank back.

The priest paused, and waited for the temple to grow silent. Julia could hear the faint noise of the street. He gave a nod and the drumbeat started again as the priest did a series of complicated motions with his hands over the scroll. He gestured to one of the acolytes who brought a shiny bowl filled with a red liquid. The priest nodded. And the drumming ceased.

'As to your questions about where to seek a match, the omens assure me that you are best seeking an alliance with someone who has been restored from death.'

The temple went silent. Julia felt a curl of cold trace down her backbone. How could anybody be restored from death? The priest's prophecy made no sense. Who had her father picked out?

'Restored from death! Are you positive that is what the omens say?' Julius Antonius questioned. 'Don't you mean restored to health?'

The priest stared at him with cold eyes.

'If you would like me to re-examine the entrails, it will be another fifty *denarii*.'

'I thought when we discussed my intentions…' Julius Antonius blustered.

The priest pressed his fingertips together, forming a temple. His eyes flashed cold fire.

'When we talked, I agreed to read the entrails once for you. I told you then that the goddess moves in mysterious ways. Do you question my word as priest? The price of knowledge is not cheap.'

'I told you this augur is a charlatan!' Sabina exclaimed. 'How can anybody be restored from death? Julius Antonius, I told you that we ought to—'

'I will have silence in my temple,' the priest roared. 'You were warned to keep silent. Escort that woman out!'

Julia watched as Sabina was forced to leave the temple. Every limb felt tired. But the one thing she knew was that she would not have to marry Mettalius. She'd worry about the other part of the prediction later.

'Shall we go, Father?' Julia asked as the priest finished the ceremony and departed.

'What?' Julius Antonius shook his head. 'Julia, the priest's second prediction was entirely unexpected. It appears the goddess must speak to him after all.'

'I am not sure I understand you, Father.'

'Dealing with augurs can be a tricky business, Julia. I had rather thought he would say something different.' His lips gave a queer half-smile. 'I dare say your stepmother thought it would be something else again.'

Julia tilted her head and look at her father, trying to assess what he was saying. 'Surely the priest speaks for Venus, Father.'

'Sometimes, daughter,' Julius Antonius said, giving her shoulder a gentle squeeze, 'sometimes, but don't fret, Julia, I shall find the right match for you. One that honours the family and brings you happiness. I need to ponder the phrase—restored from death. The goddess moves in mysterious ways.'

'Very mysterious ways,' Julia agreed and listened to her father's suppressed chuckle.

'Shall we go rescue Sabina Claudia before she starts shrieking the temple down?'

Her father took her arm and Julia felt like they were father and daughter again, as they had been before her mother died. He was very different from the austere father of only a few weeks ago.

The blow from Tigris's sword hit Valens squarely on his right shoulder, causing him to wince and nearly drop his shield. Valens wiped the back of his hand across his mouth and eased the shield back up his left arm. With the blow his shoulder had just received, the shield felt twice as heavy as it normally did. Valens crouched down, balancing on the balls of his feet, watching for the next feint by Tigris.

'You need to pay attention,' Tigris said with a wide smile as Valens barely blocked the next blow. 'You normally see that particular trick coming before my sword is halfway to your shoulder.'

'Shall we begin again?' Valens said, ignoring the comment as he rotated his arm.

'That's the third parry you've missed this morning, Valens.' Strabo's voice rang out across the Julian compound. 'What is the matter with you, boy?'

'A slight shoulder pull.'

'Then see the doctor immediately after this session and concentrate. A *tiro* could do better than that,' Strabo said, coming over to Valens to test his shoulder. 'The opening day is less than a week away and I want you fit and well. All mental faculties concentrated on the games.'

Valens gave a brief nod and wiped the sweat from his brow. Concentration. It was all very well to say it, but he discovered it was hard to find. He knelt down and rubbed the sand between his hands, feeling the grit stick to his palms. A symbolic act to show he was now part of the arena, his other life had no meaning. He balanced on his toes and gave a nod to Tigris.

'Are you going to tell me about her?' Tigris said after Strabo left to harangue another set of fighters.

'What nonsense are you spouting now, Tigris?' Valens blocked the blow by moving his shield with great speed.

'The reason you only just made the start of practice, the woman you are not interested in taking to bed. I assume she has a name.'

Tigris blocked Valens's move and countered with another blow. Valens could feel the anger beginning to build within him, his concentration starting to slip once more.

'You have a vivid imagination,' Valens said and brought his shield up. 'I told you I had to make an act of worship at one of the temples. I felt a sudden calling.'

'Since when did you come religious?' Tigris remarked. He touched the brim of his helmet and then brought his sword back for the next attack. 'You should take her to bed instead of skulking around temples. A much more pleasurable activity to my mind at any rate.'

Valens watched for the next swipe of the sword and knew what he had to do. He and Tigris had practised this easy but showy move a thousand times before. Valens brought down his shield, intending to strike Tigris's sword, but Tigris's remarks about Julia distracted him. The shield came down a fraction too late and connected with Tigris's hand with a bone-jarring thump.

'Sorry about that,' he muttered, staring at Tigris's reddened sword arm. It was basic mistake. Had this been in the arena, he would now be dead, as the opposing gladiator's sword would have sliced through his unprotected midriff. A mistake worthy of an untried *tiro* rather than a very experienced gladiator.

Tigris flexed his hand several times.

'It will be a nasty bruise, but not much more than that,' Tigris said.

'Shall we go and see the doctor, just to make sure? I have no wish to be the cause of your pulling out of the games,' Valens said with a teasing note in his voice, but his insides churned. He had come within a whisker of seriously injuring his friend through his own lack of attention.

'What is her name?' Tigris remarked as they walked towards the infirmary. 'A hurt sword arm deserves at least a name.'

'You're incorrigible, Tigris.'

'The name.'

Valens glanced around the dusty sand-strewn court-yard. It was only a practice of the Thracian and other small shields. If Tigris's gentle teasing made him make a mistake like that, how much more damage could Aquilia do?

'Julia, Julia Antonia,' he said quietly as Tigris continued to stare.

Tigris whistled. "I thought you were only interested in her dog.'

'Be serious, Tigris.'

'I'm always serious in matters of the heart.' Tigris gave an elaborate bow. 'You should take her into your bed. It will cure you. It always has before. I find it difficult to think of one woman with whom you have had a long-term relationship. One tumble and you are off and on to pastures new.'

Valens rolled his eyes. He had wondered if the time they shared might decrease his desire for Julia. But his slow reactions today were proving otherwise. He had lost his essential focus.

'I had already thought of that one,' he said, raking his hand through his hair. 'What if it only increases the desire?'

Tigris roared with laughter and clapped Valens on the back. 'Then you keep taking the girl to bed. Eventually one of two things will happen: either you tire of each other or you marry.'

Marriage—the word hung in the air. Valens knew it was what he desired, the only cure for Julia. He forced back images of her lying in his bed, with her hair spread out on his chest, their limbs entwined. What man alive would not want to spend the rest of the time allotted to him in that way? What would a child of theirs look like?

'Marriage is forbidden between patrician women and slaves, you know that,' Valens said through clenched teeth.

'I fail to see that as a problem.'

'I'm still a slave, not a contract gladiator like you.'

Tigris's face sobered. 'Since when has a little thing like that stopped you? Go and buy your freedom. You are then a freeman and a rich one. If you need the money, I am happy to loan you some until you sell one of your estates in Capua. Stop putting non-existent obstacles in your way. You may name your first child after me.'

'Next you will have me believing in fairy stories.' Valens gave a nod to the surgeon and allowed the surgeon's assistant to start rubbing salve into his shoulder while the surgeon bound Tigris's arm. Tigris had little understanding of Roman society, what doors would be forever closed to Julia, but he knew Julius Antonius knew. And he knew he was right. The only way to go forward was to continue with his plan and hope. 'It is amazing what these doctors can do with a bit of medicine, instead of resorting to chants and superstition.'

'You are stubborn,' Tigris said and his next words quashed Valens's hope that he would take the hint and change the subject. 'Strabo would have allowed you to buy your freedom years ago. He made the offer at the same time I purchased my freedom.'

'I told you then and I tell you now, I want to win my freedom. Purchasing my freedom means nothing to me.' Valens leant his head back against the rough-hewn plaster of the infirmary and closed his eyes.

The argument had nearly led to the break up of their friendship. Tigris refused to understand why Valens was content to be a slave. He did not understand that, without honour, Valens had no standing in society and his sons, if he should have them, would always be looked down upon, sneered at. Without the honour the wooden sword would bring, it was unlikely Julius Antonius would ever agree to ally his family with Valens.

'You would be purchasing it with your winnings,' Tigris argued back. 'I know how wealthy you are, Valens, and shutting your eyes will not make the force of my argument go away.'

'How's Maia and the children?' Valens asked, blatantly trying to distract Tigris.

He watched Tigris throw up his hands in disgust and knew he had won. The prodding was over.

'Maia arrives tonight, if all goes to plan.'

'But I thought you were worried about Aquilia.'

'I will worry a lot less if they are under my watchful eye. I have rented a house in the Aventine. It has a good view of the Circus. They will be able to watch without the jostling of the crowds.'

The Circus Maximus where the games were to be held nestled in the hollow between the two most important hills in Rome—the Palatine, where Valens had grown up, and the Aventine, where the masses lived. It symbolised the meeting of the two halves of Roman society for the games and for the chariot races—two passions both sections of society shared.

Valens thought, with a pang of nostalgia, of how he'd loved watching the games at the Circus, and how one day he'd made the mistake of voicing his love for the games and rousing his father's anger. It was why, when the ransom had not arrived, it had been confirmation of something he'd always known. His father preferred death before dishonour.

'I look forward to seeing Maia.'

Tigris's eyes grew grave.

'Valens, you need to fight against something. I need to fight for someone. Maia and the children we have are those people.'

'Did I say a word?' Valens tried to push the thoughts out of his mind. With Julia, he had lost the will to fight. His desire to stay alive was greater than his desire to win. Valens stooped and picked up a handful of sand, allowing it to trickle through his fingers. He had to find a way, otherwise all hopes for the future were doomed. He gave an ironic laugh. His future depended on his fighting as if he had no future. 'The situation is very complicated.'

Tigris clasped Valens's arms. 'You can always stay with us.'

Valens shook his head. To see the love Tigris and Maia had for each other would only increase his need to be with Julia. It would tear at his soul and show what he had lost. But he could not explain this to Tigris, not now. Instead he opted for a laugh. 'I have stayed with you before. I will just get in the way.'

'The door is open and the offer is there.'

'I'll remember that.' Valens stood up and rotated his

shoulder, intending to let the offer quietly drop. 'Shall we go out and brave the practice ring again?'

Julia put down the scroll and moved to the window, but the courtyard was virtually empty, just two of the household servants cleaning the fountain. She let out a soft breath. The words of the augur kept ringing in her mind—returned from the dead. Who was a modern-day Orpheus?

If only Valens was a Roman… Julia put a hand to her throat. Of course he was a Roman, but one in disgrace. Disgrace was not the same as death. But what if his family had thought him dead? They had left him to die in the pirate's hold. And what if she could effect a reconciliation? She could give him back his past.

She started to pace the room. Where to start? She needed to have a plan, a place to begin. Bato nudged her hand. She bent down to stroke him, but sighed. He had something in his mouth. 'Give.'

Bato placed the figurine of Valens on the floor with a sheepish look. Julia picked it and regarded it. The day they met, Valens had said that she knew him because of the figurine. But the figurine was wearing a helmet. His features were familiar from somewhere else. Julia shut her eyes and willed it to come to her. At the edge of her mind she saw it—a death mask, one that hung in the Gracchus compound. A clue? Her heart beat faster. She needed more than a feeling.

'That's it, Bato, you are a marvel.'

She walked down the corridor and pushed Valens's door open. The room still held his faint smell, making her limbs tremble. She hesitated, her heart thumping louder than the drums on the Campo Martial in her ears, then walked purposefully over to the small wooden trunk.

As she hoped, it was unlocked. With a loud creak, she opened it and stared at the items: several tunics, a cloak and another box. She picked it up. This one was locked. She tightened her lips and made a face.

So much for great ideas.

One by one she replaced his garments, taking care that each was put back exactly how she had found them, the smell of him clinging to her fingers and enveloping her. She felt a warmth engulf her as she remembered how his arms had held her tightly against his body. As her hand brushed the cloak, smoothing out the final wrinkles, a pin pricked her.

She put her index finger into her mouth, making sure no blood dropped on the dark blue cloak, then took a closer look at the brooch fastened on the collar, expecting to see the lion from Strabo's school, but it wasn't.

She stared at the two greyhounds on either side of a three-pointed rock. It reminded her of her ex-father-in-law's signet ring. Her hands started trembling. Senator Gracchus's son had died about five years ago, shortly before his wife. Could it be?

She sat back on her feet, dismissing the idea as being ludicrous. The more she thought, the more it refused to go away.

She tried to remember if she had ever seen a grave. Or was it simply a death mask? Was his death mask the one she remembered? The reason she thought she knew Valens?

He looked nothing like her ex-husband. Lucius had been the son of the senator's wife's sister, the nearest male relation who was willing to be adopted—it was important that the Gracchus name continue. Senator Gracchus had to have an heir. It was the Roman custom.

Julia put a hand to her throat, playing with her beads. What to do? Her body trembled with excitement. She had to know. She had to grab the chance, as slight as it might be.

She should have visited Gracchus a long time ago, listened more fully to his stories. She didn't even know what the son's name had been. Gaius? Gneus? Julia sighed and shook her head. The precise name escaped her. Every time she had visited with Lucius and the question of his son had been raised, Lucius had behaved strangely, changing the subject as soon as possible.

Julia smoothed the cloak one last time before replacing it in the trunk. Finding out about the son's death might be difficult, but it should be relatively straightforward to see the death mask that hung on the back of Gracchus's atrium. It would take but a glance and she could rest her mind. She had to be certain. And once she was, she'd solve all her problems. For the first time in a long time, Julia thought she saw the glimmer of light. But before she could do anything, she needed an excuse to visit.

'Come on, Bato, your old master should have a bone or two for you.'

The Gracchus compound was on the lower slopes of the Palatine. Unlike the winding narrow passageways of Subura, where houses of ill repute stood next to patrician villas, here nothing was allowed to spoil the tranquillity. Julia walked along the leafy lane, enjoying the sounds of birds instead of the shouts from the market.

She stood in front of the Graccus villa, rehearsing her speech, a pleasant fiction about Bato missing the senator.

Her hand trembled as she knocked on the solid oak door.

After a brief conversation with the porter, she went into the dappled shade of the large courtyard to await the arrival of Senator Gracchus. Julia walked slowly amongst the death masks and various statues, looking for Gracchus's son. Her heart sank slightly. The one she wanted was missing. She could see the white patch where it had hung, but the mask was gone.

Julia made a face. Why were things never simple?

A movement caused her to turn from the wall. She watched as Senator Gracchus made a grand entrance, frail but resplendent in his snow-white toga with its large purple border.

'Julia Antonia, how good it is of you to call on an old man,' Senator Gracchus said, holding out both his hands, gold rings glittering on every finger. His hair was thinner and his face much more lined than she remembered. He appeared to have lost a great deal of weight, but his bearing showed he had not lost much of the presence that had intimidated two generations of senators. 'It has been too long since your charm graced this garden, Julia.'

'Far too long since I have had the pleasure of enjoying your hospitality,' Julia agreed and her eyes scanned his face, searching for any resemblance to Valens. There a vague resemblance in the way he held his head and moved, but little in the way of matching physical features. 'Bato wanted to come to see you.'

She pointed to Bato who immediately lay on his back and wriggled. Gracchus laughed and reached down to tickle the dog's tummy.

'Dogs always remember those who have been kind to them,' he said. 'I remember this one as being a particular scamp. Perhaps the cook can rustle up a ham bone or two.

He clapped his hands. Two servants appeared and led Bato towards the kitchen.

'Was Bato your dog?' Julia tried to make her voice casual.

'No, my son's.' A shadow passed over Gracchus's face. 'Gaius left him here when he was posted off to Zama in North Africa—called him something, I can't think of the name, but Lucius changed it when I gave him Bato. I thought Bato would cement my ties with Lucius, but the dog did not take to him in the same way.'

It would do no good to tell Senator Gracchus that Bato disliked Lucius because he had hit her and the dog had tried to protect her. He had never wanted to hear the reasons before, believing Julia's lies about walking into doors.

Julia forced air out of her lungs. She had to concentrate and not allow her mind to be distracted. Gracchus's son had been posted off to Zama, in North Africa. Valens had not said where he had been stationed. North Africa was large. It could have been anywhere. She closed her eyes, willing her heart to be still, not to race ahead. She wanted to be calm.

'I forget. How did your son die? Captured by pirates?' Her hairstyle felt heavy against the back of her neck.

Gracchus gave a small sad smile. 'I only wish. I would have been only too happy to pay any ransom legitimately demanded. He perished in an assault on a rebellious town. A needless waste as the town was unimportant.'

Julia felt like a foolish girl who believed in dreams. With a few words, Gracchus had extinguished the small flicker of hope.

'I thought there was a tale about pirates,' she said, trying to recover and not to let her disappointment show.

'Child,' Gracchus said, putting his hand on her shoulder, 'a request for ransom arrived, but they sought to play on an old man's desire for his son. Your latest suitor, Mettalius, saw him fall. He brought back Gaius's brooch pinned to the bloody cloak that Gaius wore. My son would never have freely given that up. It had been in my wife's family for generations. My wife faded away after that. Lucius was so attentive to her in the last few days. Always here, always finding something to cheer her up or some sweetmeat to tempt her appetite. Of course, when she died, I knew I was too old to take another woman, and I made Lucius my heir. He was the closest male relation who was willing to be adopted.'

Julia swallowed hard and closed her eyes. It had

been too easy, too much like a fairy tale. At least she had had the wit not to come in and proclaim to Gracchus that his son was alive.

'I am so sorry.'

'The Fates decreed that I outlive my son and wife, but don't put ashes on your head or allow your eyes to fill with tears for someone you did not know. He had done his military service. He ignored my pleas to stay at home, and would go adventuring, lusting after glory.' Gracchus clapped his hands. 'And now, I think a bit of cool mint tea to revive our spirits. You do have time to stay.'

'Only if you desire it. I have no wish to tire you.' She watched the servants bring the table and jug of mint tea. With great ceremony, the servant poured a beaker for her. She took a sip and felt the cool sweetness slip down her throat, easing it.

'Good, you must tell me all that has been happening to you since you last graced this garden.' Gracchus waved his hands expansively and his rings threw beams of light across the garden.

A servant brought Bato back and he flopped down at Julia's feet, with a bone large enough to feed a family of five, let alone a greyhound. 'We have a gladiator staying with us. One of Caesar's troop. The one called Valens the Thracian. You may have seen the notices or his figurine on street corners.'

Gracchus frowned and swirled his beaker of tea. 'Caesar has altogether too many gladiators. He reaches too far, too fast, I believe.'

Julia took another sip of her tea and watched Gracchus. She had forgotten the politics. Gracchus was a senator of the old school, one who believed in the Republic and its ancient ideals. 'My father seems pleased with the gladiator. He is helping my father improve his sword technique.'

'Your father is much like my dead son in that. He too was fascinated by the gladiatorial life. There was nowhere he was happier than in the ring.'

'You did not approve?'

'No,' Gracchus spluttered. 'We, patricians, are born into a position and have a duty to hold that position up. Little good comes from associating with people like gladiators. I can remember as a young boy when such shows were strictly for funerals and not spectacles for mass entertainment. I despise everything to do with them. They show how far Rome has fallen. In my youth statuettes of gods were sold at street corners, not figurines of *infamia*.'

'I will keep that in mind.' Julia felt the prick of a headache start between her brows.

'I heard about your escapade with the gladiators, Julia,' Gracchus said, his face turning even graver. Julia shifted uncomfortably in her chair. 'It saddened me to think my ex-daughter-in-law was mixed up with such ruffians. I thought you were more modest than that. Many times, I have said how much you remind me of my dear departed wife, a true Roman matron. Such a pity you and Lucius never had any children.'

'It was never my intention to be involved, but Bato had other ideas,' Julia said stiffly. 'Thankfully, Valens rescued Bato or else he might not be here to beg treats from your hand.'

The senator harrumphed, but fed Bato another sweetmeat.

Julia set down her empty beaker and stood up. She needed to go now before she said something she regretted. Valens might be a gladiator, but he was a far better man than Lucius could ever be.

A door slammed and Lucius strode in. As his gaze fell on her, he frowned and his eyes became ice-cold. Julia's stomach twisted and swayed as she remembered the beating that had followed the last time she had seen him look like that. Bato raised his hackles and growled.

'What are you doing here, Julia Antonia?' Lucius squeaked out, not bothering with pleasantries. 'What sort of poisoned gossip are you spreading?'

He can't touch you, she repeated, hoping to stem the rising tide of bile in her throat.

'Julia Antonia is here to visit me at my invitation.

Now calm yourself, Lucius, and behave like a Roman. Have some mint tea.' Gracchus rang a silver bell. 'Some fresh mint tea for my son.'

'I must go,' Julia said, ignoring Lucius. She leant over and gave Gracchus a kiss on the cheek. 'I have enjoyed our visit. Perhaps sometime you will show me the brooch that your son valued so much.'

'It is here.' Gracchus held out a brooch that bore more than a superficial resemblance to the brooch Julia had seen on Valens's cloak. 'I wear it all the time to remind me of my dead son.'

'I can see why he wore it until his death,' Julia said, trying to be casual, but feeling her heart start to pound. She rose gracefully. 'I enjoyed my tea.'

'Come again soon.'

'I plan to.' Julia curled her fingers around Bato, and started towards the door. As she left, she heard Lucius complaining to Gracchus.

Chapter Eleven

Julia sat on the stone bench in her father's atrium. The twin scents of lavender and rose filled the air. The late afternoon sunshine cast elongated shadows over her and the scrolls of poetry she had by her side, as a cover. Instead of thumbing through the well-loved lines, Julia kept her eyes focussed on the outside door.

Valens would have to pass this way and she'd explain all that had happened with the augur, but she would keep her visit to Senator Gracchus a secret. There was no need for Valens to know about her clumsy attempt at finding his family.

She'd save it for a surprise. After she had found them, told them of Valens's miraculous escape, then she'd tell him. She'd give him life again and bring happiness to his estranged family. It had to work. She hoped it would. She had promised Venus that she'd control her impulsiveness and then she had done this.

And she had met Lucius again as well. Seeing him was never good. Somehow, he always contrived to make matters worse.

At first, her stomach knotted with each sound. Was it Valens's footstep? But so far, it had only been Clodius the porter or one of the other servants. She had even tried taking a bath, hoping he'd appear. Her hair curling softly about her shoulders bore testimony to the amount of time she had spent in her bath. Still he had not returned from practice as far as she could tell.

'I still cannot understand why your father chooses to believe that charlatan of an augur. Anyone with half an eye could see that the man was mad.' Sabina stopped in front of Julia and blocked her vision of the courtyard and the door.

'Caesar believes in him.' Julia kept her voice neutral. This morning seemed so long ago. She conspicuously rattled the papyrus of the scroll she was currently reading, hoping Sabina would take the hint. The augur had to be right. Her life had to be about to turn for the better.

'The more fool him. Returned from the dead, indeed. Do you know what trouble I've been to to find a suitable alliance? Only for that priest to undo weeks and weeks of unstinting effort. Perhaps your father might be persuaded to visit another more sensible augur.' Sabina gave a slight smirk. 'I understand you have decided to increase your chances of a good alliance and have renewed your acquaintance with Senator Gracchus.'

'News travels fast.' Julia turned again to the scroll, pretending the news did not perturb her. How did Sabina know? She thought she had kept the visit a secret.

'You used the litter.' Sabina tapped a perfectly shod foot. 'Next time ask permission first. I was forced to walk to Flavia's. However, I find it impossible to be cross with you as you visited Gracchus. Your father will be pleased.'

'I fail to see how my visiting Gracchus will help Father.'

'You never know what lawsuits he might put Julius's way, now that he has fallen out with Lucius.' Her face bore all the hallmarks of a woman who found true satisfaction in the latest tidbit of gossip.

'I wasn't aware Gracchus had fallen out with Lucius,' Julia said carefully, watching Sabina, whose cheeks flushed. 'Rome is rife with rumours.'

'I heard Lucius is a disappointment to Gracchus. He is proving less adept in the Senate—four years the heir and yet to win an election. More spendthrift than Gracchus expected. He's already gone through his real father's fortune, you know. Now, Gracchus's invitation to you proves the rumour mill wasn't working overtime.'

'The invitation had more to do with Bato…'

Sabina's clawlike hand grasped Julia's arm. 'Just think of what this could mean. Clever you to have spotted the chance. Perhaps there is more to you…'

Julia shifted uneasily on the stone bench, pressing her hands into the seat. She hated to think that she might be seen to be like Sabina, playing games and barely hiding her ambition. 'He seemed pleased to see me and asked me to visit again. Lucius was less than pleased.'

'You're a dark horse, Julia. Perhaps that augur wasn't entirely mad after all. Perhaps he was right. The signs for a betrothal with Mettalius, who has had close links to Lucius in the Senate, are not good. We may have had a lucky escape. Restored from death could mean many things. Didn't Sulla sentence many senators to death? Or perhaps an elderly man whose doctor's had all but given up hope…'

'Who am I to question the whims of the gods?' Julia pursed her lips and silently vowed she'd find a way to bribe the augur before she consented to marriage to someone older than her father. Valens restored to the place she knew he belonged was what she wanted.

'Quite, and now we need to develop a plan…'

The great oak door swung open and Valens entered. Her eyes devoured him and traced the line of his shoulders. She noticed small things. The way a small drop of water clung to the base of his throat. The way his hair gleamed with the faint sheen of the freshly washed and his tunic swung, revealing a bit more of his muscular legs than it should. Julia's breath caught in her throat. She tightened her hold on the scrolls and attempted to appear nonchalant, but her mind raced. She had to discover more about his past. She had seen his face on a statue somewhere. She simply need to discover where.

When he reached the fountain, Valens stopped, listening. Then he turned towards them, a smile playing on his lips. Julia sat paralysed. How to begin with Sabina next to her?

'Excuse me, ladies, but you look so comfortable sitting in the sun, would you mind if I joined you?' Without waiting for an answer, he sat down beside Julia, leant back, with the sun on his face and closed his eyes. His eyelashes made dark smudges on his tanned cheeks.

Sabina made little shooing motions. 'Julia, there are things we need to do. Things we have been discussing.'

'As soon as I have finished this poem.' Julia fought to keep her voice steady. How could she bring the conversation around to his boyhood? Maybe if she did, she'd be able to convince him to go and make peace with his family.

'Which poem?' Sabina's voice was sharp with suspicion. 'You are reading something appropriate, aren't you, Julia? Something sensible rather than the rubbish you normally read.'

'The one I was reading when you interrupted me. Senator Gracchus recommended it to me,' she finished with sudden inspiration. She felt Valens's leg tense against hers as if the name disturbed him. But it happened so briefly, Julia dismissed the idea.

'If the senator recommended it…' Sabina said, and stood up. She straightened her *stola*, and stalked off. Julia could hear her voice screech several orders at the servants.

Julia waited until Sabina's voice had died away before she risked a proper look at Valens. He had not moved since he closed his eyes. Julia watched his chest as he took deep steady breaths, a lock of black hair falling down over his right eye. All her ideas deserted her. She opened her mouth and closed it again. Very quietly, she began to roll up the scrolls, fastening each one with a bit of cord. When she had finished, and he had still made no sound or move, she started to stand up.

His hand caught hers, lacing her fingers with his. 'Stay, please stay.'

'Sabina will be back shortly,' Julia explained, but his fingers remained closed around hers. Julia swallowed hard and her heart thumped in her ears. Her heart demanded she press her face close to his, touch his lips with her, regardless of who might see. She had to hang on to her sense of propriety. Things were too finely balanced to risk her father's wrath. She had had a reprieve this morning, but there was no telling for how long. 'We will have barely any time to talk.'

She withdrew her hands and placed them primly on her lap. The skirt of her gown brushed his bare calf. She reached down and smoothed it away, but her hand felt the heat of his leg.

'Shall we talk about poetry—unless you want to tell me about your day?' he asked, breaking the silence. 'Are you to be betrothed to Mettalius?'

'The augur did not approve. The omens had changed.'

'Did he say anything else?'

'You know how priests are.' Julia gave a little wave of her hand. She had to get the subject away from this morning and towards Valens's boyhood without him realising why. She did not dare take the risk that he might stop her. After all, he had not contacted his family before now. 'They enjoy speaking in riddles. Do you find them helpful?'

A smile tugged at the side of his mouth. 'At times, they have their uses. But you must be careful. One told my father I was destined for great things.'

Julia's body tensed. He was doing it without her prompting. He was speaking of his childhood. 'Was the augur correct?'

'Not in the way my father hoped.' Valens folded his hands behind his head. 'But in my own way, perhaps he was right. I, Valens the Thracian, have achieved greatness.'

Back to gladiators. Julia bit her lip. She wanted to hear about before, not now. She had to try one more time. 'But are you worried about disappointing your father?'

'Julia, my past no longer concerns me. I live only for the present.' The planes of his face were shadowed. 'Shall we discuss something more agreeable. Poetry, perhaps?'

He reached towards the scroll she had been reading and unwrapped it. His smile faded slightly and Julia wondered if somehow she had hurt him. Could he read Greek?

'You are going through a Sappho stage,' he said with a small quirked smile. 'I liked her just before I reached my manhood, but I thought her a bit *risqué* for a properly brought-up young woman. My tutor once said she was primarily read by people who had recently discovered sex and enjoyed it.'

Julia laughed, a high-pitched laugh of relief. They could talk about poetry for a while, then, when the time was right, she'd try again. 'Lucius always refused to let me read her and he can no longer forbid me.'

'An act of rebellion?' Valens raised an eyebrow.

'If you like, but I wanted to be able to make up my

own mind about her. I was tired of Lucius's dictates.' Julia shifted uncomfortably. He made it seem as if she only liked Sappho out of spite. She enjoyed the cadence and the rhythm. 'I tried reading her and found that I liked her use of imagery. Have you read any of her work?'

'You need not look so surprised. I did have a traditional Roman education. To study philosophy properly one must know how to read Greek. My father despaired of my liking for poetry. He felt it frivolous compared to speeches of the great orators and generals. Carthage must be destroyed and all that.' His eyes bore into her soul and Julia dropped her gaze. She hardly dare breathe. Might this be the way? 'Is there something wrong with a gladiator who reads?'

Julia felt her cheeks flush. Anything she said would be misinterpreted.

'Oh, I see you fell for my physical rather than mental charms.' A dimple showed in the corner of his mouth. He handed her back the scroll with a glint of regret in his eyes. 'You need not be ashamed. It is why most women support the games.'

'I think perhaps I had best go.' Julia stood up. This was all wrong. Any explanation she gave now would be wrong. How could she explain when he now thought she was like the other women supporters? 'I confused the situation.'

Valens's hand shot out, keeping her there, imprisoning her in its grasp. She pulled gently and he released her. 'I asked you to stay.'

'You want to make speeches. You should be in the Senate, not in the arena.' Julia put her hand over her mouth. Why could she never think, then speak?

'I wanted to discuss your reading with you, and to learn more about you.' His voice was low but firm. 'I thought you wanted more than a pretty face.'

Julia stared at her hands. Her mind raced. She was making a complete muddle of this. 'Stop distorting what I said. I just had never considered it.' She tilted her head and peeped at him through her lashes. 'You will have to admit, you were not spouting poetry yesterday.'

He leant forward. His face was far sterner and more serious than she had seen before. 'Are you sure Senator Gracchus recommended Sappho to you?'

'Gracchus? What does he have to do with…? Oh, you mean the story I told Sabina.' Julia toyed with her bracelets. 'He is my ex-father-in-law, Lucius's adopted father. Sabina is in awe of him. When he decided to adopt Lucius, she could not believe her luck. Senator Gracchus, however, has refused all of her invitations to dine, but she lives in hope and doesn't dare say anything against him. Why?'

Julia watched his face for any sign, relieved in a way that he had brought up Gracchus. She felt that perhaps she should explain about earlier today and her mistake. Perhaps then he would see that she wanted to help and he'd trust her with the name of his father. His face became inscrutable, a blank slab of marble on which she could read no emotion.

'He was a man I used to know, and, if you were seeking an alliance with him, I thought to warn you.'

'Warn me?'

A humourless smile played on Valens's lips. 'Yes, he despises liars and Sappho. He does not consider her poetry fitting reading for any right-thinking Roman. Let alone a Roman matron.'

'How do you know this?' Julia rolled the scroll tighter. She hated being caught in a lie. A quiver rose in her stomach. How did Valens know? Her heart beat faster. Maybe she had been correct.

'I served with his son in North Africa. He, if I remember correctly, had the same fondness as I do for poetry and he also had to battle with his father.'

'You served with his son?' Julia breathed and her mind raced. Perhaps Senator Gracchus would tell her who his son served with. Or there were the military lists. She tried to keep her mind on what he was saying.

'And you are his ex-daughter-in-law. It is a small world. I hadn't realised your husband was a Gracchi.' His voice was smooth, too smooth. 'I should have paid more attention when Caesar offered me this billet.'

Julia thought she could hear faint undercurrents, some emotion he wished to keep hidden. She kept her voice steady and held back the questions that threatened to tumble out.

'Who my ex-husband is has no bearing on me! I want nothing to do with him or his family. In light of the divorce, my father no longer receives any work from Senator Gracchus.' Julia peered more closely at Valens, but no muscles moved in his face. She drew a deep breath and plunged on, before she lost her nerve. 'Can you tell me how Senator Gracchus's son died? You said you were in North Africa, I believe. Were you with him in the assault that led to his death?'

Valens did not reply. His eyes grew hard as he stared unseeing into the middle distance.

'He died in a pirate's hold,' he said, biting out each word. 'A death Senator Gracchus would not have approved of. By my hasty actions and uncontrolled temper, I ensured he perished dishonourably.'

'I thought Gracchus said he died fighting some insurgents,' Julia said, confused. 'My ex-suitor Mettalius brought back the brooch. Senator Gracchus showed it to me this afternoon. He said his son had died a hero's death.'

'No, he died in a pirates' hold. I should know. I was there. Perhaps it was the best thing to do. He saved his father the embarrassment of having to be ransomed.' He gripped her arm and forced her to look at him. His gaze seemed to burn into her soul. 'Was there any special reason you were talking to Senator Gracchus about his son? You said that you wanted nothing to do with the family. Why now? What game are you playing, Julia?'

Julia stood up and started to pace the garden, hugging her waist with her arms. She had been wrong, oh, so wrong. In the late afternoon heat, she shivered. Who was he that Gaius Gracchus had been punished for things he had done? She had to figure out a way to ask, and get around his defences.

'Julia, Julia, I want to talk to you.' Lucius's querulous voice carried across the courtyard. 'I refuse to be manhandled by this oaf of a porter.'

Her stomach twisted, knotted and then untwisted. Not here, not now with Valens present. She had no desire to be dragged back into the mire of her marriage. She had escaped from that.

Julia crossed the courtyard to where her ex-husband stood. She gave a nod and Clodius released Lucius, bowed low and left. Lucius's face was redder than this morning. His toga bore spots of red wine and food stains. Julia felt her arms begin to tremble as she remembered the other times when she had seen Lucius like this and the beatings that had ensued.

'Julia, is everything all right?' Through a fog, she heard Valens speak.

She gave a brief nod, but refused to look at him. Lucius had her full attention. Lucius's face wore that special grin he always had, right before he attacked her. Her blood ran cold. This day was becoming a disaster.

'What do you want, Lucius?' she asked, her voice sounding more forthright than she thought possible.

'I want to speak to you about your sneaking little ways, your unasked-for visits to my father. You are trying to make trouble.'

'You're drunk.' Julia looked him directly in his eyes. 'I refuse to speak with you when you are in this state. We have nothing to say to each other.'

Lucius straightened his toga, swayed, repositioned his feet and swayed some more.

'I am perfectly sober,' he spat. 'I want to know why you went to see my adopted father and tried to spread your poisonous lies. Stirring up long ago happenings, Julia. Gaius Gracchus is dead. I had nothing to do with his murder.'

'I beg your pardon?' Julia toyed with her necklace as her courage started to desert her. She had not expected this full-frontal assault. Lucius was usually more content with verbal barbs. She felt the brush of a tunic and knew without looking that Valens stood behind her. A small glimmer of hope filled her. She had support.

'Don't play the mealy-mouthed innocent with me, Julia Antonia.' Lucius positioned himself as if he was preparing for a fight, hands balled at his sides. 'You went to see Gracchus deliberately to undermine me. I want to know who sent you and why. Parroting tales of long-dead sons indeed. As if I had anything to do with Gaius Gracchus's death! I was in Rome, when Gaius Gracchus breathed his last, ask anyone. We had not met in years, since we were children. Ask Mettalius Scipio. He was the one who found the brooch when he stumbled on the mutilated body.'

'I never said anything…'

'You implied it, you implied that there was something untoward. I will not have it, Julia. Show me the proof first.' He took a step towards her. His hand quivered, upraised.

Julia wanted to shrink down to the stones, but forced her back to stay upright. What had she done?

'Is there some sort of difficulty, Julia?' Valens's low voice rumbled.

'My wife and I were having an amicable discussion,' Lucius replied. 'She is in no need of…protection.'

'Your ex-wife,' Julia corrected. She drew a deep breath. She could do this. Lucius would not dare hit her here, not while there were witnesses. 'Stay, Valens. Anything Lucius has to say, he can say in front of you.'

'Since when do you need protection from me, Julia?'

Julia stared at the ground and longed for the courage to say the words detailing her injuries. But she found it impossible to speak. A rushing noise filled her ears. She closed her eyes, hoping that the nightmare would go away.

'Since you started threatening and intimidating her,' came Valens's firm answer.

'What do you know about it…Gladiator?' His eyes raked Valens up and down, but Julia fancied Lucius seemed less sure. Almost as if he had seen a ghost.

'I know enough. You are divorced and therefore have no rights over this woman.'

'She only understands one thing, Gladiator. And she appears to have forgotten her lesson.' Lucius raised his hand a second time.

'I think you had better go now.' Valens caught Lucius's wrist and forced his hand away from Julia.

'How dare you! I can behave how I like towards my wife.' Lucius aimed a blow at Valens's midriff.

In a blur, Valens had Lucius's arms pinned behind his back and Lucius screamed like a stuck pig.

'She is no longer your wife. You have no right to touch her.' Valens looked as if he might strike him. Then he seemed to think better of it and let him go.

Lucius staggered back a step. He rubbed his wrist.

'We'll meet again, Gladiator,' he said with a curling

lip. 'Julia, remember what I said—no more visits to Gracchus or I will make your life akin to Hades, protector or no.'

Julia watched as Lucius staggered out of the courtyard. She closed her eyes and wished she had restrained her impulses this morning. Now Valens had witnessed the full sordidness of her life, had seen what a coward she was.

'Julia.'

She became aware that Valens was calling her and had called her several times. She turned towards him. The tenderness in his eyes shone out at her. She longed to stumble a few steps and lay her head against his chest. She wanted to feel his strong arms about her. But that was impossible here in the open courtyard. The only thing she could do was to stare and draw strength from his eyes.

She brushed an errant lock of hair back from her forehead.

'I am sorry about that little display, Valens. My ex-husband is… well…not right in the head.'

'He seemed to blame you for some mishap.' There was a questioning expression in his eyes.

'I went to see my ex-father-in-law about some other matter—about Bato, if you must know—and Lucius leapt to the wrong conclusion.' Julia pressed her hands together. There was no need to confide her mistaken ideas. It could only inflame the situation. She wanted to forget that. It seemed so...so misguided somehow. 'I never accused him of killing Gracchus's son.'

She felt Valens's eyes on her, piercing her, and shifted.

'Have you told your father about Lucius's behaviour?'

Julia released a deep breath.

'I will,' she answered.

'You must do—I may not always be around to protect you.'

Julia nodded. A stab of pain coursed through her heart as she stared at his implacable face. She knew he was only acknowledging the truth. Their affair was finite. It would end. She had no desire for it to end or to think of the ending, but he obviously had.

'I will do.'

'Julia, you are shaking. If you would like, I'll give your excuses to Sabina and your father. You mustn't let him upset you like this.'

She took the coward's way and nodded. It was much easier to let him think her trembling was down to Lucius than to losing him.

'If you would be so kind...I think I shall retire to my room. Perhaps you could ask one of the servants to bring up a cup of mint tea.'

Chapter Twelve

The sound of silence filled the corridor. Valens hesitated, looking at the solid door that separated him from Julia. His natural inclination would be fling open the door and demand to know if she had recovered. But after witnessing her white-faced reaction to Lucius, he had no wish to frighten her further. He rapped his knuckles softly against the wood and waited.

At Julia's muffled reply, he pushed the door open.

Julia lay on the bed, her eyes covered by a cloth.

'Put the tea on my dressing table, please.' She waved her hand.

Valens closed the door with a click before he set the tray down.

'Shall I pour you some tea or would you rather do it yourself?' he asked, watching the rise and fall of her chest.

'Valens?' Julia sat bolt upright, the cloth falling

from her eyes. Her cheeks took on a rosy hue. 'I thought it was the servant with the tea.'

Her voice trailed away. Her dark eyes looked gigantic in her ashen face. His insides twisted. The rivulets of memory he had managed to stem earlier had swollen and crashed through the barriers of his mind. It would be easy to lose his temper and go after that misbegotten man Lucius Gracchus, demanding old wrongs be righted. But Strabo had taught him control and patience. He would make sure Lucius suffered for what he had done, but first he had to fulfill his obligations to the arena.

One enemy at a time.

'Are you hurt?'

'You stopped him.' Her voice held a note of wonder. 'I prepared my body for the blow and you stopped it.'

How could anyone raise his hand against her? Valens resisted the temptation to pull her into his arms and kiss the shadows away. Since this morning's practice with Tigris, Valens had been trying to convince himself that what had happened yesterday evening was a unique event. The attraction to Julia would have faded as it did with all the rest.

In this room together, he felt his desire for her rise higher with each passing breath he took. He thought himself only concerned for her safety, but he knew, looking at her tousled hair and heightened cheek colour, he felt something more for this woman. Feelings he thought he would never feel for any woman. Her vulnerability terrified him because the need to keep her safe seemed to dominate his thoughts, loosening the arena's hold from his mind. He raked his hand through his hair as her reddened lips caught his attention.

'Lucius always upsets me. I should know what to expect by now.' She gave a feeble laugh and half a shrug. 'Old habits die hard. Please don't say anything to anyone. It will only cause upset.'

Valens reached out and brushed her cheek with his hand. To his relief, she sat there, unflinching. A faint smile flickered at the corner of her lips before dying.

'I've spoken with your father. I explained about Lucius's unprovoked attack,' he explained as gently as possible. Having seen Lucius's anger and her reaction, it became his duty to tell her father.

Her eyes looked even more terrified. Valens cursed the hold her ex-husband had over her and longed to draw her into his arms. *Patience, he needed patience.*

Myriad emotions flitted across Julia's face—surprise, anger and fear, but mostly fear. 'Why? Why did you that? I told you those things in confidence. You had no right to do that.'

'Because you deserve some measure of protection. He had to know about Lucius Gracchus's threats. If not for your sake, for the rest of your family's. A senator's anger can have many repercussions. Your father knows that. He appreciated the news.'

Valens placed his hand on her shoulder, seeking to calm her. He could see the rapid beating of her heart in her throat's hollow.

'Did you tell him everything?' she asked in a small voice. She flinched away from his hand. Her face became as white as newly made toga, and her dark eyes seemed to swallow her face.

'I told him what he needed to know—that Lucius had threatened you and his manner appeared to be verging on lunacy this afternoon,' he said soothingly. 'The porter would have told him in any case.'

She pushed a lock of hair back. A patch of colour returned to her cheeks and her breathing seemed easier.

'I suppose you are right. Clodius does tell my father everything. My father trusts him, even though he is getting on in his years.'

'There is no suppose about it. You are no longer Lucius Gracchus's wife. An attack on you is an attack on your family. Your father should know his enemies. It is your father's duty to protect you.'

'What did my father say?' she whispered, twisting a tendril of hair around her finger.

Valens stared at the narrow slit of a window and wondered how best to describe Julius Antonius's explosion. Julia's shoulders were beginning to ease, and the pinched look about her mouth.

'He has given strict instructions to the porter and the other servants that they are to refuse entry to him. They will look after you, Julia, if you stay within the house and its gardens.'

Julia's eyes drank in Valens's features. The concern on his brow. She looked at his huge arm muscles and thought of how they wielded a sword and yet had gently held her last night. She released a long breath and gave into her desire to rest her head. His arms came around and held her tight. The wool of his tunic felt rough against her cheek. The thump of his heart echoed hers. She allowed her hurt and anger to drain away. Nothing much mattered except Valens had taken her in his arms. He wanted to help her.

'It is such a new thing to have anyone care enough about me to want to help,' she said, trying to explain the turmoil inside her. She looked into his eyes, trying to assess his mood, trying to discover why he was there. 'Thank you.'

She lifted her hand to his cheek. He turned his head slightly and his lips brushed her palm.

'I want to make sure you are safe, that no harm comes to you.' The rich timbre of his voice held her and caressed her senses. 'I am a guest in your house.'

Her heart dropped a bit. Was it only because his obligations as a guest? She'd worry about it later. Right now, all she knew was that she wanted the feel of his lips against hers. She needed to feel that what they had shared last night had not been destroyed by Lucius. She had worried that the disgust she had seen earlier in Valens's eyes was for her.

'I can look after myself,' she whispered and her hand touched his hair. She ran her fingers through the silky strands, burying them deep, and pulled his face nearer to hers. 'I survived three and a half years of marriage to Lucius.'

'You are married no longer.' His voice rasped in her ear. 'Sometimes you need help.'

He pushed the material off her shoulder and traced the faint scars of Lucius's beatings with a finger. Where they had once ached with pain, they now ached with another sensation, a burning that made her body press closer towards him.

As her body arched, she encountered the hard unyieldingness of his chest. A tremor ran from the pit of her stomach to the ends of her fingers as her body remembered the passion they had shared yesterday. As if he could read her mind, he bent his head and softly touched her mouth with his—a butterfly kiss. She opened her mouth and allowed him to explore, his tongue entering to tease and torment.

She felt her nipples harden as they strained against

their bindings. Hot and swollen. His lips started to trail down her neck. She tried to drag her mind away from the vortex of sensation that promised to engulf her. She brought her hands up to his chest to hold him off. She had to be sensible. She had to think of more than the immediate warmth in her belly. 'My father will be expecting me.'

Valens's lips curved upwards. 'Gone out. He and Sabina have a dinner engagement. We decided it might be a bit much for you. He will speak to you in the morning. The servants will be in the kitchen should you call for your tray.'

Julia nodded, hated the thought of another deciding how her life should be ordered, but she refused to quarrel with the result. 'You decided?'

In answer, his hands cupped her breasts while his thumbs made small circles over her nipples until they tightened to small points of exquisite sensation. Her spine arched and he eased her backwards until her head encountered the soft yielding of the bed.

'I rather thought this would be easier for you.' His eyes were dark with passion. 'Julia, I want to be with you. I want to chisel away all traces of that man in your mind.'

He undid the discs holding her gown and pushed the material down to her waist. His fingers moved aside the strips of cloths to release her breasts. As each nipple was freed, his lips captured its peak, suckling. His tongue drew small circles, teasing the nipple to a tighter and tighter point, sending wave after wave of sensation through her body, making her writhe and wriggle as each new wave hit. 'Valens…'

Valens raised himself on his elbows. His darkened eyes met hers. Her body shivered in response to the depths of promise she saw there. He smoothed a tendril of hair away from her forehead. 'I'm seducing you, showing you what it should be like between a man and a woman, so you know and understand what pleasure truly is.'

This time the word *pleasure* evoked anticipation rather than fear. Her body trembled as she remembered the sensations of the evening before. 'I believe that could be arranged. There is a soft bed here, and, as you say…no one will disturb us.'

'We are of one mind,' Valens said as relief swept through him. Until he heard the invitation in her voice, he had been unaware how much it meant to him that her passion equal his. He wanted to lock away her memories of Lucius as surely as he had locked his own memories away. He wanted her to realise it was the present that mattered, not the chains of the past.

He ran a hand down her bare arm, drawing lines on her flesh, lines that his tongue followed. Her hands captured his face and brought his lips back to hers.

A surge of excitement ran through him as her tongue boldly entered his mouth. She wanted his touch.

Valens kept his own passion in check. Despite his body's urging, he wanted to go slowly and bring her to the heights of ecstasy before he indulged in his fulfillment.

He gave a wholly male laugh before his mouth slid down her body, following the path of his fingers. Her hands gripped his shoulders and plucked at the hem of his tunic.

'Please let me see you,' she whispered. 'I must see you.'

His mouth paused in its search. He lifted his head from her belly.

'As my lady requests...' With one movement, he divested himself of clothes, his body and his desire displayed for her. 'You see what you do to me.'

She ran a trembling hand down his chest and stomach until she reached his soft hardness. He groaned in the back of his throat as the need to possess her threatened to overwhelm him. He'd sworn that he'd hold back, that their coupling would mean as much to her as to him. But she only had to touch him and his seed was threatening to spill.

'Julia, you will unman me,' he rasped as her fingers curled round and the heat of him infused her fingers. 'Shall I show you what you are doing to me?'

'The same as you are doing to me.'

She wanted him. Her body was made new for him. He felt more powerful than he had ever felt in the ring and more vulnerable as well. This woman was doing things to his insides that he had never dreamed possible. Valens stroked both his hands down the length of her body and then up again until they reached the apex of her thighs. His fingers hovered, tantalisingly close, but not touching her curls. Her body bucked upwards. She gasped as they touched, tangled and tormented, sliding between her thighs and out again, softly stroking her until he could see her start to reach the crest of her desire.

Julia's hands plucked at his shoulders, pulling him upwards, but his fingers continued to stroke and circle until her head thrashed about and pleading noises came from her throat. Then and only then did he permit his shaft to bury itself deep within her. Her body stretched, and welcomed his full length.

Valens raised himself up on his elbows and looked at her passion-darkened eyes. Then she started to move her hips and he allowed his passion full rein.

In the aftermath, Julia lay with one leg over his hip, with Valens still buried deep within her. Each breath she took matched his. His tenderness and consideration filled her with a warm glow. It was hard to believe that the man lying next to her was a hardened gladiator who fought for his life in the arena. He had never pushed her or hurt her. As he had promised, there had been only pleasure.

The coming together had been no less passionate than before. Yesterday had been fast and furious, but today they had taken their time. She felt cherished in his arms.

Her hands touched the sheen of sweat on his brow and his eyes came back into focus. His lips placed a gentle kiss on her cheek.

'You should never doubt your ability to give pleasure.' His mouth curved in a smile and there was a teasing lilt to his voice. 'You are a warm, vibrant woman. Let that be a lesson to you.'

'It may take me a few more lessons before I get the essence of it,' she replied with a grin and reached a lazy hand up to stroke the soft stubble of his cheek. She felt like nothing bad could ever happen to her again. Her whole life had been building up to this and this man. There had to be a way of keeping him here in Rome.

'A demanding woman.' His hand cupped her bottom and pulled her closer. 'Give me time.'

'I am willing to wait…' She pressed her breasts against his chest, arching her back. As her nipples brushed his naked chest, she felt him grow inside her, filling her once again.

'It may be less time than I thought,' he said, nipping her chin and beginning to move against her body.

Late the next morning, Julia inclined her head as Senator Gracchus came into the room, dressed in an immaculate white toga with a large bright purple stripe. He had sent word earlier that morning that he would be calling. The excitement and curiosity of the message took some of the disappointment off the fact that Valens had left before she had woken up. Her deep regret was that she forgot to probe more about his boyhood. There was that one tantalising clue that he served with Senator Gracchus's son. But it could wait. Everything could wait.

Julia's fingers curled around the little figurine of Valens she had placed by her work basket, for luck and for courage, but she also intended on showing it to Senator Gracchus and asking him for ideas of where to take her search.

Bodyguards and servants carrying a statue and his chair flanked the elderly Senator. At a wave of his be-ringed hand, the servant placed the chair in the centre of the room, and draped a deep purple cloth over the top. Gracchus sat down, surveying the room in the same manner she supposed a general surveys the battlefield.

'Senator, it is so good of you to call on our humble

household…' Sabina breathed, making a show of placing her spindle down.

'Sabina Claudia, it does my old heart good to see that some Roman matrons remember the old ways and keep their hands busy by spinning rather than their tongues wagging with gossip. No doubt you are making your husband a new toga.'

'Spinning means so much to me,' Sabina cooed, patting her elaborate curls. 'I only wish Julia would derive the same pleasure as I do from it, but these young women, Senator.'

'I have things I would like to say to Julia in private. It was easier if I came here. Thank you for your hospitality.'

'Perhaps later you might have a glass of honey wine with us?'

'If there is time.' The senator's tone implied there wouldn't be. 'If you'll excuse us. I am sure your other duties call.'

Sabina left the room in a rush, muttering about senators who took their status for granted.

'Senator, you do me a great honour,' Julia said, breaking the silence that had descended on Sabina's departure and trying to refrain from flinching under his steady gaze. There could be only one reason for his visit. Somehow, Lucius had twisted the story of what happened here yesterday.

His face stern, he motioned for her to sit. Julia sank gratefully down on her stool as her knees had started to tremble. She crossed her ankles and resisted the urge to pick up the discarded spindle.

'I understand you suffered an unpleasantness yesterday,' he said gravely after exchanging pleasantries about the weather and Rome's recent success in Asia. 'My son came to see you. I understand his behaviour left a good deal to be desired. It was not the actions I would expect of a Roman, let alone someone who is the heir to the Gracchus name. His behaviour is disappointing.'

One by one the knots in her stomach began to release. Julia drew a long breath, filling her lungs with cleansing air. She could take her revenge on Lucius now and tell the senator everything. But Valens was correct. She needed to live in the present. Senator Gracchus must have known what Lucius was like before now. Her words would not change that.

'Think nothing of it.' Julia waved her hand. 'I assure you. I have forgotten the incident.'

Again the steady gaze from the senator. Julia tried to read his face, but failed. She gripped her hands together to keep from asking—what did he want?

'Nevertheless I have not. Brawling in public with a woman and then a gladiator.' Gracchus's voice condemned Lucius. 'He becomes more ungovernable by the day. I can only offer my sincere and abject apologies. I was horrified when I learnt. He behaved worse than the most mean slave in my household. I expect my son to maintain certain standards of behaviour. If we lower our standards to that level, what will Rome become?'

Julia plucked at the sleeve of her gown. Let Lucius be the cause of his own downfall. 'No harm was done. The so-called brawl stopped before it started, thanks to the swift intervention of the *gladiator*. Please forget it as I intend to.'

A smile broke over the senator's face, transforming it, making it seem much younger. Julia caught a glimpse of the devastatingly handsome man he must have been in his youth.

'We shall mention the subject no more then. It is a wrapped and sealed scroll.' He folded his hands in his lap and showed little sign of departing.

Julia reached down and gave Bato a stroke. What else did the senator want? He did not come all this way to smooth over Lucius's transgressions.

'Can I offer you a drink?' she asked, breaking the silence. She clapped her hands and a servant appeared. 'Some cool mint tea? Or perhaps sweet wine? Sabina is sure to have ordered the honey to be mixed in.'

'A cup of mint tea would do nicely.'

'Is there some other reason for your visit, Senator?' Julia asked after she had ordered the tea and the senator still sat there. 'I am honoured that you chose to come and visit, but feel your visit may have some other purpose.'

Gracchus beckoned to one of his servants. The man dressed in whortleberry-purple brought the cloth-covered statuette forward and placed it on his knee.

'Apologising was my main purpose, but I did have another one,' he said, with his hands moving over the statuette as if he sought to draw strength from it. 'You asked me a question about my son yesterday. A question I regrettably had no time to answer. You wanted to know what my son looked like.'

'Yes, I did.' Julia edged forward on her seat and wondered if she should tell the Senator the story Valens had told her about the manner of his son's death. She wanted him to know there was someone who was with his son when he died.

'This is my son, Gaius, as a young man.'

The servant pulled the cloth from the statuette. Julia's mouth dropped open. Her hands trembled. Had Valens not told her he had seen Gaius Gracchus die, she would have been convinced this was a younger version of Valens—the nose and mouth were similar. She rubbed her eyes. Who was Valens?

'I don't recall seeing this before.' Julia reached out her right forefinger to touch the statuette's face.

'It resides in my bedroom, beside one of his mother.

He was such a paragon of Roman virtue—honourable, unselfish and public-spirited. He would have gone far if his life had not been cut short by Fate.'

'He doesn't look very much like you.' Julia glanced at the Senator with his hooded eyes and then back at the statuette of his son, spear in one hand, dressed in military garb.

'My son took after my dead wife in many ways,' Gracchus said with a smile. 'May the gods grant their shades a pleasant time in Hades.'

Julia toyed with her bracelet. He had given her a slight opening for her tale about his son's death. She felt she had an obligation to tell him that someone had been with Gaius Gracchus when he died, and could tell him precisely about the manner of his death.

'I have met a man,' she said carefully, 'a gladiator who claims he was held in the same pirate's hold as your son. He saw your son die.'

Gracchus's eyes turned grave. He made a motion, dismissing his bodyguard and servants. Julia watched in silence as they departed, her stomach knotting tighter and tighter.

'Dear sweet child,' Gracchus said at last, 'you hardly know what you say. I showed you yesterday Gaius's brooch. Mettalius laid it in my hand. He tore it from Gaius's body. I have his solemn oath on it. Why would he lie to me about the manner of my only son's death? Besides, the ransom note was a forgery. Lucius spotted the errors straight away. Blinded by love for my son and concern for my wife who was suffering her first bout of severe illness, I missed them the first time I read the note, but Lucius noticed how the code had been altered. Rage filled me that someone should play such a shabby trick and that I should be so gullible to believe it.'

Julia turned her head towards Bato, staring at the dog's grizzled muzzle, but not really seeing it. She had to find a way of making him believe. She had to do it for Valens. Maybe if he spoke to the senator, it would give him the courage to seek out his own father. 'That may be true, but the gladiator—what reason would he have to lie?'

Gracchus leant over and patted Julia's hand. 'I know not of his purpose, but I never trust an *infamis*. They are not honourable men and have forfeited their right to be believed. How can I begin to guess what he might have hoped to gain from this tale? But mark my words, he will have wanted something, they always do.'

'I…' Julia stumbled over her words. If only Valens were here, she would drag him to Gracchus and demand him to repeat the story. It would force the issue out into the open. But she had no idea when Valens would return, nor could she ask Gracchus to stay.

A noise made her look up. In the shadow of the doorway, she saw Valens standing there, pale as a ghost, his face a mixture of thunder and pain.

The soothing non-committal words she had been about to say dried on her lips.

She was sure she had made a sound because Gracchus half-turned and followed the line of Julia's eyes. The statuette of his son tumbled from his grasp as he rose in his seat. Julia caught the statuette before it crashed to the floor.

'Gaius?' Gracchus croaked. 'Can it be you?'

Chapter Thirteen

Valens stood in the doorway, unable to move, his eyes taking in every detail of the scene. Julia was crouched on the floor with the white statuette held gently between her hands. The man was seated in a resplendent chair with his arm raised as if he were making a speech in the Senate. His face was older and more lined than the last time they had met, but his toga was still as brilliantly white, the coloured stripe still as broad.

The coils of the past finally had reached out to ensnare him and Valens waited for the final thrust of Fate's trident. He should have left when he first learnt of the Gracchus connection, or before that, when he first felt the tugs of memory.

He heard the whispered *Gaius*, and felt it pierce his soul. The temptation to walk away was overpowering, but he appeared to have lost all movement in his feet. He wanted to rage and cry. Yesterday had been bad enough, facing his cousin who innocently had taken his place, but here was the man who had allowed it all to happen. This was the man who had refused to pay his ransom and who had condemned him to this life of infamy and his men to their death. That compartment of his life had to remain shut and locked forever.

'I am Valens the Thracian gladiator,' he heard his voice say from a long way away. 'Not Gaius Gracchus.'

He watched the old man intently to gauge his reaction. Would he deny the words and insist on the truth? He had to know the truth. What parent would not instinctively know his only son?

Gracchus's eyes peered at him, burned into his soul. Valens drew on all his gladiatorial training to force his feet to stay still. He returned the gaze without flinching. Then his father's shoulders shrank and his face grew more lined before Gracchus turned his head away.

'Forgive an old man's fancy—in the half-light I thought my son had returned from the dead.' His father's voice sounded tired and over-burdened with age. 'An old man's folly.'

The desire to run and bury his face in Gracchus's toga as he had when he was a small boy and had broken his favourite toy filled Valens. He wanted to be that son again. He wanted to have his whole future in front of him, a future that could include Julia.

He started to form the words, to beg his father's forgiveness. Then the anger returned, surging through him. How dare his father not pay the ransom! How dare he condemn his only son to an infamous death! He had behaved in a way no father should. He had forfeited any right to be comforted. The last remnant of Gaius Gracchus died when he took the gladiator's oath. Valens bit back the words.

'Valens is the gladiator I told you about. See, here is his figurine.' Julia reached forward and touched Gracchus's hand, indicating a small figurine on a shelf next to his father's chair. 'He saw your son die and can tell you about the manner of his death.'

Gracchus made an irritated noise and signalled for a servant to take the statuette from Julia. Valens felt his blood run cold. He knew the statuette, but he needed to know why his father had brought it to Julius Antonius's house.

What was Julia's part in this? Had she guessed? She should have asked him first. She should have asked him if he wanted this. He did want Julia, but not this way. She had to want him for who he was, the man he had become, not the patrician he had been.

'Julia, I have already told you. My son died in Zama in North Africa. I have his brooch. I know how he died. Mettalius told me and Mettalius is an honourable man. Yes, there was a ransom note, but it was a crude attempt at exploiting money, preying on a sick woman's fancy.'

Valens found it impossible to contain his anger.

'Six men perished when your refusal arrived,' he stated bluntly. 'That note was no forgery. He was alive when the pirates captured him, injured but alive.'

Gracchus turned towards him, a look of disdain on his face. Valens knew in that heartbeat of time that his father was determined not to believe the evidence of his own eyes. That it was more convenient for him to believe his only son was dead than to face the truth. All the hope he had had that somehow it had been a mistake, that Gracchus would forgive him for not being Roman enough to put honour before death, was gone. When had his father forgiven any act he considered less than honourable?

'You ask me to believe the word of a gladiator above the word of a senator—two senators? I have the evidence.' His father's voice was ice-cold. 'I held my son's cloak in my hands. I wear his brooch. He would not have given up either without a fight. The note was a forgery. Lucius showed me the errors and how the code had been changed.'

Valens winced as he remembered how Aquilia had pulled the cloak from his shoulders. We have need of this elsewhere, he had said. He had always assumed that it had been sold. That the attack had been random. A twist of Fate's spindle. Had he been mistaken? What could have Mettalius hoped to gain from his death? And the note. Aquilia's smile when he said that it was to make sure that there were no mistakes. How could his father say that it was a forgery, except to provide salve for his own mind?

'You may believe what you like,' Valens said stiffly, refusing to beg. His father had repudiated him once. He would not give him an opportunity to do so a second time.

He looked at his father who clapped his hands, summoning his servants.

'I shall go now, before I insult your hospitality, Julia Antonia.' His father stood up and draped his toga over his arm, the senatorial stripe proudly displayed. 'I will not have my decisions questioned by an *infamis*!'

'Yes, you are always right and hate being proved wrong.' The bitter words poured from Valens's mouth before he could stop them. 'You never change, just as you always were. The pride of the Gracchi before everything. Remember you misplaced your speech on Sulla and you blamed your son for it, beating him to teach him a lesson. Later you discovered the speech in a pile of scrolls you had put away. You were wrong then and you are now.'

His father's dark eyes met Valens. The look in them was terrible, but Valens returned it, never flinching. This was it—the moment of truth. He had never intended it to be this way. He had planned on confronting his father after he had regained his honour through winning the *rudius*. And it was never to be in anger. But the gods had decreed otherwise.

His father had to know who he was. He had to put the bonds of blood and love before the ties of family honour.

His father took a half-step towards him and Valens felt a great welling up of emotion. All these years, these five long wasted years, had he misjudged his father? His father's hand reached out and toppled the Valens figurine. It rolled across the floor and came to rest at Valens's feet.

'My son would have died before he was captured, I know that in my heart of hearts,' he said with each word ringing out through the room. 'My son would have never become a slave. He would never ever have fallen so low as to become a gladiator. He would have preferred death. He would never have disgraced the family's honour. He would never have risen to the heights of that profession.'

'As you wish, Senator Gracchus, but we both know the truth,' Valens said and gave a bow.

He had his answer. His father had put honour before

death. And despite the evidence of his eyes, Gracchus would continue to insist on his version of the events.

Valens stumbled to his room, a mixture of rage, anger and despair filling his body. Any last doubt about his father vanished. There was no turning time back. His father had denied him.

Waves of silent spasms racked his body and for the first time since he was a child and his dog had died, Valens cried.

Julia sat quietly on her stool after Gracchus and his entourage left, watching the little figurine on the floor. The image of Valens's face when the senator had said that no son of his would become a gladiator warred with the image of the senator when he had first glimpsed Valens's face.

When Sabina came back and made some remark about the senator leaving in a temper, Julia answered her, but refused to say more. Sabina had swept away to prepare for the dinner party she was attending. The servants came in, cleared the tea things, lit the lamps and still Julia sat, hands motionless, spindle lying at her side. Bato came over and laid his head on her knee and her hand automatically stroked him.

A noise made her open her eyes and she stared at Valens who was dressed in his travelling cloak.

Despite his ravaged features, his face seemed as remote and cold as the statuette she had held in her hands. All warmth had vanished. Whatever growing feeling there had been between them, she knew she had inadvertently destroyed it. She had wanted to save him, to give him back his life.

'You are Gaius Gracchus,' she said in the silence before her nerve gave way.

'I should know who I am.' The words were said in a low voice, but one that was intended to quash all dissent. 'Who I was is not important.'

Julia stood up and hugged her arms about her waist. 'Then who are you?'

'Valens the gladiator,' came the swift reply. 'I told you so when we met. Nothing has changed to alter that fact. The arena is my whole life. My past has no meaning.'

'But who were you before? You had to have been somebody. Were you Gaius Gracchus?'

'You seem determined to think I am.'

'That is not an answer, and you know it. You cannot pretend you never had a past. Every Roman has a family and you deserve to have yours back.' He had to see she had acted out of the best motives. She wanted a reconciliation between father and son. Gracchus mourned for his son and Valens needed a father, or at least need to make peace with his father. He deserved to have his family and his past back.

Valens continued to stare at her with eyes made out of cold black ice.

'Tell me what sort of man you were,' she pleaded. There had to be a way of going back, of undoing the harm she had unwittingly caused. If she had explained about the augur's prediction in the first place, before she contacted Senator Gracchus, would none of this have happened?

'A Roman and not a very good one, according to my father. Certainly not worth paying a ransom for.'

'There are many types of Romans. You were a patrician.' Her arms trembled as if she had been in a long race. 'People grow. They change for the better. You were his only son.'

'Don't you think I know that? I know what my father wanted from me. How I could never live up to the glittering future he desired for me. And when it was taken from me, rather than dying honourably, I chose to live dishonourably.' Valens stared at her, stony-faced, his arms crossed and his feet planted firmly. She saw a muscle twitch in his jaw. Julia wanted to shrink, but her feet refused to listen to any command. She stood rooted to the spot.

He bowed his head and she saw his shoulders shake. 'Julia…'

'Please tell me I wasn't wrong,' she whispered.

He raked his hand through his hair and his eyes

fastened on the middle distance. 'You must understand, Julia, when you become a gladiator, you are
reborn. There is no past, no future only the arena and
the spectacle. The man I was perished back in the
pirate's hold. I am Valens the Thracian. I have no
wish to revisit the past. It is not where my future lies.'

'And what about me?'

'I trusted you, Julia, to keep my secrets, not to go
prying into my past.'

Julia hugged her arms about her waist, longing to
run into his arms and longing to do anything to
turn back time.

'I was only trying to help,' she said in a small voice.
'I wanted to reunite you with your family.'

'When I need your help, I will ask for it. My family
now is the Strabo's gladiatorial school. And will be
until I retire honourably from the sport. Then I will take
a name of my own choosing and live my life the way
I have chosen as the honourable man I know I now am.'

He turned towards the door, and Julia knew he was
about to walk out of her life. The memories of the
long hours she had spent at Gracchus's, listening to
him talk about his son, assaulted her. She felt she had
to try again, even if it meant losing Valens. She felt he
had to understand that his father did love him, that it
had all been a terrible mistake. She kept thinking about
how she'd feel if her father behaved in that fashion.

'Senator Gracchus makes offerings to the gods every day in his son's name…in your name.'

Valens turned back towards her, his face savage.

'Not in my name. I can never be the son he wants. You heard him. His son died fighting in North Africa. He has the brooch to prove it. I have this.' Valens tore back his cloak and shoved his forearm towards her, the tattooed lion gleaming up at her. 'My only value to him was to carry on the glory of the family name— in the Senate. I am an *infamis*, Julia. I can never hold public office. I am tainted. My being alive will not bring back his dreams.'

'He wants his son, Valens, the child he held in his arms. I know he does. He is a proud man and won't beg, but I was there. I saw his face. He hungered to see you.'

Valens slammed his fist into the wall.

'He wants someone to carry on the family name. Day after day when I was growing up, I had to look at the busts of my ancestors and listen to how great they once were. How I had to match up to their ideals…'

She drew a deep breath and walked over to Valens, laid a hand on his arm.

'He has changed, Valens,' she whispered. 'He loved his son. He used to talk about you all the time, to praise what you had done to Lucius and to me. Someone lied to him…'

A look of anguish passed over Valens's face, but then

he straightened and stared out into the middle distance. His face became as impassive as a death mask.

'If he cared about me, why did he leave me to die in a pirate's hold?' he asked in a voice filled with rage. 'I can still hear Aquilia's laughter as he read out the words—my son is dead, no amount of money can bring him back. Then he ordered the remaining six men of my patrol and me beaten. None survived that beating except me. Six men died because my father chose honour above his son. They were good men, Julia.'

His face contorted in pain at the memory. She did not deny he had suffered. But his father had suffered as well. Julia hugged her arms about her waist and tried to remember the stories.

'He was lied to. That's obvious. Mistakes were made. There were tears in his eyes when he showed me the brooch you always wore. He said Mettalius had brought it back along with a bloodied cloak. He had no reason to distrust Mettalius. Someone told him that your note was a forgery. Someone had tampered with it. Who benefitted? Who stood to gain everything?'

Valens gave his head a shake. 'Julia, you would have me believing in nymphs and fables next. You have no proof. My father taught me to demand the utmost proof.'

Julia laid a hand on his arm, but he pushed it away. 'Talk to him.'

'Why? Why should I debase myself in front of him? You heard him—no son of his would ever become a gladiator. He knew who I was. What sort of father does not recognise his own flesh and blood? If he had wanted me for a son, he would have made a sign. And Hercules help me, I would have gone to him and laid my head on his toga, begging his forgiveness.'

Julia felt her stomach begin to shake with pain. She hated this. She hated confrontation, fighting. With each passing breath, her knees became weaker and the temptation to flee grew. She was scared he would turn his anger on her, but she had to say it. She had to try to save his life and to fight for their future.

'Your father could restore you to your life, Valens. He is a wealthy man. He could purchase your contract and you would not have to fight in the arena. He was angry and hurt. Your appearance was unexpected. He wasn't prepared for it. But his anger will disappear. I know he loves his son. Talk to him, explain what happened—for my sake, if nothing else.'

Valens felt the anger flare uncontrollably through him. How dare she! He had never asked to be freed from being a slave, not in that way. To go to his father in the way she suggested would be unthinkable. He would have no pride or honour left. He stared at Julia. Her face was turned up to him, her eyes glowing with unshed tears. It would be easy. Valens swallowed hard and drew on all of his self-control. His voice emerged as a ragged whisper. 'Let me regain my honour in my own way.'

'Valens,' she said, coming over to him, touching his hand with a gentle finger, 'I care about you.'

Valens shrugged the hand off and tried to ignore her siren's call. It would be so easy to give into her demands, to do what she asked. Already he could see the image forming before his eyes. But he also knew that to do what she asked was to condemn their life to one without honour, one where he would eventually despise her.

'If you cared at all for me, you would not ask this. The way you suggest is the coward's way, the way without honour. It will not solve anything. Your father will not accept me because I am free. I would still be an *infamis*. I am sorry, Julia, but my life doesn't work that way.'

She turned from him and Valens grabbed her arm. The red mist curled at the edges of his vision. How dare she interfere with his life! He was trying to make her see why he couldn't go back and all she could do was demand he speak with his father.

'You're hurting me,' she gasped, pulling away from him, her eyes wide with fear. 'Let me go, you brute.'

His hands dropped to his sides and his face reddened. For what felt like eternity, they stared at each other, chests heaving with each breath.

'Please…' she whispered. 'Please don't hurt me.

You said you would protect me, but who will protect me from you?'

'I would never hurt you.' He could see the angry red marks on her forearm, and heard Bato's soft growl. He felt ashamed of his actions. He had grabbed her in anger. His anger was with his father, not with her, and he had been about to take all that hurt and anger out on her. How had it come to this?

'Julia, I am sorry…'

'Would you go, leave?' Julia straightened her back, hating him and her heart. She wanted to agree to his demands but not if he was going to force her. 'When I left Lucius, I vowed I would not bow to any man's force.'

'Julia, I didn't mean to…'

Venus help her, she wanted to lean her head against Valens's chest. She wanted to feel his arms about her. But he frightened her as well. When she had argued something from her heart, he had tried to bend her to his will. He obviously cared nothing for them, for her. She wanted to sink down into a ball, but she refused to give him the satisfaction of seeing her cowed. She forced her head higher, her back straighter. 'Please just go. We had something, but it is over. It is better this way. I am a Roman matron and you are a gladiator.'

'I had come to tell you that I was going. My form in

the arena has suffered. I find it impossible to concen-trate on my work here. Tigris has taken a house in the Aventine. There it will be easy to remember who I truly am—Valens the Thracian—and to concentrate on the only thing that means something in my life, the arena.'

Julia closed her eyes. She would be strong. She refused to beg.

'That is what I want. What we had is over,' she said in a quiet voice.

He gave a bow and was gone.

Chapter Fourteen

Over the next two days, Julia tried unsuccessfully to forget she had ever met Valens. She spent time offering prayers of thanks to Venus and the other household gods while her father and Sabina seemed more intent in creating a list of possible suitors than noticing her distress. Once again, she had become invisible.

Claudia, however, was another matter entirely when she arrived unannounced on the morning of the third day. She bustled into Julia's room as she sat, her hairbrush in hand, gazing through her narrow window. Claudia refused to accept any of Julia's explanations for her shadowed eyes and pale face, dismissing each with a small wave of her hand.

'You may want me to believe that, Julia, but I have seen the end of an affair too often. I'd have to be blind and deaf not to know the signs.'

'Is it that obvious?' Julia asked and wondered if she

should put another layer of powder on her face to hide the dark circles.

'Only to someone who has been there before— many times.' Claudia placed her head close to Julia's as she gave her a hug. 'You slept with Valens.'

Julia dropped the brush.

'I thought—' she began, her heart pounding. If Claudia knew, how many other people had guessed? 'I thought we had been careful.'

Claudia picked the brush up and started to stroke Julia's hair, piling it high on her head and pinning it with several hairpins.

'The affair is over. Why are you worried?' she asked after she had finished. 'That style suits you, Julia.'

'It could cause a scandal.'

'Public displays cause scandals, not private passion,' Claudia said, tapping the brush against her lips. 'In private, everything is permissible. You will cause a scandal if you withdraw to your room for days. You must go out and face the would-be gossips down. Show them you are not concerned by this. If anyone whispers, it will be just whispers. Look at how Servilia behaves. Or the Clodiae. Rome whispers, but no one can prove a thing.'

'I am not sure I want to become notorious.' Julia gave a small hiccupping laugh. 'I have seen what Sabina and her harpies can do to people.'

'You will become more notorious if you stay in this room much longer. People will begin to question.'

'What do you suggest?'

'I suggest you go to the baths with me. A new one has opened on the edge of the Aventine. It has a series of good exercise rooms and treatments. Plus it allows for mixed bathing. And some of the men there, well…they will drive all thoughts of Valens from your head.' Claudia kissed her fingers.

Julia drew a shaky breath. She refused to think about other men. The only man she wanted was Valens. She wanted to go back to the closeness they seemed to be developing. 'It is too soon.'

'Nonsense. It will do you good. The best way to cure a broken heart is to find another object of affection. The bathing suites will open at five hours, but we can exercise, and perhaps play a game of *trignon* if we can find someone else, or perhaps hoops until then.'

The Aventine baths were a complex of marble-fronted buildings, gardens and exercise areas and a small library. The covered portico outside the baths teemed with small shops, market traders and their customers. Everything from monkeys to silk seemed to be on sale here and each trader seemed to be vying with the other as they shouted out their wares.

Julia and Claudia waited in a short queue to pay

their quarter of an *as* and then went into the baths. The first thing Julia noticed was the absolute quiet of the courtyard after the noisy throng outside. The only sound was the splash of the fountain.

After changing into short exercise tunics, Claudia led the way towards the gymnasium. Julia looked at the men dressed in short tunics or loin cloths who were engaged in a variety of games and exercises and tried not to compare their physical attributes to Valens's. Two or three might have better legs, but none had his stature. She doubted if she could feel safe in any of these men's arms.

'You see why everyone is talking about it,' Claudia gushed, pointing to the marble bathing complex. 'It is a splendid addition to Rome. A true mark of civilisation. And, as promised, enough men to satisfy your eyes for days.'

'When you said the Aventine baths, I thought you meant the one Sabina and her friends often use. It is luxurious, but nothing on this scale.'

'I knew you would like it. It opened on the last Ides.' Claudia started to signal to another woman. 'Look, there's our third for *trignon*—Poppea Scipia.'

Julia winced as the small woman whose hair was piled high in a Greek fashion hurried towards them. Poppea and Claudia attended gladiatorial matches together. She was even more dedicated to the games than Claudia and made it a point to compete against men whenever possible. The whisper in the Forum was that her husband had requested a posting in Cyrene to escape her.

'Claudia as I live and breathe and Julia Antonia as well. What a surprise,' Poppea said, racing up to them. 'I was about to start exercising with a dumb-bell, but if you are here we must have a ball game.' She paused and eyed Julia up and down. 'That is, if Julia knows the rules. I know how she hates all things to due with any form of physical activity.'

'I know the rules to *trignon*,' Julia said through clenched teeth and stared at Poppea. 'There are three players. Each takes a corner of the triangle. You catch the balls with one hand and throw with the other. The person who drops the green ball gains a point. At the end of the game, the person with the least points wins.'

'Very good, Julia.' Poppea clapped her hands together briefly. 'And now let's see if you can actually play it. Or will it be like the time you tried to play *harpastum* and were unable to snatch the ball from anyone?'

At the sound of Poppea's loud voice, several men dressed in short tunics turned round. Julia wished the ground would open up and swallow her.

She hesitated, about to withdraw from the contest. Then she saw the small smirk on Poppea's face.

'Poppea, an active spectator in the gladiatorial arena

does not necessarily mean you are good at *trignon*. I look forward to beating you.'

The game went better than Julia dared hope. After ten rounds she and Poppea were tied with Claudia only a point behind. A trickle of sweat snaked down her forehead. Julia wiped it away and reflected that perhaps Claudia had had a point after all. It was a relief to get her frustrations out by throwing the ball as hard as she could at Poppea and seeing her wince as she caught it.

She deftly caught Claudia's underarm pass of the green ball and pivoted to throw it at Poppea. Standing directly behind Poppea was Valens.

Julia froze. She blinked, hoping he might be a figment of her over-active imagination. When she opened her eyes, he was still there, feet planted, hands on hips, watching her. She swallowed hard and tried not to concentrate on the way his mouth looked or the shadows in his eyes.

'Come on, Julia, throw the ball,' Poppea called.

Julia tossed the ball wildly. It hit the ground and then rolled to within a few feet of Valens.

'There was no way I could have caught that,' Poppea complained with her hands on her hips. 'That's Julia's point. Don't you agree, Claudia?'

'I'll get the ball,' Julia said with a faltering voice.

She wiped her palms on the skirt of her tunic and

started forward. She kept her eyes on the ground, hoping against hope he had decided to ignore her.

As she reached the ball, his long fingers closed around it and lifted it up. Her eyes followed the progress of the ball, from the ground past his calves to the bottom of his crimson tunic and up to his face.

'Are you searching for this?' he asked, tossing the ball in one hand.

Julia's mouth went dry. This was not how she had planned on meeting Valens again—hot and sweaty from exercise, her hair held back by a simple tie. If she met him at all, she had intended to be perfectly turned out, dressed in her most fetching clothes.

She tucked a strand of hair behind her ear and tried to look unperturbed. But her breath came in short sharp gasps that had nothing to do with the ball game she had been playing.

'We need the ball to continue the game,' she said after what felt like for ever and held out her hand.

He made no move to give the ball back. Instead, it seemed his eyes roamed her features, pinning her. Julia swallowed hard and tried to think of something witty to say. The only thing she could think of was how much she had missed him, how much she had missed hearing his voice and how frightened she had been of never having a chance to speak to him again.

She wanted to apologise and to ask if they could begin again. But she found it impossible to utter any words.

'Julia—' he said thickly.

'Valens, there you are.' A cool, impeccably coif-fured blonde appeared and tucked her arm in Valens's. 'I searched everywhere for you. Give the woman her ball back or we'll be late.'

Julia felt a knife stab her heart. He had found another. But she refused to hide her face like some misbehaving child. She held out her hand.

'My ball, please, Valens. My friends are waiting.'

He tossed the ball and Julia caught it, closing her fingers around its faint warmth.

'Enjoy playing your game, Julia,' he said and allowed the woman to drag him away.

She watched them go, heard the woman's trilling laughter and her heart sank. She kicked the ground in disgust.

'Is something the matter, Julia?' Claudia's voice pierced through a haze of misery. 'What did he say to you?'

'Probably realised that she has no hope of winning the game,' Poppea said. 'Hurry up. Time is wasting.'

Julia shook herself. She had to accept and to carry on. Valens was an interlude, nothing more. She had been foolish in the extreme to want more than what she had. She should be going down on her knees and thanking Venus that their affair was mercifully short.

Gladiators were for one night, she reminded herself of Claudia's words. The trouble was that her heart refused to believe it.

'I am perfectly fine,' she lied as Claudia continued to look at her with a strange concerned expression. 'It is hotter today than I thought it would be. But it looks like the baths proper are now open. What I would really like is a nice spell in the dry bath, sweating out everything, and a plunge in the cold pool.'

Claudia came over and patted her shoulder. 'Poppea doesn't mean to be so forthright, Julia. It is just her way. When you're ready, we can talk.'

Julia offered a silent prayer up to Venus. Claudia was not pressing for more details about Valens.

'The last few days have taken more out of me than I thought,' she said with a faint rueful grin, wiping her hands on her tunic. 'Hopefully these baths will be the last word in luxury as the sign over the portico said.'

When Julia finished her bath and started putting on her make-up, she had stopped trembling. The bath suite with its marble columns, and mosaic-covered floors and walls, had lived up to its promise, but it had also been a bit more crowded than she would have liked.

Also, the price for being dried off and massaged was far steeper than at any of the baths she had been to.

Still, the massage had made her muscles tingle and she had to agree with Claudia's assessment that a bit of pampering never hurt. The warm glow from the exercise, bath and rub down made her feel like she was floating on clouds. As she tried to decide if her cheeks needed wine dregs or not, she allowed Claudia and Poppea's conversation to flow over her.

'They are harder to come by than Tyrean purple unless you know the right people, but I have two extra tickets,' Poppea said. 'Would either of you two like one? Claudia? Julia?'

Julia stopped gazing at the mirror and turned towards Poppea, brush in hand.

'Tickets to where?'

'To the Gladiatorial Last-Night Feast,' Poppea replied as she fastened up a disc on her gown. 'Not that you will be interested, Julia, but it is when the gladiators say goodbye to their supporters and their families. It can be quite moving. For many of them it might be their last night on earth. It is something no true supporter wants to miss, but Lucia has a cold and Serena's husband has just come back from North Africa. Claudia, are you interested?'

'I already have mine, thanks, and I am sure Julia has better things to do.'

Julia's stomach dropped as the brush slipped out of her grasp and hit the counter with a small crash. She had completely forgotten about what day the games started. A queasy feeling washed over her. Tomorrow Valens would be out there, fighting for his life, and, if his prediction was to be believed, against Aquilia.

She looked at the large statue of Fortunata that dominated the changing room. Tomorrow the goddess would reveal which one she favoured. She stared at the statue's bland features and knew she needed to see Valens once more, if only to wish him good luck. She had been so wrapped up in her own misery and problems that she had forgotten he faced probably the toughest challenge of his career. She should have said something, something that resembled an apology, instead of merely asking for her ball.

'I will take a ticket, Poppea,' she said before her courage failed her.

Both Claudia and Poppea turned towards her with astonished faces.

'Are you positive about this, Julia?' Claudia asked in quiet voice. 'There are public places and public places.'

'I am more positive about going than anything else I have ever done before.' Julia felt her confidence grow with each word she uttered. 'I want to go tonight and then to the arena tomorrow. I need to go.'

Claudia gave a small clap of her hands.

'Have you been to a feast before, Julia?' Poppea asked. 'It is very dramatic and you should see what some of the women wear.'

'I thought the point was to go to see the gladiators and wish them good fortune,' Julia replied, careful to keep her emotions from showing on her face.

'It is, and for the gladiators to see you.' Poppea giggled. 'But fashions are often started at these feasts. I have had a new emerald-green gap-sleeve gown made for the occasion. I think the hint of flesh is so much more elegant than the plain old-fashioned gowns that covered everything.'

The exhilaration drained out of Julia, leaving her feeling limp and weak. The enormity of what she was about to do washed over her. Having made the promise, she had no idea of what was expected of her, what she should wear. She wanted to look her best, but knew if she wore her usual party clothes—green gown and *stola*—she'd probably look like a dowdy moth in an array of butterflies. She felt Claudia put an arm around her shoulders and give her a quick squeeze.

'Fear not, Julia,' she whispered in her ear. 'I will make sure you are dressed properly and that Valens will be stunned by your appearance. He will see what he has casually discarded.'

Julia nodded. She had to see him at least one more time, and try to explain.

'Julia may not have been to a feast before, but I have, Poppea. She will not disgrace you. What time shall we meet?'

The banqueting hall of the Aventine baths flickered in the light of a hundred lamps. Valens stood in the doorway, surveying the feast teeming with food and people. From the corners came the just-audible sounds of dice clicking as groups of men huddled over gaming boards.

The central tables groaned with a spread of food fit for the gods: roast wild boar with two baskets containing dates hanging from its tusks, bearded mullet floating in a sauce in such a way that they looked as if they were still alive and rich pastries dripping with rose petals and honey. A pyramid of exotic fruits and berries stood next to a fountain of wine.

Women dressed in brightly coloured gowns drifted about, draping themselves over the nearest male. These were no courtesans, but women with enough money to indulge their appetites. Who knew how many patricians had been sired by gladiators?

One woman caught Valens's gaze and patted the couch beside her, licking her lips in a suggestive manner.

Valens shook his head and passed by. It was not something he needed—meaningless coupling in one of the cubicles thoughtfully provided by his host.

There was only one woman who haunted his dreams, and he very much doubted that Julia Antonia would be in a place like this.

He should have said more this afternoon when he saw Julia at the baths, but there had been no time. A thousand words had crowded into his mind, and her friends had been waiting for her. He could hardly drag her away without causing a scene and more scandal.

The one thing he had been conscious of was the huge gaping hole where his heart normally resided. The argument need never have happened. He knew he had been searching for one, trying to find a way out, and the worse part of it was that she was right. He was a coward for not contacting his father. He should have tried. He should not have shut the door on his past.

He wanted his honour back, but he also wanted Julia. Despite everything, it looked like it would be impossible to have both. Honour was a cold bedfellow.

Valens took a glass of wine from a silver tray and tried to concentrate on the scene before him. The buzz was quieter in here where the gladiators of the first hall had gathered than in the other rooms. Unlike the frantic wailing or gorging on food that he had seen in the other rooms where the untried gladiators and the ones who had only won a single bout feasted, here most behaved with dignity.

The gladiators of the first hall were survivors, and, while they might perish because of an injury, it was doubtful that they would be killed at the crowd's request—their price was too high for the giver of the games to pay to the *lanistra*. Or at least it was what they told themselves. Valens lifted the cup of honey-sweetened wine to his lips and avoided the outstretched arms of a cloyingly perfumed beauty in lavender.

'Valens, you are here at last,' Tigris said, clapping him on the back. 'Come to partake of the wine, women and song. Eat, drink and be merry, for tomorrow we may die.'

'Something like that,' Valens said and tried to keep his mind away from the horrors with which he knew tomorrow would be filled. Time enough for nightmares in the small hours of the morning. He gave a brief laugh and gestured at the gladiators who lounged on the couches. 'I come to watch and make sure you and the others stuff your faces. It will make my job easier tomorrow afternoon.'

'No, seriously, why are you here? You generally avoid these gatherings like the plague. Your views and Maia's are the same—maudlin overblown spectacles that demean the dignity of the gladiator.'

'I've made an exception, at Strabo's insistence. He is our manager after all.' Valens raised his cup to the *lanistra*, who waved back from where he lounged, surrounded by young men. 'These parties are not the way I want to relax before a bout. But the paying guests will want the top of the bill, according to direct orders from Caesar. Who am I to disobey?'

'You delight in talking riddles.' Tigris poked a finger at Valens's chest. 'You may want to believe that, but I know you are here for another purpose.'

'Believe what you like,' Valens said and put his cup down on the table, disturbed that Tigris had read him that easily. 'Now, if you'll excuse me, I'll leave. I have fulfilled my contract, Strabo has seen me and I can now look forward to the bout tomorrow without worrying about my fee being docked for non-attendance at the feast.'

Valens looked around the hall at the gambling and the women. He counted at least six men who could recognise him from his youth. The only thing that might prevent a confrontation was the story of his death. 'There are too many shades of my misspent youth here.'

'You might have cause to linger.' Tigris leant forward and whispered 'She's here, you know. I saw you searching for her earlier. You can't fool me, old friend, with your talk of counting gladiators and orders from Strabo, I know you too well.'

'Who's here?' Before he finished forming the words, Valens knew who Tigris meant—Julia.

'Julia Antonia, the woman you proclaimed you were finished with. The woman you stood transfixed by this afternoon, or so Maia tells me. I recognised her from Maia's description. Shaking your head in disgust at me will do you no good,' Tigris laughed and then sobered. 'But if you want her, you'll have to move fast.'

'Why?'

'It appears Aquilia has taken you at your word and is treating her as fair game.'

Valens's jaw clenched as he followed the line of Tigris's finger. There in a knot by the door stood Aquilia speaking to a vision in rose-pink.

Despite the stylised hair and the gown so thin it left little to the imagination, he knew from the way she tilted her head that it was Julia—a suspicion confirmed when he heard the echo of her laughter over the din of the crowd.

As he watched, he saw Julia try to disentangle herself from Aquilia's heavy grip, only for the former pirate to wrap his arm around her waist.

Their eyes met, and Valens fancied he saw desperation in them. Why had she approached Aquilia? She knew what he was like. Aquilia was not the sort of man to pay attention to any woman's wish. Nobody would come to her rescue, not here, not at this feast. More likely they would be wagering on whether or not she'd manage to take him to bed. Anger at Julia, at Aquilia and most of all at the system washed over him. He squared his shoulders and started towards the pair.

'Valens, what are you going to do?' Tigris grabbed on to his arm. 'Remember, Strabo gave you clear warning to stay away from Aquilia. He will find another to amuse him shortly.'

'Would you be so quick to find excuses if that was Maia?'

'The lady might welcome his attention...' Tigris began. 'You did say you two were finished. Perhaps she merely wants a gladiator...'

His voice fell silent as Valens glared at him, feeling the anger surge through him. He was uncertain whose neck he wanted to wring more—Aquilia's or Julia's. Although he was pleased to see her, she should know better than to be here.

'That is what I am going to find out.' Valens shook off Tigris's arm and took another stride towards the couple. 'She appears to be in need of assistance and I intend to offer it.'

Chapter Fifteen

Julia tried to disentangle her hand from Aquilia's broad one for the third time. Talking to this overgrown cretin had been Poppea's idea. *Ask him where your gladiator is,* she had hissed with a giggle and a hard shove to her back.

Before Julia could explain or interrupt Claudia's discussion with a soldier about the merits of extra armour on the torso to ask her to explain, Poppea had simpered up to the man, spoken to him and then had pushed her forward. With a flick of his wrist, his paw had closed around her arm. His eyes glittered with the same intensity as they had after the weapon-giving ceremony.

She felt her backbone begin to give way, then she thought of how he liked to see women cowed. She refused to allow him that satisfaction. She lifted her chin into the air and stared directly back at Aquilia.

'Please release my hand,' she said through gritted teeth.

Aquilia showed no signs of granting her request. His meaty breath assaulted her nose, and his eyes held a distinct leer to them.

'Do I need to repeat myself? Let my hand go.' She heard her voice rise and a tremble of fear appear in the last word. This whole feast idea was a grim mistake. Between the crowds, the noise and now Aquilia's behaviour, she would be hard pressed to think of a less pleasant way to spend an evening. Thus far, she had not seen one glimpse of Valens.

Her heart sank further. Perhaps he had already been and left. Her entire journey would be for nothing. The only thing she would be able to do would be to perch in the stands and pray that she would have a chance to explain and to put things right between them.

Aquilia seemed to notice her discomfort and laughed. He put his hand on her waist.

'You are very pretty. I am a gladiator. We go somewhere, yes?'

'No. I need to find my friends. They are in the crowd. I told you that.'

Julia jerked her hand away, and the force she had to use propelled her into a large object. She put out her hand to steady herself as warm fingers grasped her elbow.

'We meet again, Julia Antonia.'

Julia looked at where her fingers were—not grabbing on to a marble pillar as she had first hoped, but clutching on to fine wool material. Her heart sank to the tops of her sandals at the sound of his rich voice. She froze, refusing to believe that this could be happening to her. She was supposed to be calm and poised when she met him, not grabbing on to his tunic for dear life.

Her whole body trembled at his light touch. She swallowed hard and attempted to regain some dignity. The way she had imagined they would meet again, her carefully planned speech about why she was here, the one she had practised three times in front of the mirror, vanished from her mind, leaving only a feeling of overwhelming happiness that he was here.

'Valens, what an unexpected pleasure,' Julia said and forced her hands to let go of his tunic. She raised her chin a notch. 'I was hoping to see you.'

Valens gave a brief nod of his head, but his eyes remained cool, assessing her.

This evening is the biggest mistake I have ever made, Julia thought.

'The evening is made all the more pleasurable by your presence.' Valens captured her hand and raised it to his lips.

Julia tried to ignore the sensation that ran from his lips up her arm, infusing her whole body with warmth, a body which remembered each touch of his fingers and the taste of his skin. She could see the faint shadow of stubble on his chin and remembered the feel of it against her cheek.

'Charming party, don't you agree?' Julia heard her voice say from a long way away. She waited for a heartbeat before continuing. 'So many gladiators all in one place…'

'Mine. I saw her first,' Aquilia grunted, drowning out the last part of her sentence. 'You find another woman, Valens. You are finished with this one.'

'I think you are making a mistake here, Aquilia.' Valens's tone was even, but his eyes glittered gold. 'The lady and I are already acquainted. Intimately acquainted.'

Several people turned towards them. Julia saw one woman whisper behind her hand to a fat senator, pointing directly at her. With a few simple words, the gossip would be revived and Sabina would have her reason to find another marriage for Julia.

'I beg your pardon,' Julia said quickly, trying to ignore the thump of her heart. 'What in the name of the Good Goddess are you talking about?'

'At last you arrive, Julia. I have been looking everywhere for you.' Valens put his arm around her waist and drew her close. His lips brushed her hair and his scent of sandalwood enveloped her, reminding her body of all that they had shared. 'I have been counting the hours until we could meet again.'

'You, his woman?' Aquilia asked, his eyes narrowing as he fingered the knife that hung from his belt.

Julia opened her mouth to protest, but decided to smile enigmatically instead. 'I know Valens. Why should I deny it? He was billeted at my father's house.'

Valens's eyes darkened. She found it impossible to tell if the emotion was passion or anger. He placed a possessive hand on her shoulder and drew her close.

The veins on Aquilia's neck bulged. 'I remember you and your dog. Greyhounds have such slender necks.'

Julia went cold, despite the warmth from Valens's body.

'I believe you were warned, Aquilia,' Valens growled. 'To stay away from me and mine.'

Julia glanced from one gladiator to the other. Where she had been afraid of Valens, now she realised his anger was directed towards protecting her, not hurting her. Her breath stopped in her throat. She watched Aquilia's hands to see if he would draw his eating dagger. Aquilia blinked and seemed to reconsider. Julia felt the tension ease out of her.

'I look forward to meeting you in the ring, Valens,' Aquilia said before he turned on his heel and stalked away. 'You will not be able to hide behind the skirts of your woman then.'

Julia waited until Aquilia had moved off before she removed Valens's hand from her waist and stepped away from him. A slight amused male grin played on his lips, giving him a distinct resemblance to Bato after he had thieved and eaten an entire leg of lamb. Her earlier anger and fear returned as she realised she was no longer in physical danger. How dare he treat her like that! There had been no need to say those things.

'What do you think you are playing at?' she asked, crossing her arms.

'Rescuing you.' Except for the twitching corners of his mouth, his face was the picture of injured innocence. 'What does it look like?'

'Rescued, is that what you call it?' Julia raised her eyes to the bronze gilded ceiling. Her lips ached for his touch, but not like this, not here. 'Proclaiming to all and sundry I am your woman! Feeding the gossip-mongers' insatiable appetite.'

'I never said that. I implied we were acquainted,' he answered quietly.

'I was playing along,' she said quickly as she felt her heart begin to race. 'Aquilia frightens me and I wanted to be rid of him as quickly possible. Now that he is gone, I can drop the pretence, go about my business and try to determine just how much damage has been done, if anyone has started to gossip. What we had was a brief meeting.'

She turned to go, but his hand reached forward and grabbed her elbow. Julia's heart thudded in her ears and her throat went parched from Valens's look. A look that devoured her. A look that bored deep into her soul.

'Why are you here, Julia? This is the last place I would have expected to see you, particularly dressed like that.'

Julia looked down at the rose pink gown with its gold belt looped just below her breasts. Normally, she'd have worn a white wool long-sleeved undertunic with it, but Poppea had assured her that the fashion at these parties was to wear gowns on their own. Her arms felt bare, exposed. She didn't want to expose her heart. She tried to think of a suitable explanation, one that would not give a lie to her statement about not being his woman.

A scantily clad serving girl came by with a tray of cups filled with wine. Grabbing one, Julia took a long drink of the wine and felt the fiery sweetness trail down the back of her throat, giving her courage. She refused to tell him her true feelings, and risk being laughed at or, worse, pitied.

'The same reason everyone else is here—to see the gladiators as they feast for one last time,' Julia said with far more conviction than she felt. She gave a slight cough as the wine went down the wrong way.

His eyes became hardened points of rocks. 'Why do I have a difficult time believing that?'

'Isn't that why everyone is here?' she whispered, looking into Valens's incredulous face. 'It is why Poppea and Claudia told me they came and to join in the merry-making.'

Julia bit her lip. He had to believe her. Her daydreams of this afternoon were just that. He had made no attempt to contact her. He probably had only come over to rescue her because of his hatred towards Aquilia. He had been seeking a reason to confront Aquilia.

Her heart whispered she was lying, but she refused to pay attention.

'Do you understand why these women, these upright senator's wives, are here?' Valens asked. He nodded towards various expensively dressed women. One was feeding a gladiator a grape and giggling. Another had her hands on a gladiator's back, giving him a massage. And a third was slowly twirling to music as several men watched. 'There is more to a gladiator's feast than food.'

Julia allowed her mouth to drop open. With every passing breath, the intimate scenes in the room increased. Everywhere she looked, there was something more to be embarrassed about. Now she understood the whispers about gladiators. She could never behave like that.

If that was what Valens was looking for, she could never be like that. What they shared had been private, between them, not this mindless coupling. She felt her cheeks grow cold and then start to burn with an intense fire.

'I think I made a mistake,' she said around the lump in her throat. 'I should go. There has been a grave misunderstanding. Sabina! My father!'

'But I thought you came to see gladiators feast. You have done nothing improper.'

'I've seen enough. Being here will be a scandal in my father's eyes, if he hears it from Sabina's honeyed tongue. Who knows which ageing senator Sabina has her eye on?' Julia whispered to the floor. 'I need to find my friends, Claudia and Poppea. I need to go home.'

'Not before you tell me why you are here.' He put a finger under her chin and lifted her gaze to his. 'I know you, Julia Antonia, and you are not like these women. Tell me the truth—why are you here?'

'I wanted to apologise to you for what I said. You were right. I had no business trying to interfere in your life. I should have allowed you to make your own decisions and to contact your father in your own way. It is your life and not mine.'

His face gave her no encouragement. Julia took a deep breath before continuing.

'Since I divorced Lucius, I have resented anyone trying to interfere with my life. Why I should have thought it different for you, I am not sure. Please understand I did it from the best of motives. I wanted you to be reconciled with your father. My own family means so much to me. Without my father, I would not be the person I am. I did not intend it to shame you or to dishonour you. If you thought that, please accept my humble apologies.'

Julia held her breath, waiting for his answer. Except for the twitching of his jaw, his face was inscrutable.

'I have said what I want to say now. And I will depart,' she said, attempting to maintain her dignity

She looked over her shoulder and spied Claudia engaged in an animated conversation and Poppea draped over a gladiator. An intense pain developed between her eyes. She had said these words, intending to sweep out, now she would be stuck, milling about. She wanted to throw her winecup down in disgust.

'I'll take you home,' Valens's rich timbre washed over her.

She stared at him, wondering if he could read her thoughts. 'I wouldn't want to put you to any trouble.'

'It's no trouble. I was on my way out when I saw you.' He gave a nod towards Claudia. 'I assume you came with your friend…Claudia. She looks like she could be here a while longer.'

Julia felt her mouth drop open. How could she be that transparent!

'How…I mean…can you read thoughts?'

He gave a small laugh. 'Let me remind you, being able to read people is an asset in my profession. I remembered you had appeared at the practices with Claudia before. And the woman you were playing *trignon* with this afternoon is rather entangled with Leoparda and won't take kindly to the interruption.'

A small prickle ran down her back. He had even noticed whom she was with at the baths. Julia pressed her lips together to prevent the questions about the blonde she had seen him with from tumbling out.

As Valens predicted, Poppea had not minded that Julia was leaving. Claudia had given Julia's hand a hard squeeze and her eyes seemed to question if this was what Julia wanted. Julia had nodded back and had given a thumbs up. At that, Claudia leaned over and touched her arm, saying that she would offer a prayer to Venus.

The orgy lessened as they walked towards the entrance to the baths. By the time they had reached where the untried gladiators stood, the party atmosphere had vanished. The crowds had thinned to one or two curious onlookers. Several of the gladiators were openly weeping while one or two sat blankly staring at a wall.

'The first time is always the worst,' Valens said, noticing her gaze.

'Were you like that?' Julia found her eyes drawn to a near-hysterical gladiator who was hugging a small child and wailing in a strange tongue.

She felt Valens place a hand under her elbow and turn her away. In the shadowy light, his face had gone grave and the planes of his cheeks had been highlighted. Julia found it impossible to detect anything but grim determination.

'For me,' he said, 'it was a chance to begin to regain my honour. Death held no fear. Unlike that man, I had nothing to lose. My life had no meaning outside the arena.'

'Surely living without honour is better than being dead.'

'I have found to my cost that a coward dies a thousand deaths…a hero only need die once.'

Julia concentrated on putting one foot in front of the other and listening to the tapping of her sandals against the mosaics and the steady pounding of his sandals as he kept pace with her. She held back the question she longed to ask—did he have something to lose now?

Through the portico and out into the streets they walked. Despite the lateness of the hour, the streets were filled with litters, carts and people. They wandered through the maze of streets, neither speaking. Julia kept one eye on the uneven cobblestones and the other on Valens's stern visage. He had to regret offering to see her home, she thought as his expression appeared to become grimmer by the footstep.

'It is quicker if we turn down this way,' Julia said, pointing to a nearly black alley. 'This road will take us past the Quirinal but if we go down here we will reach a small square where there is a road off to Subura.'

'We'll go this way by the Senate House and the Forum,' Valens replied.

'Why?'

'For one thing, there is less danger of being attacked. The streets are very different at night, Julia. I promised to see you safely back to Subura and I will.'

'Why are you doing this?'

'Because I want to,' he said.

A shaft of moonlight illuminated Valens's face. It had a fierce intent look. Julia tore her gaze away, but her heart started to beat faster. She allowed Valens to take her arm and lead her towards the Forum.

With each step he took, Valens was aware of the small figure by his side.

He had been unprepared for her, unprepared for her appearance at the feast and unprepared for her apology. His eyes drank in her form and the way that her whisper-thin mantle covered her hair. He had missed her. When he had said earlier that his life had no meaning outside the ring, he knew he had lied. She gave his life meaning.

His overconfident statements to Maia and Tigris about how he was indifferent to her were lies. One soft look from her eyes and he melted. He realised his life was empty without her, but there was too much between them. He worried about taking her away from her family. She had admitted tonight how much her father meant to her.

As their footsteps turned past the Temple of Concord, and the Senate House that was still under reconstruction after the ravages of Sulla twenty years before, he thought about using these places, places that were sacred to Romans, as a way of explaining, but each time he rejected the idea.

When they were but a few steps from Julia's house, he stopped in the narrow street and turned her to look at him. Her face was solemn but dignified, much as a *tiro*'s face is before he enters the arena for the first time as a gladiator.

The words Valens had been about to say died on his lips. His heart constricted. He drew her into his arms and rested his head against the silky softness of her hair. Each breath enveloped him in rose-scented perfume. He listened to the thud of her heartbeat and knew it echoed his.

'Julia—'

She laid a finger across his lips and gave her head a slight shake. 'Hold me. There is no need for words.'

He held her for another breath and then put her away from him, tilting her head so he could stare into her dark eyes.

'Julia, I understand what you tried to do, but you need to understand—I must fight tomorrow.'

'But you—'

He cut her off. 'I have to fight. Beyond anything else, I have signed a contract and it is what I want to do. My fighting in the arena will distress my father. He cannot admit that his son could ever become an *infamis*. For his sake, it is better that Gaius Gracchus is dead.'

He saw her stiffen.

'Gaius Gracchus need not have died,' she said slowly. 'It was all a plot by Lucius and Mettalius so that Lucius could inherit. It has to be. He is the one who stood to gain the most. I know my ex-husband and the things he was involved in.'

'You are guessing. You have no proof. It could have easily been a hideous mistake. You have no idea of who Gaius Gracchus was.' He put his hands on her shoulders. 'The games have changed me beyond all recognition. You would have not liked hot-headed Gaius who was always off gambling, or whoring, and had exaggerated ideas of his own greatness. My father sees his son through the rosy-tinted glass of memory. Do you want some idea of a man or do you want me?'

Her mouth trembled. Valens felt his heart stop as he waited for her response. He had to know.

'I want you,' she whispered. 'The man I know, the man who held me, who made me laugh and taught me what pleasure was, who made me feel like I was important.'

He released his breath. Relief invaded his limbs. The canker that had been eating at his soul vanished. She wanted him, not some dream lover. He ran his hand down her spine to convince himself that she was not some sort of vision about to evaporate in the morning light.

'Then you have him.'

'But I want you to live,' she whispered. 'Is that so wicked of me?'

He raised her hand to his lips and kissed each of her fingers one by one.

'I have no intention of dying,' he assured her. 'And every intention of fighting for you after I have regained my honour.'

He bent his head and captured her lips. He felt them part and tasted the honeyed sweetness of her mouth, drinking from it as if it was his last chance. His arms came around and pressed her close, her curves moulding to the hardness of his body. Then he recaptured her mouth and continued his exploration.

Everything he wanted to say in words, he tried to say with his kiss. She answered back with a fever and a frenzy that matched his. She seemed to drink the very soul out of him.

He heard a noise behind him. The slightest movement. A footfall. He lifted his head, but Julia recaptured it, her warm hands burning his cheeks.

'Don't stop. Kiss me again, Valens.'

He found he was powerless to resist her plea.

'Looks like the boss guessed right, the rats do return to the nest,' he heard a voice say, then felt the first blow to the back of his head.

Unprepared for the pain, he staggered and reached for his dagger. The second blow came before he could unsheathe it. He heard Julia start to scream and then blackness gathered him in its cloak.

Chapter Sixteen

Julia felt a scream rip through her. As the heavy weight of Valens's body sagged against her, she glimpsed the attacker's heavy cudgel. Julia tried to hold Valens upright, but her knees began to buckle under the weight and she was forced to set him down.

In the dim light, she could just make out the white of the attacker's tunic and his snarling scarred face. He lifted his cudgel, preparing to strike Valens again.

Julia's heart stopped. Everything seemed to slow down. Each movement took an age. A rushing noise filled her ears as the cudgel started to come closer. An evil grin split the attacker's face. This was it, the time of her death.

She felt another scream build within her, then escape with a fury. The attacker checked. She crouched low and made a grab for Valens's eating dagger, which hung off his belt. Her hand curled around the hilt and she pulled it with all her might. The dagger arched upwards and hit the neck of the cudgel with a crash that shook her arms. Instinctively she moved the dagger away from her, trying to force the cudgel backwards.

It refused to move. Julia braced her feet against the wall and resisted the attacker's attempts to bring the cudgel down. Neither gave way. Her arms ached and she wondered that she could hold out for this long. The fetid stench of the attacker's breath was overpowering. Gagging, she locked her elbows and used the wall to push her feet off and drive the dagger forward.

The cudgel moved with a suddenness that made her gasp. She saw it fly out of the attacker's hand and bounce to her right. The attacker then ran down a darkened alleyway. She stepped over Valens's prone body and looked up and down a twisting street with its shadowed doorways and narrow darkened alley entrances. Only the faintest of moonbeams pierced the high tenement buildings where several flickering oil lamps showed in the slitted windows.

'Valens,' she muttered under her breath. 'Stand up. Move. We have to leave.'

Her ears strained to hear. Nothing except a low moan, so soft that Julia thought she had misheard. Then it repeated, louder. Julia's heart leapt. Valens was alive.

She used a hand to wipe the sweat from her brow

while the other made a slow sweep with the dagger in front of her. The weight grew heavier with each pass. Her shoulder muscles screamed. She wanted to change hands but her fingers were glued to the hilt.

A small movement to her right and Julia used her last ounce of strength and lunged forward. Her arm jerked as the blade hit something soft and bounced back. She heard the cry, the clatter of a dropped object and then footsteps.

She felt her arms begin to give way and lowered the dagger with a heartfelt sigh. She had done it! She had seen off the attacker.

When Valens gave another low moan, Julia immediately knelt by his side, her hand probing his head for any injury. A noise from the alleyway in front of her made her pause and raise the dagger again.

'Who goes there?' she cried, hoping it was a rat. The attacker had to have fled. She was certain she had heard running noises disappearing down the alleyway. 'Show yourself.'

Keeping the dagger trained straight ahead, she stooped down, picked up several pebbles from the road and tossed them in the general direction of the noise. A faint cough made her blood run cold.

'Quite the tigress when you are aroused, Julia.' A cold voice from the alleyway sent shivers down her spine. 'Pity I only learnt of it now.'

'Lucius,' Julia said. Cold sweat started to drip down her back.

'Who else?' Lucius stepped from the shadows. She felt the bile rise in her stomach. She had seen that look on his face all too often. 'You have been a most annoying problem, Julia Antonia, but in the end, you had your uses.'

Julia tried to lash out with her dagger, but missed.

'What are you talking about, Lucius?' she said forcibly, trying not to show her fear. 'I will never do anything for you.'

'But you have, my dear, you led me straight to Gaius Gracchus. I had thought my cousin dead five years ago, dead of an…unfortunate…accident. It grieved his father so and I was able to comfort him and his wife whose illness I had learnt of from my mother. Did you know the senator would have married my mother, but then he saw her cousin? The Gracchi wealth is great and it should have been my birthright. Only one person stood between me and its inheritance. So simple, so easy. Why, I never even had to meet the man. How was I to know that the pirate would double-cross me? He took my money, sent me the ransom note and then failed to kill Gaius. Instead, he sold him on.'

'Never trust a pirate.'

'Indeed.'

She glanced at the dark alleyway where the first attacker had disappeared. Her mouth went dry. How long until he would be back with reinforcements?

'Clodius,' she screamed, hoping the elderly porter would hear her through the oak door. 'It's Julia Antonia, help me.'

'All the pleading in the world won't help you.' Lucius leant forward and Julia could see the strange glowing light in his eyes. 'You know it only makes me angry. You and I know Clodius is deaf when he chooses. I took precautions.'

'You are evil,' Julia said between gritted teeth. 'You won't get away with this. My father—'

'The gods have decreed it, Julia Antonia. Such a fitting end for the two people I dislike most in the world dead…killed by a footpad as they attempted to copulate in the alleyway.'

'I don't think so, Lucius. I have a dagger and I am determined to use it.'

His hand snaked out and closed around her wrist like a vice. He tightened until she found the knife slipping from her grasp and falling to the street with a loud clang.

'Correction—you had a dagger.'

Julia swallowed hard and refused to curl up in a ball and wait for the next blow. She brought her arm to her teeth and clamped down on his fingers with all her might.

'You bitch,' he swore and she felt his hand connect with her face, sending her reeling back against the wall.

She collapsed down to the cobbles and her foot kicked the abandoned cudgel. She dropped to her knees and grabbed it.

'Correction, I have another weapon.'

'You have changed, Julia. The mouse has learnt to roar. A pity that.'

He brought the knife down on the cudgel. The reverberations shook her teeth, and she felt the cudgel grow slippery from sweat. Her fingers struggled to maintain their grip and knew she would not be able to hold out much longer.

A pool of light formed in the doorway.

'What in the name of Hades is going on out there! Honest people want to sleep!' she heard Clodius call.

'Clodius, come quickly!' she called out.

'What sort of shade calls my name? Back, you creature of the night.'

'It's Julia Antonia,' she replied. 'I need help. We're being attacked!'

Clodius swung his oil lamp towards her. She blinked in the sudden glare, she could see Lucius frozen in the pool of light.

'What are you doing out there, Julia Antonia? I thought you were spending the night at your friend's.'

Lucius's wolfish grin increased. He took a step closer to Julia. 'Deaf and blind…when he chooses, Julia.'

'Get my father quick!' she yelled, raising the cudgel with the last ounce of her strength and prayed fervently that some god might see her plight and help. 'Please, Clodius.'

'Exactly what is going on out here!' her father roared.

At the sound of her father's voice, Lucius dropped the dagger and started to run. The cudgel slipped from her gasp and fell to the ground with a thump.

'Father, thank Venus you are here!'

'Julia, I thought I heard your voice. Why in the name of Jupiter are you screaming like a Fury?'

Julia wiped her hands on her gown, swallowed hard and made sure her voice was clear and firm.

'I've been attacked,' she called. 'Come quickly.'

'Who attacked you?' her father demanded. 'An armed gang of thieves, my political enemies, who?'

'Lucius,' she stated flatly, staring into the shadows where he had vanished. She raised a hand to shield her eyes against the glare of her father's lamp. 'Lucius and his henchmen attacked me.'

Her father lowered the oil lamp he was carrying.

'Lucius! I refuse to believe that. He'd never do a thing like that—not to you. Not to my family.'

She heard a slight moan from Valens. Without stopping to think, she knelt down and cradled his head in her lap. She fancied that his eyelashes fluttered and his lips turned up in a weak smile.

'Believe what you like!' she said, looking up at her father. 'I have no reason to lie. And Valens has been injured. These were no shades of the night that attacked us.'

'There is no reason for Lucius to be here. He lives on the Palatine and I warned him away not more than four days ago. Your imagination is playing tricks on you, daughter.'

'I think I should know my ex-husband.' Julia said between clenched teeth. 'I know what he did, what he is capable of doing.'

'Lucius was here earlier, master,' Clodius said, plucking at Antonius's sleeve. 'He and his servants brought an amphora for me to apologise for his behaviour the other day. He said you knew all about it. Right chatty he was. He wanted to know all about what the family had planned. Whether or not Julia was going to the Gladiatorial Feast, whom I thought would do well in the games. That sort of thing.'

'Did he, indeed? And where is this amphora, Clodius?'

Clodius hung his head. 'Julia's dog came bounding up and pushed it over, shattering it before I had a chance to drink a drop. I thought there was no harm in it.'

'Next time, you will tell me about it.' Her father's

voice was full of ice-cold fury. 'You know what they say about Greeks bearing gifts. Lucius is no friend of this family.'

Clodius hung his head and scuffed his sandal. 'I didn't think a broken amphora was worth mention-ing, not straight away like.'

Julia heard Valens groan again and saw him struggle to raise his head from her lap.

'You're hurt,' she cried. 'Don't move. Lie still, and we'll get help.'

'I knew you had the makings of a gladiatrix,' he whispered with more than a hint of pride in his voice. His hand caught hers and giving it a brief squeeze before he rolled over onto his side, taking his head off her lap. 'The way you faced Lucius down with that cudgel. I owe you my life.'

'Pure fear and stupidity, I am afraid,' she said, but her heart glowed. She smoothed her gown out, touching the spot where Valens's head had lain.

'Fear and courage are closely linked, Julia. Not many men would have done that.' He started to stand up, but sank back down to the ground and placed his head on his knees, groaning.

'It will be fine,' she said soothingly, touching his shoulder with her hand.

Valens gave a groan in reply and waved his hand above his head as if to say he understood.

'Who do you have with you, Julia?' Antonius asked, lifting the oil lamp again and sending shadows across Julia's face.

'Valens,' she said. 'He saw me home from the Gladiatorial Feast. Lucius attacked us without any provocation.'

'Why should your ex-husband do that? Tell me the truth, Julia. What are you trying to hide from me?'

She wondered how much she should tell her father. She ought to explain about what Lucius had done, but she also knew Valens wanted to keep his past, a secret. She had promised him. She knew what she wanted. She had to let Valens do it his way.

The world started to tilt and her legs grew weak. Suddenly she sat down on the cold ground and drank in gulps of cold air.

'Her experience has overwhelmed her,' she heard Valens say from a long way away. He took her wrist in his hand, his fingers curling around, probing. Julia gave a small tug and they released.

'If we can give her some air,' Valens said with a perplexed look in his eyes, 'she will recover. It is the aftershock of the fight. You should have seen the way she wielded the dagger. Without her bravery, you would have had two corpses by your door.'

Julia pressed her hands together in an effort to keep from speaking. She wanted to protest and say that it had nothing to with that and everything to do with her fear about what would happen now that her father was bound to guess something had occurred between her and Valens.

'Are you telling me that my daughter fended off Lucius's friends on her own?'

'She saved my life. Lucius was intent on killing us both. Only the gods know the true reason.' Valens rubbed the back of his neck. 'It is lucky I have a hard head.'

Julia felt her whole body begin to shake. He had made his choice. She ran her hands up and down her arms.

'It's so very cold,' she said, 'Funny, I thought it was warm before but now the night air has turned bitter.'

Antonius snapped his fingers and Clodius disappeared briefly, only to reappear with a coarse woollen blanket that he handed to Antonius. Antonius draped the blanket over Julia's shoulders.

'We need to get you both inside the compound. The night air is not good for anyone,' Antonius said. 'We can talk about your exploits later, Julia. But inside first, out of this night air. I'll take Julia; Clodius, you support Valens.'

The few hundred yards to the porter's lodge seemed like climbing Mount Vesuvius to Julia. Without her father's hand under her elbow, she was certain she would have stumbled and fallen. She carefully kept her eyes from Valens, but found it impossible not to wonder if this completely drained feeling was what he felt after a bout in the arena.

At the sight of Clodius's small stool, she sank down. Her feet refused to move any further.

She held her hands over the tiny brazier and tried to get them warm. When she thought she had control of her emotions, she turned towards Valens. He was sitting on the floor. Legs sprawled out in front of him, eyes trained directly on her. At her glance, he gave a small smile and raised his thumb upwards. Julia found her face breaking into a wide smile.

'How are you feeling?' she asked and her hands gripped the edges of the stool to prevent her from hurrying over and exploring his injuries.

'My head feels like it has been hit by a cudgel but other than that I'll live.'

'Good,' Julia breathed. Her eyes met his and she allowed herself to be swallowed up in his deepening pools of brown. The world seemed to narrow down to the two of them. Nobody or nothing else mattered. She half-rose and swayed towards him.

'Clodius, I want you to get me a runner.' Her father's brusque voice cut across Julia's thoughts, making her start. She had forgotten he was there.

Julia felt her cheeks begin to burn. She abruptly sat down and covered her face with her thin mantle, pretending to be overcome once more. She clenched her fist, hoping that her father had not noticed what had just passed between Valens and her.

She risked a glance upwards. Her father's impassive face gave no clues.

'I want that runner now, Clodius,' her father's voice commanded. Grumbling, Clodius left the room. He continued in the same tone of voice. 'And now I would like to know what I am supposed to do about all this?'

'What do you mean all this, Father?' Julia asked, holding her palms upwards. 'Surely it is obvious that you must file suit against Lucius and prevent him from attacking me again.'

Her father waved an impatient hand. 'That is immaterial to what I am talking about, Julia. I want to know what I am supposed to do about you two and your affair. There will be no hushing up the scandal this time. All Rome will know and they will realise that it has been going on for a while.'

Julia's heart stopped. He knew! She glanced up into her father's hard, grizzled face. There was no merriment or sentiment in his countenance.

Out of the corner of her eye, she saw Valens stand and move closer to her. She only had to reach out her hand to brush his. She tightened her grip until her knuckles shone white against each other.

'Father, you are jumping to conclusions.'

Her father's face contorted. 'I am no fool, Julia, please refrain from treating me like one. If I had not known before tonight, Lucius's actions make it abundantly clear what is going on.'

'Julius Antonius—' Valens started to say.

Her father's face grew beet-red before the words exploded from his mouth.

'You be quiet! Look at the trouble you have caused. Sabina was correct. We should never have had an *infamis* in the house.'

Julia buried her head in her hands. Her father was treating Valens as if he were some object, as if he were a slave. She felt Valens's reassuring touch on her shoulder.

'How long?' she whispered and raised her head to look at her father. "How long have you known?'

'Long enough.' Her father's face softened and he touched Julia's hand. 'I am neither blind nor an imbecile. You have blossomed ever since this gladiator arrived. When he abruptly left, you wilted like a flower starved of sunshine and water.'

Julia tilted her head and looked at her father. The explosive anger appeared to have vanished.

'Blossomed?' she questioned.

'Became more like the way you were as a child. Not jumping at every noise. Back to being my little Julia.'

'I hadn't realised you noticed.' Julia stared at her

father in disbelief. She had thought her father never bothered, that she was an encumbrance, a pawn to be used by Sabina; now she discovered he did care.

'I am your father, Julia,' he said quietly and patted her hand. 'I notice you.'

'Then you approve?'

'Approve?' her father roared, his face growing red again. All tenderness vanished as if it had never been. 'No, I most certainly do not approve. How could I approve? He is a gladiator. I could never approve of such a relationship. While you were discreet, I had no reason to interfere.'

Julia stared at her father's forbidding face. He had to understand. She offered up prayers to Venus to intervene. 'But you like him. You said you liked him. You said you liked the way I have been blossoming.'

'If I did not like him, I would have stopped this much sooner, but, like a sentimental fool, I allowed you to keep seeing him. I thought it had all ended when he left the other day, but now I see it has not. And the incident tonight means I shall have to take action.'

Julia tried to ignore the growing pit in her stomach. 'Why has it changed?'

'Lucius obviously came upon you two and reacted with the appropriate rage. He was well within his rights, Julia. A Roman matron consorting in a public street with an *infamis*. No jury will convict on such evidence. The story will be all over Rome within hours. Our family and our standing in the community will be ruined!'

'What do you intend to do?' Julia stared her father directly in the eye.

Her father reached out a hand, but she brushed it away.

'You will have to make a choice, Julia—either your life with your family or exile.'

Julia's body trembled from rage. Her father had no wish for her future happiness. Her only use to him was a rung in Sabina's pathetic attempts to climb the social ladder.

'I choose—'

'I refuse to let you make that choice, Julia,' Valens said firmly and put Julia's hand in her father's. 'You stay with your family.'

All the feelings of anger, elation and rage disappeared from Julia's body. She drew her hand out of her father's and turned to stare at Valens. Had she mistaken everything? Her lips still ached from his kiss.

'I understand,' she said quietly, summoning her last reserves of dignity. 'I thought we had something, but obviously I was mistaken.'

'Julia, I do have feelings for you, but I know you love your family. And I also know what it is like to lose your family, to become one of the damned.'

'But I—'

'Hear me out, Julia, and you too, Julius Antonius. We could be happy, very happy at first, but there will come a time when regret like a snake grows and coils around your heart, poisoning it with its whispers. You would grow to resent me.'

'I could never resent you!' Julia cried wildly. She had to make him see. 'I care nothing for my life here.'

Valens shook his head. His eyes looked grave.

'You have no idea what your father is asking you, Julia. You will not leave your family, your home, your life because of me. I forbid it. I refuse to let what we have shared become mired in bitterness and resentment.'

'Most impressive, young man,' her father said. 'Spoken like a true Roman.'

Valens made an ironic bow and his eyes warned Julia to keep silent. Julia pressed her fists into her mouth. She wanted to hate Valens for taking away the decision from her, but a little part of her argued he was right. She was not ready for exile.

'Will you give me a little time alone with Julia to say my goodbyes?' Valens asked. 'The games begin in a few hours' time and I wish to bid her farewell.'

'Yes, of course.' Her father turned to go. 'I can give you that much, but no more.'

'Julius Antonius, one other thing before you go… Had I not been a gladiator, what would you have felt about my suit?'

Her father turned with his hand on the doorknob.

'You are an honourable man, Valens, despite your profession. I will answer the question when the time comes, should Julia Antonia still be free. I feel obliged to warn you though—I have had several other offers for her hand. Offers that would advance this family's standing considerably.'

He strode from the room.

Julia looked at Valens. She wanted to weep, but all the tears had long since fled. She felt numb. It was ending here. This was the last time she would see him alone. And he had refused her father's offer to let her go into exile.

Valens drew her into his arms and she felt his lips nuzzle her forehead. At his touch, she looked up.

'You must not weep, Julia,' he said with a tender smile.

'You are about to go out of my life, to fight in the arena. You refused to let me make my decision.' Julia lifted her chin. She was determined that nothing should show on her face.

Valens reached out and smoothed tendrils of hair off her face. The gesture nearly caused her bottom lip to tremble. She forced her mouth to smile as she tucked her hair behind her ears.

'Your father has not said no. He has said not right now. You must believe in his words.'

'Valens—'

'Julia, I have to fight tomorrow. I need to know you are safe.' He rubbed a hand over the back of his head. 'I cannot be worrying about you and fighting at the same time.'

Julia stared at his pale face and her heart constricted. His injuries were too great. Claudia had warned her that he needed to be in top physical condition to make some of those rolls and parries with his sword.

'But you are hurt. Surely they won't make you fight with your injuries.'

'I have received worse knocks in training practice.' He knelt by Julia's side. 'Strabo would never excuse me from the games for such a minor thing. I would never ask.'

'But—'

'I am doing this for both of us, Julia.' He lowered his head to hers and touched her mouth with his lips. 'If I win the *rudius*, your father will welcome me into the family, you will see.'

Chapter Seventeen

Julia shivered in the pale rose light of dawn as she waited with Claudia, Poppea, and a small group of other onlookers and well-wishers, just outside the Aventine baths. The square had been deserted when they arrived, but now it was rapidly beginning to fill up with excited boys hanging on their fathers' hands and vendors selling all sorts of gladiatorial memorabilia.

It felt as if Julia had barely closed her eyes before Claudia had banged on her door this morning. She was pleased she had left Bato with Clodius. The old porter seemed to have a genuine affection for the dog.

She had also breathed a sigh of relief that neither her father nor stepmother was about when Claudia came to collect her. Her father had not actually forbidden the games, and she knew in her heart that she would have disobeyed him in any case. She had to go.

She had to watch. She had to be there for Valens. She had to know what happened when it happened.

'Explain to me again why we are here?' Julia asked Claudia as the crowd started cheering and stamping its feet.

'We are here to see the start of the gladiatorial parade. The gladiators will ride through the streets of Rome in their chariots with the servants marching behind, carrying their armour. It starts here and then winds it way across Rome through the Forum and down to the Circus Maximus where they will arrive at about four hours.' Claudia waved a scroll under Julia's nose. 'You see the whole timetable is in here—from parade route to starting times for each of the events.'

'Events?' Julia looked blankly at the document. 'I thought there were just the games.'

Poppea gave a hoot of laughter. 'This is entertainment on the grand scale, my novice supporter. After the parade, there is the grand entrance, the warm-up matches, the fights with wooden swords by gladiatorial hopefuls.'

Julia unrolled her scroll and peered at the long list of events. 'When are those fights? Before or after midday? I don't see them listed.'

'Julia, Poppea means the *lusio*. They are listed just here.' Claudia unrolled the scroll and showed Julia the spot. 'They give the illusion of fighting. After one or two matches to warm up the crowd, the beast fights are at midday. After the midday interval, the real fun begins—there is the drawing of the names, the testing of the swords and finally the games themselves. I understand Caesar has thrown in everything from chariot fights to a pair of gladiatorix from Gaul.'

'When do you expect the Thracians to fight?'

Claudia gave her a sharp glance and Julia kept her face resolutely blank.

'Towards the end of the afternoon.'

'Do you think anyone will win the *rudius*, the wooden sword you were talking about?'

'You mean be able to retire from the profession with honour? No stain on his character from appearing in the ring? A man who symbolises the best in Roman heroics?' Poppea broke in. 'I think Caesar would dearly love to award one, but you know it is rare. I have only seen wooden swords given out a dozen times, Julia, in all the hundreds of matches I have been to.'

A blare of trumpets saved Julia from answering. She tightened her grip on her scroll and watched as the horses and chariots were led from the baths. Another blast of trumpets and the gladiators marched out.

Julia strained to see Valens through the growing throng. As soon as the gladiators had mounted their chariots, the crowd surged forward.

A hand touched Julia's elbow. 'Julia Antonia,' a heavily accented voice said, 'there is someone who wishes to speak with you.'

Julia turned her head slightly and saw a grey-haired man dressed in livery from the Strabo school.

'Just me or my friends?'

'Preferably just you.'

'Go on, Julia,' Claudia said, giving her a push. 'We'll meet you at the entrance to the Circus Maximus.'

She nodded and followed the man a little way into the shelter of the portico.

'Apollonius was able to find you,' Valens said behind her.

Julia jumped, and then allowed herself to be drawn into his embrace. The only thing that mattered was the safe feeling she had when his arms were around her.

'I thought you were out there,' she whispered against the white wool of his tunic. 'With the rest of the gladiators.'

'I will be in a little while. Maia, Tigris's wife, caught a glimpse of you and thought you might want to see me on your own.'

Julia turned her head slightly, trying to ignore the feeling of disappointment that grew in her chest. Following the line of his finger, she saw the blonde from the baths standing next to Tigris. Two young children clung to her skirts. Maia laughed up at Tigris and ruffled his hair. Julia was amazed that she seemed so calm about the proceedings. Her insides were churning and the games had not even begun.

'So that is Tigris's wife—I had wondered.'

'She is expecting their third, Tigris informs me.'

'He's a lucky man.'

'I am the lucky man.' Valens's lips curved upwards like a bow and his arms tightened around her. 'For I have you in my arms.'

A shiver of delight ran down Julia's back, followed closely by a shiver of apprehension. She wanted to be brave and not beg.

'How's your head?' she asked.

'It hurts, but I will survive. Luckily your ex-husband's henchmen were not as accurate as some of the gladiators I have encountered or I would not be here.'

'Maybe I should be cursing them. If they had injured you more, you would not be out fighting.'

He shook his head. 'The only way I wouldn't fight today is if I were dead. You must understand how much it means to me, to us.'

'Why won't you just let me be like Maia? She has not gone into exile and she is Tigris's wife.'

He put his forefinger under her chin and lifted her eyes to his. 'Because you are not a slave. Maia was a slave when Tigris first met her. He bought her, freed her and married her. You are different. Your father would demand your removal from Italy.'

'But—'

Another blast of the trumpets sounded and Valens's face changed. Gone was the easy smile of a heartbeat before; now he wore an intent look.

'I shall have to go and climb into my chariot,' he said. 'That's the signal for the second halls to depart. The first-hall gladiators are the last ones to set off. They release the gladiators in waves. That way each hall of gladiators is properly cheered and the excitement builds.' Valens put his hands on her shoulders and she saw his eyes darken.

'Julia, will you do something for me? Will you give this to my father if I should not make it?'

He took the brooch with the two racing greyhounds from his cloak and placed it in her hand. Julia turned it over and stared at it.

'But you will survive.'

'Take it to my father and tell him that my mother's eyes were grey and that underneath the third brazier in the dining room is his secret store of gold coins, the one he once beat me for finding. Our family code is based on the first letter of every seventh word. I had this brooch made with my first prize money. It is an exact duplicate of the one I lost. Will you do that for me, Julia?'

'I will,' she said, the brooch dangling from her fingers. 'But there will be no need. You said you will survive. You will be able to give it to him yourself.'

His hand stroked her cheek and then fell to his side. He took the brooch out of her palm and pinned it to the cord of her *stola*. 'It has helped keep me safe and has served to remind me what I am fighting for. Now I don't need any reminders. I know what I am fighting for.'

'And that is…' The world was blurring in a mass of tears. Julia blinked rapidly.

A trumpet sounded again.

'I shall go now. Be a Roman matron for me and let us have no tears.'

He gave her hands one last squeeze and then strode away, laughing and joking with one of the School's servants. Julia whispered a prayer as she touched the pendant still warm from his skin.

'It is always the same,' a low musical voice said next to her. Maia had glided up. Her laughing face was now solemn and a tear glistened on her cheek. 'They think it is a big joke and we are left behind to worry.'

'You are Tigris's wife?'

'That is right, and you are the woman who has captured Valens's heart.'

'For now at any rate…'

Julia felt her cheeks colour as the woman's cool eyes assessed her.

'You are the first woman he has ever allowed to wear his brooch. It is very precious to him.'

Julia put her hand to her throat. She stared across to where Valens's chariot had stood. There were so many questions she wanted to ask him, things she should have said. Her insides were torn apart with a mixture of happiness and rage. 'I am just looking after it for him.'

'If you would like, you may sit with us, with the rest of the gladiatorial family.' Maia shifted her toddler on to her other hip.

Julia shook her head. The temptation was almost too great but then she thought of her father and of what Valens had said. Valens had refused to let her make that choice. He had not asked her to sit with the other women who belonged to gladiators. He had forbidden it. For now, she had to respect his wishes and show him that she was worthy of his trust. 'That would be impossible. I am here with friends, friends I need to find.'

Maia nodded, but then produced a small ticket stamped with a lion. 'Should you change your mind, give this ticket to the porter, and he will show you the spot.'

She was gone before Julia had a chance to give the ticket back. She stared at it for a long time and started to walk towards the Circus. The crowds had thinned, but the atmosphere was still one of a public holiday.

* * *

'You took your time about getting here,' Poppea said crossly when Julia found them in the crowded street outside the Circus Maximus. 'I thought you were lost. I was about to send one of my servants to find you.'

'The streets were blocked because of the parade route,' Julia said, gasping for breath. She wiped a trickle of sweat from her forehead and refused to think how she had gone down several blind alleys and had taken several wrong turns. 'Has the procession arrived yet?'

'We and the rest of humanity would be inside if it had,' Poppea commented. 'I can hear the trumpets now.'

Julia caught Claudia's eye and shrugged. She had not anticipated there would be so many people here. It seemed as if the whole of Rome had turned out for Caesar's games. She thought of the faces of Maia and her children after Tigris left and contrasted it with the happy excited faces of the supporters. The families had the nervous anticipation of death and the supporters would only see the spectacle. Julia shivered despite the heat and readjusted her shawl. She knew which she would see and offered another prayer up to Venus that Valens might be safe.

With each step she took up the steep staircase to the wooden stalls where their seats were, she said a prayer.

'You are not afraid of heights, Julia,' Poppea said as they sat down. 'Your face is as white as a ghost.'

'Heights, crowds—this is not my idea of an ideal day out,' Julia replied, sinking down on to the bench. She looked down and saw the sandy oval curve away from her. The few men who were raking the sand smooth looked more like figurines than people. 'How can you see anything up here?'

'It is one of the best views...for women,' Claudia said and laid her hand on Julia's arm. 'Don't worry, Julia, Valens will win. He has not lost a match yet.'

Julia gave a brief nod. If she started to confide in Claudia, all her fears would pour out and she'd become a gibbering wreck. Valens hadn't even arrived at the arena and already her stomach was knotted so tightly she could barely breathe. Her programme had been twisted and rolled so much she could no longer read the order of the spectacle.

The trumpets blew a long fanfare.

'It is about to start,' whispered Claudia. 'See, Caesar and his family are taking their seats along with the Vestal Virgins. Sometimes I wonder if becoming a Virgin would not have been a better life. At least I would have had a front-row seat at every chariot race, play or gladiatorial bout.'

'Claudia, you like men too well. You would not have lasted a day,' Julia said with a laugh.

Claudia made a face of mock contrition. 'Too true. I suppose there has to be compensations. Just think what those women give up.'

The entire arena fell silent, waiting for the next act in the spectacle to begin.

Valens heard the crowd grow hushed, holding its collective breath, waiting for the grand entrance. In the gladiator's tunnel, everyone was busy with the final preparations.

Gone were the nervous lamentations of last night. All around him he could see pale resolute faces. Even Aquilia's face had lost its usual sneer.

Another blast from the trumpet.

The sound of buckling armour and the snapping shut of visors filled the tunnel. Valens glanced over and saw that Leoparda, the young gladiator who had been punished at Aquilia's request had not put his helmet on, but in fact looked green under his dark skin.

'It will be fine, lad,' Valens said. 'This is what you have trained for. This is your hour of glory.'

'I hope so, Valens.'

'Let's put it this way, lad.' Valens gestured to the group of condemned criminals huddled in the corner waiting for the beast show. 'You have a chance, those poor devils don't.'

Leoparda nodded.

'Once you are in the ring, Leoparda, it will all come back to you. It always does.'

Valens jammed his ceremonial helmet on his head. 'Right, lads, we may have been slaves, prisoners of war and criminals in our past lives, but who we were counts for nothing. It is who we are that matters. The Romans out there are waiting for the chance to sneer and laugh at us. They like to think they are better than us, but we have a chance to prove they are wrong. We are better men than they are. We have gone through hell and back again in our training. Let's show the Romans what we are made of—that we know how to fight and how to die like men!'

A ragged cheer erupted from the gladiators. Valens stepped out on the sandy floor and into the blinding light of the sun.

He touched his cloak where the brooch usually lay and met nothing. He frowned, then relaxed as he thought of Julia. He had no need of a talisman. He knew what he fought for, who he fought for.

He gave a nod to the other first-hall gladiators and squared his shoulders. The training had ended. The spectacle was about to begin.

The crowd erupted in cheers as he appeared in the entranceway. He gave a brief glance at the bright array of colours, hoping to spot Julia, but gave up; it was enough knowing that she was there.

He took measured steps across the arena and stopped in front of Caesar's box. The sound of a hundred pairs of marching feet echoed around the arena behind him, then stopped.

The last cheers of the crowd died away. Except for the fluttering of paper, the entire arena was silent, holding its breath, waiting.

In unison with the others, Valens brought his hand to his chest. He looked towards the patron's box, resplendent in bright rich purple. The cost of the cloth alone would feed an army for six weeks. Standing behind Caesar was Julius Antonius. And next to him stood his own father. Valens tightened his jaw and stood up straighter as their eyes met. Then Valens concentrated his entire being on the tall slim man with greying hair who had brought about this entire spectacle.

'Hail, Caesar! We who are about to die salute you!'

The crowd erupted.

Caesar raised his right hand, acknowledging the salute and the cheers. 'I, Julius Caesar, Aedile of Rome, acknowledge you. Let the games in honour of my father's death begin!'

Then Valens walked back towards the gladiators' holding pen. Just before he left the arena, he bent down and let the sand dribble through his fingers. 'Fortunata, be with me now in the hour of my greatest need,' he prayed.

Valens took a deep breath and once again tried to make out Julia, but without success. As he stepped into the pen, he undid his sandals and left them placed neatly against the wooden wall. His time as man was over. His time as a god was over. His time as fighter was about to begin.

Julia watched the mock fights with growing apprehension. The weapons were only made of wood, but already she had seen one fighter dragged off by the guards after he had fallen. She heard the crowds, growing ever louder, baying for blood.

'What comes next?' she asked Claudia as the parts of the crowd started to stand up and move around.

'The beast fights come next. It is after that the real action begins.'

Julia's stomach churned. She found it impossible to imagine anything less appetising—watching condemned murderers and other enemies of the state being torn apart by lions and tigers.

'I think I will have a wander about and see what the latest betting is.' Without waiting for a reply, she stood up and made her way to the exit. Once there she took great gulps of fresh air before climbing down the steps.

On the concourse, people milled around, chatting about the fights and the likely pairings, placing bets and happily munching food. One man belched and rubbed his fat stomach as he proclaimed to his companion about the chances of Aquilia beating Valens. Julia clenched her fists and hurried her footsteps past.

On her right two security guards, their tunics emblazoned with Strabo's lion badge, stood guard. Julia hesitated, torn about what she should do, then common sense reasserted itself. She knew if she went in there, she'd be proclaiming to Rome, to all the world, where her allegiance lay. Valens had refused to allow her to make her decision, a decision she had no desire to make.

Everywhere she heard conversations about gladiators, comparing them as if they were things, not people with feelings.

'Julia Antonia, you are the last person I expected to see here.'

Julia spun around and met the warm gaze of Senator Gracchus.

'You as well, senator. I thought you had little love for the games.'

'I wanted to see what young Caesar was up to.'

The brooch cut into the side of Julia's neck and she thought of Valens's words, how she was supposed to take it to Gracchus should Valens die. She swallowed hard. Her hand closed around it. Then she stopped and forced her fingers to release it. Until the time came, she had to be brave. She had to respect Valens's wishes. 'Is that the only reason you are here?'

The senator's face turned grave. He laid a hand on her shoulder. 'Child, we both know why I am here. There are many sins I have committed in my life, but none so grievous as that one. He is my son, my own flesh and blood.'

Julia looked at the cobblestones. 'He insisted that he fight.'

Gracchus did not bother to pretend. 'He would. He is stubborn like his father.'

Julia tried for a smile, but her lips refused to curve upwards. 'He's a survivor,' she said with greater conviction in her voice than she felt in her heart.

'I hope with all my heart, child. I greatly wronged him the other day. I was angry that he had not contacted me. He had chosen to fight. In five years, he must have had opportunity after opportunity to come to see me.'

'He is proud. He did not want to face you as an *infamis*.'

'He gets that from his father, too.'

A blare of trumpets sounded and the crowd started to head back into the arena. Julia's heart leapt to her mouth.

'They are about to draw the pairings for this afternoon's fights. Would you like to join me in Caesar's box? Your father and stepmother are there already.'

Julia hesitated. She couldn't sit there in that box with all eyes on her, pretending she had no interest in the outcome.

She shook her head.

'I have another seat,' she said.

'You've missed the pair draw,' Claudia remarked as Julia reached them. 'The first bout is about to begin.'

'Who is it between?' Julia forced the words from her mouth.

'Tigris and Hylas,' Poppea answered without looking at her.

Julia sank down on the bench. Her legs refusing to hold her upright.

'Do you know who Valens is paired with?' she whispered.

Claudia leant over and patted her hand. 'Aquilia,' she said simply. 'They are the last bout of the afternoon. If I didn't know better, I would say the ballot was rigged.'

Nausea rose in Julia's stomach. She had no idea how she would last. She glanced over to the area where Maia and her children and knew what they must be going through.

The trumpets sounded again. This time solemn and mournful. Then the match began. Julia could barely keep up with the flashes of swords and clanging of shields. Despite her nerves, she found herself yelling with the rest of them.

Suddenly the crowd gave a collective sigh as Tigris's

sword fell again, striking the other gladiator fully in the chest. The gladiator raised his finger and the crowd started to chant, '*Habet, hoc habet.* He's had it.'

At a sign from Caesar, the crowd rose as one and started cheering.

Julia gripped Claudia's arm. 'What happening?'

'Tigris has won!' Claudia turned to her, her face glowing with admiration and pride. 'I can't believe it. That was an absolutely brilliant performance. Caesar has awarded him the *rudius*.' She clapped her hands and cheered. 'Oh, bravo. Well done! Marvellous fighting!'

'Tigris has done what?' Julia asked, straining to hear Claudia above the cheers.

'He's won his freedom! It was an absolutely stunning performance and to happen on the first match as well. He will never have to fight again!'

'You are lucky, Julia,' Poppea said. 'I had to wait for seven whole games before I ever saw a *rudius* being awarded.'

Julia's heart pounded in her ears.

'Do you think this will be the only *rudius* to be awarded this afternoon?'

Poppea gave a short laugh. 'I know Crassus is bank-rolling Caesar, but even he does not have that type of money to release two gladiators in one games. Very doubtful, if not to say impossible.'

The others around them murmured their agreement.

Julia sat down and put her head in her hands. Her world had crumbled before Valens had even stepped into the ring. She hadn't realised until that instant how much she had been counting on him winning the *rudius* and becoming free. It was her secret fantasy and had sustained her throughout the night. Nothing had mattered much because Valens was bound to win the *rudius* and be covered in honour. Now, that dream lay in the dust.

She looked across to the box where her father sat cheering with the rest of them as Caesar presented the wooden sword to Tigris and crowned his head with palm leaves.

She had to make a choice. Sitting there, patiently waiting for the outcome, was no longer a choice. She drew out the ticket Maia had given her then stood up and started to walk away.

'Julia, where are you going?'

'I am going to where I should have been in the first place. Where I belong.'

Chapter Eighteen

In the gladiator's enclosure, Valens listened to the cheers for Tigris and tried to be happy for him and Maia. All the years of long hard work had paid off. He had won the ultimate prize.

On any other day, he'd be happy for Tigris, but not today. Today it gave Fortunata another chance to laugh at him. Once again, he had encountered Fate's slippery pole. Just as his hand reached out to grasp the final ring, it had been pulled from him. Valens gave a bitter laugh.

Last night, he had refused to let Julia make a choice, afraid of what she might choose. It now came back to haunt him. Yes, he could purchase his way out of the profession by selling everything he owned—but what then could he offer Julia?

He heard the cheers as Tigris came back in, wooden sword held aloft for all to see. He carefully composed his face and strode over to Tigris, hugged him tightly to his chest and then released him. 'Absolutely marvellous. I am so proud for you and for Maia.'

Tigris clasped Valens's forearm. 'Thank you kindly, my old friend. Without you, I would not be here today to enjoy this honour.'

His eyes said words that his mouth did not.

'I am truly happy for you, Tigris,' Valens repeated. 'I can't think of anyone who deserves it more.'

'And you? What will you do?' Tigris nodded towards where Aquilia lounged, the only gladiator not to have congratulated Tigris on his good fortune.

'I'll fight.' Valens held up the palms of his hands. 'It is in the lap of the gods but I have a job to do.

'He will be tough, but I will find his weakness, you can count on that. He will not turn me to stone. Tonight we will be raising our winecups in celebration of your freedom.'

The trumpets sounded and another pair of gladiators walked out into the arena. Valens began his final preparations, taking comfort in the small automatic rituals of checking his equipment.

Julia stared at the two security guards, standing with their axes crossed, preventing her from entering the area.

'I had a ticket, I tell you,' she said searching through

the folds in her shawl for a third time. 'Maia, Tigris's wife, gave it to me this morning before the parade.'

The security guards exchanged a look.

'That is what they all say.'

'No, honestly.' Julia felt the panic rising in her throat. She had lost the ticket. All her plans were going to be ruined. She had decided to make a stand and now these two oafs blocked her way.

She started to readjust her *stola* and her hand touched Valens's brooch. She undid it and held it out to the security guard.

'You say you work for Strabo, but do you recognise this? It belongs to Valens the Thracian gladiator. He gave it to me…'

She waited as the two guards consulted. One went off. The trumpets blew, signalling the start of another bout, and Julia stood on her tiptoes, trying to see. Each glimpse was precious. She felt sure Valens would look towards the family enclosure. He had to see what she had done. That she had made her decision in the most public way possible.

'All right,' the burly guard came back. 'I've spoken to the boss. You can go in. He has seen Valens wear that brooch. No trickery, mind you. They are about to signal the last bout.'

Julia clasped her hands together, took a deep breath and started forward. The trumpets blared a complicated fanfare and she began to run. She made her way to the edge of the enclosure, pushing past various people, trying to see what was going on in the arena. When she reached the front, she looked directly at the box and nodded to her father.

A small stab of pleasure filled her as she watched Sabina notice and point. She waved back and watched Sabina's face grow redder and redder. She saw her stepmother start to make angry gestures. It felt wonderful to watch Sabina impotent for once, reduced to merely opening and closing her mouth.

There was no point in thinking about what might have been. She had reached her *discrimen*, her dividing line, and gone beyond it. Now she could only go forwards.

'The die is cast,' she whispered, quoting the line from Meander's famous play. 'Let my die fall where they will.'

She noticed a man gesturing towards her.

'I'm Strabo, the owner of this school and you are…' The man in a badly fitting wig leant towards her.

'Julia Antonia.' At Strabo's hooded look, she hesitated. Then she tightened her hold on the brooch. 'Valens's woman.'

'Bah, he has no woman. He is a lone wolf.'

Julia held out the brooch. 'He does now.'

'Just so.' Strabo touched the side of his nose and his

lips stretched to the briefest of smiles. 'Afterwards we talk, but now the fun begins.'

Julia's breath stopped in her throat. She watched Valens stride out of the tunnel, looking every inch the perfect warrior. This morning's brilliant splendour of silver had been replaced by much more mundane steel. Even from where she sat, Julia could see the hammered-out dents from previous battles. She had expected Valens to come out carrying his helmet like the other gladiators had done, but his visor was firmly locked on his head.

She stood up, trying to make it easier for him to spot her, to see what she had done. He never looked her way. Julia sank down, her knees trembling too much to hold her.

The trumpets played a faint mournful tune, then a great cheer went up through the crowd.

'What does that mean?'

'It is a signal for a fight to the death. I hope Caesar understands how much this pair is worth. Whatever happens, his purse will be much lighter,' Strabo answered, leaning forward.

Julia felt ice invade her veins. She wanted to run and hide, but her feet were rooted to the spot and she was unable to tear her eyes away. Her hand curled around the brooch and she started to pray as she had never prayed before. He had to live, to survive.

* * *

At the sound of the trumpets, Valens started forward. He gave his helmet one last click and did not acknowledge Aquilia's snarl. His gaze swept around the arena again searching for Julia. If she were anywhere in the arena, she would be under the watchful eye of her father. Valens made a quick check of the purple-draped box—there was no sign of her.

His heart constricted. He had hoped to see her one last time before this bout, but the gods had decreed he would not. He gave a bow to Caesar and to the rest of the occupants and then crouched in his stance, waiting for Aquilia to make the first move.

They circled each other, testing and probing for strengths and weaknesses. Valens moved forward and slashed with his sword. Aquilia jumped away.

'You will have to do better than that, Tribune,' he called, wiping a hand across his mouth before spitting at Valens's feet.

'Why do you call me a tribune?' Valens blocked a thrust from Aquilia's trident.

Aquilia's eyes narrowed. 'Because I remember you. I remember every last detail about your time with me. The feel of the deck beneath my feet, the smell of salt and blood in my nose. There is a certain sweetness to the stench.'

The horror of the fetid pirate's hold swept over

Valens. He heard Aquilia's voice and remembered the time when Aquilia strode across the deck of the *trireme* with the power of death in his voice. He felt the cold creep of fear along his spine. How much did Aquilia remember that he had forgotten?

Valens used his shield to block a stab with the trident.

'I remember everything,' Aquilia's voice became singsong, lulling him, as hypnotic as a snake. Valens knew he should be concentrating on finding an opening, but Aquilia's voice sent out silken tendrils that caught his mind and dragged him back to those dark days. 'How you cried when your friends died, how you raged with anger when the ransom did not arrive, how you begged me to spare your life and sell you as a slave.'

The last words cut through the ropes that bound his mind. Valens straightened, lifted his shield and sword, prepared to attack.

'I never begged you.'

'You always begged me.' Aquilia grinned as he circled the net above his head. 'As you will beg me soon to end your life.'

Valens heard the net hiss, dropped to the ground and rolled away from it. Sand and grit filled his nose and mouth. He rose to his feet and stared back at the glowering gladiator whose every breath radiated menace. Aquilia slapped his thigh with the trident three times.

'I'm waiting, boy.' Aquilia took a step forward. 'Waiting to hear your mewling cries, just as you did before. Crying for your gods to save you. Guess what—they didn't answer. You have been abandoned by everyone and everything you held dear. Nobody cares for you.'

Valens wiped a hand across his face and took control of his emotions. His mind cleared. The secret of Aquilia's success was obvious now. Aquilia used the fear he had installed in his captives as a pirate captain to numb his opponents, to make them lose their concentration and start making fatal errors. Valens smiled grimly. Aquilia cast his web of lies effectively but he had neglected one gaping hole. Julia. Now it remained to be seen if Aquilia was as good with his trident and net as he was with his words.

Valens crouched low and pretended to cower. Aquilia's grin widened. He cast the net again, throwing with a lazy and practised ease.

As the net arced through the air towards him, Valens reached out a hand. He grabbed the end with its silver weights, ignoring the sting as the weights hit his forearm, and pulled Aquilia towards him.

'Next time tell the truth.'

He released the net and Aquilia tumbled backwards, fuming. Valens hit his shield with his sword.

'Let's see if you are any better at fighting than you

are at weaving stories to frighten the gullible. Let's see who is better—the tribune or the pirate.'

Julia gasped as she watched Valens's blade flash in the late afternoon sun. The arena was full to groaning now and with each slash of the sword or block of the shield, the crowd began chanting another slogan.

First Valens pressed forward, trying to strike. Aquilia parried the stab with his trident, blocking and seeking an opening for his net. Twice she had thought Aquilia would trap him, beat him to the ground, but each time Valens managed to roll away, or sidestep at the last possible opportunity.

She pressed her hands together and wondered how long Valens could keep up the nimble footwork.

The heat, his armour and the head wound from last night all had to be telling, slowing him down. Julia tried to push the thought away and concentrate on how brilliantly Valens sidestepped a trident thrust and answered it with a downward cut of his own.

The two combatants backed off and then rushed towards each other again.

She gave a small cheer as Aquilia stumbled, then Valens followed up with a sword thrust. Aquilia raised his trident and pushed away the sword.

The boisterous crowd grew silent as the intensity of the battle in the arena increased.

Julia tried to hide her eyes, to look away, but it was impossible. Every fibre of her being was intent on watching Valens battle for his life.

The net hissed, this time striking Valens on the shoulder, coiling around his midriff. Aquilia started to reel him in. Valens used his shield and knocked Aquilia sideways.

'Who's winning?' Julia whispered to Strabo. She had to know! Her nails made half-moon shapes on the palms of her hands as she waited for his answer.

'Hard to say,' Strabo answered. 'They have both scored points on the other. But it is a good match.'

A good match? It was a life-and-death struggle! The man she loved was out there fighting for his life, for the amusement of others. Julia felt sickened to the core.

The fight continued with all its awfulness. With each blow, she was certain Valens would receive a mortal injury. She tore the top of her thumbnail off with her teeth and then proceeded to chew each of her other fingernails to the quick before going back to her thumb.

'Are there rules?' she asked.

Strabo laughed. 'The rule is there are no rules. We wait until one of them makes a mistake. The power and the grace of two gladiators in their prime. It makes me proud to be a Roman.'

* * *

Sweat poured down Valens's face as he began to feel the full force of the injury he had received last night. Aquilia's last parry had hit him squarely in the back of his helmet, sending green lights before his eyes. He fought to keep his footing in the sand that was slippery from the earlier bouts.

Valens staggered, and tried to regain his balance. He heard the siren call of the ground asking him to fall down, to give up and embrace the darkness.

He stumbled to his knees, felt the net strike his back and instinctively rolled away. He heard Aquilia's triumphant laugh against the blackness in his head and he struggled to right himself. The crowd began to shout 'He's had it' and knew they were talking about him.

'That's right,' Aquilia sneered. 'Give in to me—you Romans always do. Nobody cares whether you live or die. Tomorrow I will be their hero.'

Valens wiped his hand across his mouth and tried to hang on, too exhausted to keep trying. Aquilia's words started weaving a spell around his thoughts, tying them up, making him powerless to resist.

The chanting grew louder, filling his body. Aquilia's trident was poised to strike. Valens wondered if he had the strength to roll to his side, to avoid the prongs.

A woman's scream tore through his consciousness with one word—*no*. Valens lifted his head and saw

Julia, her face pale as snow, her green gown vivid against the blue of Strabo's box. She was here! The inner reaches of his soul uncurled.

Strength flooded through him, a crazed strength from knowing that Julia was there. She had made her choice and had made it known in the most public way possible. She had chosen him. He had someone to fight for.

Valens used his shield and forced the trident back. The impact shuddered through his arm. He reached and grabbed the trident, sending it spinning from Aquilia's grasp.

The crowd stopped chanting, as it held a collective breath. Aquilia stood, stunned, a bemused expression on his face. Then he snarled and flung the net, aiming over Valens's head.

With one motion, Valens brought his shield up and around, catching the net on the edge of the shield. He pulled it out of Aquilia's arm and with a great tearing noise, the net ripped in half.

Aquilia stood, deprived of his weapons, a blank dazed look on his face.

'Now who has had it?' Valens asked, grimly advancing with his sword outstretched. He had hated the thought of attacking a defenceless man, but Aquilia had not made any sign of surrender.

He took another step forward.

Aquilia fell to his knees, grovelled in the dirt and made a gesture of supplication, putting one finger of his left hand into the air. The crowd start to chant again—this time screaming Aquilia had had it, Aquilia was done for.

Valens nodded, lowered his sword then took a step backwards. The match had finished. Aquilia had appealed to Caesar for mercy.

Turning to face Caesar and wait for the signal to tell him what to do, Valens tensed, and willed himself not to think about the job he'd have to do if Caesar decided not to spare Aquilia.

Caesar paused, hand held out, thumb held horizontal to the ground. Politician to the core, he was waiting to hear the crowd's verdict, Valens thought, struggling to regain his breath.

Time stood still. The crowd became silent. One or two white handkerchiefs fluttered in the breeze. Caesar made no move as a trickle of sweat coursed down Valens's face. His own being concentrated on Caesar's hand.

'A dagger! Valens, watch out! Behind you!' Julia's cry echoed in his ears. 'He has a dagger!'

Valens reacted without thinking and spun with his sword held out. In slow motion, he watched Aquilia hurl his body towards him, a dagger in his right hand.

Aquilia's charge led him straight on to Valens's

sword. Valens's arm shuddered from the impact and he dropped the sword as Aquilia fell backwards.

The crowd roared its approval.

Julia collapsed back down on her seat, hardly listening to the crowd. Every muscle trembled. Only her eyes shifted, following every move Valens made as he stood before Caesar's box.

She saw Aquilia's body being dragged away by the guards dressed as guardians of the underworld and shuddered. It could have so easily been Valens lying there.

She had no idea whether she could face seeing Valens in the arena again, and yet she knew, should he fight, that she would be there, willing him on.

She passed a hand over her brow and pushed the thought away. The only thing that mattered was that Valens lived and breathed. He was alive! And she would hold him in her arms again.

Caesar held up his hands, signalling for silence.

'Gladiator, take off your helmet, in order that I might look on your face and know your name.'

Valens slowly lifted the steel helmet. He held up his head and met Caesar's clear gaze. His father stood at Caesar's elbow, his visage sterner and older than Valens remembered, but there was a queer half-smile on his lips. Valens drew a deep breath and knew what he must do.

'I am Gaius Gracchus, the son of Marcus Graccus Quintus, who is sometimes known as Valens the Thracian.' His voice rang out through the arena, echoed and bounced off the seats.

A few catcalls of shame echoed around the arena.

'How came you to be a gladiator, Gaius Gracchus? I remember you as a junior tribune in Zama.' Caesar's question silenced the crowd.

'Pirates captured me and sold me to a gladiatorial school when my ransom failed to arrive.'

'A ransom should always be paid.' Caesar turned towards Senator Gracchus as if expecting an explanation.

'My father mistakenly believed I had died, Caesar. And I wished to live. There is no honour in dying in a pirate's hold.'

'Agreed, and have you avenged your capture?'

'The pirate who captured me died a coward's death.' Valens nodded towards Aquilia's body.

The crowd roared its approval. The sounds of thousands of pairs of feet stamping shook the arena. Caesar held up his hands again and waited for silence. This man will go far, Valens thought, he knows the people.

'Gaius Gracchus, I cannot give you your rightful place back in society. Our laws are such that no man who has fought in the arena may become a senator. I regret I cannot change them, even for a captive.'

'I understand, Caesar.' Valens bowed his head. There would be no miracle happy ending for him.

'However,' Caesar continued, 'after that performance you just gave, that performance that gave honour to my father and his death—ask a boon and if I can grant it I shall. An estate? Jewels? What you would like? What is it that is in my power to give?'

Valens looked at Caesar and then turned to look where Julia stood, hands clasped together, a pleading expression on her face. He knew what she wanted him to ask for, what Caesar expected him to ask for. But the wooden sword was no guarantee of Julia's hand. Valens knew with every beat of his heart that Julia mattered above everything else in his life.

'I would ask for the hand of Julia Antonia in marriage. There is no one or nothing that I want more on this earth than to have her by my side.'

Caesar frowned, and the crowd sat in stunned silence. Valens felt the prickle of sweat cascade down his back as he waited. The tension was worse than waiting for his bout with Aquilia to begin.

'I don't know if I can grant that,' Caesar said at last, his voice sounding less sure than previously.

'Why not? You are her father's patron. Surely you

can ask? My suit will hold more weight if you are backing it.'

Caesar motioned to Julius Antonius, who stood up and stepped forward. They had a brief whispered conversation. Valens could see Antonius pointing to where Julia stood and shaking his head.

'I cannot give you the answer you want, Gaius Gracchus Valens,' Antonius shouted. 'My daughter is a free woman and makes up her own mind. You will have to ask her!'

'And I say yes! Yes, I will give my hand to you,' Julia shouted across the arena, hoping her voice could be heard above the din of the crowd.

She knew it had to have been heard as Valens's face broke into a wreath of smiles. Her heart turned over when she thought of what he could have asked for. But he had asked for her. Suddenly the only thing that mattered was for her to feel his arms about her and know he was safe.

She started forward and tried to climb over the barrier. She knew a good deal of her leg would be exposed to Rome, that her behaviour would be talked about for weeks or months to come, but it did not matter. Valens was the only person who mattered.

Two security guards ran over to her and helped her into the arena. When her feet touched the ground she sprinted towards Valens's side. Her sandals slipped on the sand and she had to slow down. It seemed to take an age to reach his side, but suddenly she was there, feeling the warmth of his breath against her cheek.

Her hands touched the cold steel of his armour before encountering the yielding softness of his skin.

'I say yes,' she said again, looking into his eyes and knowing that this was where she belonged. 'Yes, I will be your wife.'

Valens touched his lips to hers. And she was oblivious to the stares and cheers.

'It appears, Gaius Gracchus, you do not need any help from me on that score.' Caesar's voice cut through the noise. 'The lady has made her own choice. But what I would say is that a free woman needs a free man.'

Caesar made a signal with a hand and two servants came out, carrying a wooden sword.

'I give you your freedom, Gaius Gracchus Valens. Long may you enjoy it with your wife!'

Julia watched as Valens grasped the sword with one hand and held it aloft. The roar of the crowd echoed in her ears.

'I love you, Gaius Gracchus Valens,' she whispered.

Valens bowed his head and whispered back, 'I love you with all my heart and all my soul.'

Epilogue

One year later on an estate outside Pompeii

The warm breeze brought a scent of thyme and roses, lifting Julia's hair and tickling her nose. She leant back against the stone wall and gave a happy sigh. With only the birdsong and the faint splash of the stream at the bottom of the terrace, she enjoyed the perfect peace of the estate. Rome with its incessant busy streets seemed like a half-forgotten dream. She lifted her eyes to the green-covered slopes of Mount Vesuvius and thought how timeless this place was.

She leant over and tucked the blanket around Marcus where he lay peacefully sleeping in his basket. Already three weeks old, and his little legs were constantly kicking the covers off. She had never realised how much love and joy a child could bring.

Bato lifted his head from where he lay resting at her

feet and gave a happy bark at the sound of approaching footsteps.

'I hoped I might find you and Marcus here. Some scrolls have arrived from Rome.' Valens came towards her and Julia patted her hand on the bench. After giving Bato a pat on the head, he sat down and stretched an arm about Julia. She lay her head against Valens's chest, savouring the steady thump of his heart as Bato settled himself at their feet, and put his nose under his paws. 'I thought to open them with you.'

He handed her a scroll with Claudia's familiar scrawl on the front. Julia rapidly scanned it.

'Claudia plans to be here for the games in September and wants the latest gossip as to gladiatorial form. She also writes that Apius, the augur who foretold our marriage, has been rewarded yet again by Caesar. His reputation for accuracy grows and grows. Claudia is thinking of consulting him about whom she should marry.'

'That old fraud. It is a wonder he has not been found out by now.'

'What do you mean, Valens?'

Valens lifted her chin and Julia was suddenly staring into his dark eyes. "There are some things too important to be left to Fate, my darling wife. I knew I could not offer for you then, but if I did well in the games, I had a chance. Luckily the heaviness of the purse had some influence on Apius and he gave the prediction I wanted.'

'Did you know how worried I was?' The corners of her mouth twitched. 'Do you know how much money he has made on the strength of that one prediction?'

Valens stroked her hair. 'I did what I had to do.'

Julia fell silent. She noticed he seemed quieter, more subdued as he read his scroll. 'Not bad news, I hope.'

'It's from my father. He was excited to learn of Marcus's birth and looks forward to meeting him next month. He plans on making him his heir, you know.'

Julia touched Valens's cheek. Even though Gracchus and Valens had patched up their differences, she knew the problem of who should inherit the senator's great wealth was unresolved. 'Do you want this?'

'It seems the most sensible solution. I suggested it to my father when I first learnt you were pregnant. And now my father agrees.'

'And what of Lucius? What does he think?' A shiver passed over Julia. The last thing she wanted was more trouble from that man. Valens knew her feelings on this. It had been the cause of their one quarrel. In the end, she had agreed that Senator Gracchus had the right to leave his money to whomever he wanted.

Valens's eyes turned grave and he put both his hands on Julia's shoulders. 'My father writes that the court case is over. Mettalius has been banished for his part. But the morning the judgement was due to be read out, Lucius's body was discovered in his prison cell, hemlock by his side.'

'Oh.' Julia stared at him, suddenly lost for words. 'We will never know then what truly happened.'

'He left a confession. It details everything—how he first conceived of the plan when he heard of my quarrels with my father, how he used Mettalius's gaming debts to pressure him into doing his bidding and how he arranged for the kidnapping by the pirates. My ransom note went to him first and he altered the code. Then, thinking the pirates would kill me, he murdered my mother by poison. He took his life rather than face the punishment.'

'Hades is too good for him.'

'His actions may have caused immense trouble, but in the end everything worked out because I found you.' Valens touched his lips to Julia's forehead, and Julia felt the tenderness of the kiss pervade her very being. Valens was correct—the past did not matter. It was their present and future together that was important. 'I have no desire for anything but being here on this estate with you and our son, and enjoying the rest of our days together. I could not wish for anything more.'

'I love you, my honourable gladiator.'

Valens bent his head and Julia tasted the sweetness

of his kiss. Except for the gurgling of the stream, the contented snores of Bato, and the gentle breathing of their child, the garden fell silent for a long time.

Historical Note

Gladiators were ingrained in the Roman psyche. From the earliest Etruscan times, gladiators would perform at funeral rites to honour the shades of the dead warriors. However, it was not until 105 *BC* that gladiator games were given officially by two Roman consuls. By the time Julius Caesar became Aedile in 65 *BC*, the sport had grown into a professional spectacle.

Caesar was the first to equip his gladiators with silvered armour and to try to harness the spectacle for his own political ends. The lavish games he gave in honour of his father would serve as a platform for his later political ambitions.

Prior to the first permanent Roman arena being built around 29 *BC,* gladiatorial games were either held in the Circus Maximus or in a hastily built wooden structure on the Forum. Given the importance of these particular games, and the absence of historical record as to precisely where they were held, I decided Julius Caesar would have used the largest venue possible, thus I chose the Circus Maximus.

To improve the quality of the gladiators, and partly to allay senatorial fears of a private army, Caesar housed his troupe amongst his clients. It is only in 53 *BC* that there are records of an actual school of gladiators being housed separately within Roman city limits.

Despite their wealth and the adulation from the crowds, gladiators, like actors and prostitutes, were considered to be outside society and lower than slaves, therefore no noble family would want to be willingly aligned with them. The stain could echo down the generations. Although the sexual appeal of gladiators is well documented, these were seen as passing fancies as long as they were kept out of the public domain.

For anyone wishing to read further on the period, I would highly recommend the following books. They have been very useful to me and I found Grant's book on gladiators and Holland's book on the end of the Republic particularly riveting.

Carcopino, Jerome, *Daily Life in Ancient Rome–The People and the City at the Height of the Empire* (Penguin 1941), London.

Croom, A.T., *Roman Clothing and Fashion* (Tempus Publishing Ltd 2000), Gloucestershire.

Goldsworthy, Adrian, *In the Name of Rome–The Men Who Won the Roman Empire* (Weidenfeld & Nicholson 2003), London.

Grant, Michael, *Gladiators–The Bloody Truth* (Penguin 1967), London.

Holland, Tom, *Rubicon: The Triumph and Tragedy of the Roman Republic* (Little, Brown 2003), London.

Woolf, Greg, ed. *Cambridge Illustrated History: Roman World* (Cambridge University Press 2003), Cambridge.

HISTORICAL ROMANCE™

LARGE PRINT

THE ROGUE'S KISS
Emily Bascom

Under cover of darkness, a highwayman silently waits.
He is soon to discover that the approaching carriage
holds a beautiful woman – travelling alone. Lady Roisin
Melville is escaping London and the fortune-hunting
gentlemen of the *ton* – only to be held up by a masked
figure. With her gun trained on this daring rogue,
can Roisin persuade him to take nothing more
than a kiss…?

A TREACHEROUS PROPOSITION
Patricia Frances Rowell

He trusted no one, and that was his strength – until a
brutal murder linked his life with that of the victim's
widow. Vincent Ingleton, Earl of Lonsdale, found himself
drawn to Lady Diana Corby's haunting vulnerability. But
could she ever really love a man whose whole life was a
tissue of deception and danger…?

ROWAN'S REVENGE
June Francis

Owain ap Rowan had sworn to track Lady Catherine down.
And in Spain he believed he had finally found her. Her guilt
was obvious – no innocent lady would disguise herself as a
boy! But could he be sure that the beautiful Kate was, in
truth, the lady he sought? With so many secrets between
them, he must not yield to her seductive spell…

MILLS & BOON®

Live the emotion

HIST1006 L

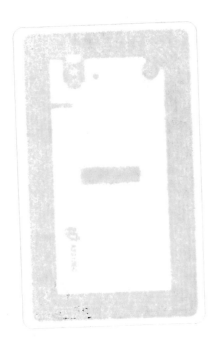